Is it possible for a book to be too successful? Sometimes a book is eclipsed by its own fame: By the time Hollywood makes the movie, people forget how good the novel really was. FIRST BLOOD is such a book—the novel that created a cultural icon in the character of John Rambo. A masterful blend of stylish prose, furious action, and a brooding mood that struck a chord with the American psyche, FIRST BLOOD reveals more about us than any other popular novel of its time. For those of you who first read this book in 1972, prepare to relive the ride of your life. For those of you who didn't, we envy you your first venture into the world of FIRST BLOOD.

—**The Editors**

PRAISE FOR DAVID MORRELL AND *FIRST BLOOD*

"Morrell, an absolute master of the thriller, plays by his own rules and leaves you dazzled."

—Dean Koontz, author of *The Silent Corner*

"A first-rate thriller."

—*Newsweek*

"Morrell delivers race-against-the-clock thrills."

—*Publishers Weekly*

"The finest thriller writer living today, bar none."

—Steve Berry, author of The Cotton Malone series

"One of the finest chase novels you will ever read."

—*Star Tribune*

"One hell of a hard, fast novel."

—John D. MacDonald, *New York Times* bestselling author

"Morrell's deft hand with thriller plotting provides copious chills and procedural satisfaction, but it is his mastery of character...and tonal sophistication that seduce and delight."

—*Kirkus Reviews*

ALSO BY DAVID MORRELL

NOVELS

First Blood

Testament

Last Reveille

The Totem

Blood Oath

The Brotherhood of the Rose

The Fraternity of the Stone

Rambo (First Blood Part II)

The League of Night and Fog

Rambo III

The Fifth Profession

The Covenant of the Flame

Assumed Identity

Desperate Measures

The Totem (Complete and Unaltered)

Extreme Denial

Double Image

Burnt Sienna

Long Lost

The Protector

Creepers

Scavenger

The Spy Who Came for Christmas

The Shimmer

The Naked Edge

Murder as a Fine Art

Inspector of the Dead

Ruler of the Night

SHORT FICTION
The Hundred-Year Christmas
Black Evening
Nightscape

ILLUSTRATED FICTION
Captain America: The Chosen

NONFICTION
John Barth: An Introduction
Fireflies: A Father's Tale of Love and Loss
The Successful Novelist: A Lifetime of Lessons about
Writing and Publishing
Stars in My Eyes: My Love Affair with Books, Movies, and Music

EDITED BY
American Fiction, American Myth: Essays by Philip Young
edited by David Morrell and Sandra Spanier
Tesseracts Thirteen: Chilling Tales from the Great White North
edited by Nancy Kilpatrick and David Morrell
Thrillers: 100 Must-Reads
edited by David Morrell and Hank Wagner

FIRST BLOOD

DAVID MORRELL

GRAND CENTRAL
PUBLISHING

NEW YORK   BOSTON

Copyright © 1972 by David Morrell
Copyright © renewed 2000 by David Morrell
Introduction © 1988 by David Morrell
Author Q&A copyright © 2017 by Hachette Book Group
Excerpt from *Murder as a Fine Art* copyright © 2013 by David Morrell

A version of the original introduction first appeared as part of an article by the author in *Playboy* magazine, copyright © August 1988 by David Morrell

Grand Central Publishing
Hachette Book Group
1290 Avenue of the Americas, New York, NY 10104
grandcentralpublishing.com
twitter.com/grandcentralpub

Originally published in 1972
First Grand Central Publishing mass market edition: February 2000
First Grand Central Publishing trade paperback edition: October 2017

Grand Central Publishing is a division of Hachette Book Group, Inc. The Grand Central Publishing name and logo is a trademark of Hachette Book Group, Inc.

The publisher is not responsible for websites (or their content) that are not owned by the publisher.

ISBNs: 978-1-5387-1137-8 (trade paperback), 978-1-5387-1136-1 (oversize mass market reissue)

Printed in the United States of America

LSC-C

10 9 8 7 6 5 4 3

to Philip Klass and William Tenn:
each in his own way

RAMBO AND ME

In the summer of 1968, I was twenty-five, a graduate student at the Pennsylvania State University. Specializing in American literature, I'd finished my master's thesis on Ernest Hemingway and was starting my doctoral dissertation on John Barth. But in my heart, what I wanted to be was a novelist.

I knew that few novelists made a living at it, so I'd decided to become a literature professor, an occupation in which I'd be surrounded by books and allowed time to write. A Penn State faculty member, Philip Klass, whose science-fiction pseudonym is William Tenn, had given me generous instruction in the techniques of fiction writing. Still, as Klass had explained, "I can teach you how to write but not what to write about."

What *would* I write about?

By chance, I watched a television program that changed my life. The program was the *CBS Evening News*, and on that sultry August evening, Walter Cronkite juxtaposed two stories whose friction flashed like lightning through my mind.

The first story showed a firefight in Vietnam. Sweaty American soldiers crouched in the jungle, shooting bursts from M-16s to repel an enemy attack. Incoming bullets kicked up dirt and shredded leaves. Medics scrambled to assist the wounded. An officer barked coordinates into a two-way radio, demanding air support. The fatigue, determination, and fear on the faces of the soldiers were dismayingly vivid.

The second story showed a different sort of battle. That steamy summer, the inner cities of America had erupted into violence. In nightmarish images, National Guardsmen clutched M-16s and stalked along the rubble of burning streets, dodging rocks, wary of snipers among devastated vehicles and gutted buildings.

Each news story, distressing enough on its own, became doubly so when paired with the other. It occurred to me that, if I'd turned off the sound, if I hadn't heard each story's reporter explain what I was watching, I might have thought that both film clips were two aspects of one horror. A firefight outside Saigon, a riot within it. A riot within an American city, a firefight outside it. Vietnam and America.

The juxtaposition made me decide to write a novel in which the Vietnam War literally came home to America. There hadn't been a war on American soil since the end of the Civil War in 1865. With America splitting apart because of Vietnam, maybe it was time for a novel that dramatized the philosophical division in our society, that shoved the brutality of the war right under our noses.

I decided my catalytic character would be a Vietnam veteran, a Green Beret who, after many harrowing missions, had been captured by the enemy, escaped, and returned home to be given America's highest military distinction, the Congressional Medal of Honor. But he would bring something back with him from Southeast Asia, what we now call post-traumatic stress disorder. Haunted by nightmares about what he had done in the war, embittered by civilian indifference and sometimes hostility toward the sacrifice he had made for his country, he would drop out of society to wander the back roads of the nation he loved. He would let his hair grow long, stop shaving, carry his few possessions in a rolled-up sleeping bag slung over his shoulder, and look like what we then called a hippie. In what I loosely thought of as an allegory, he would represent the disaffected.

His name would be…I get asked about his name a lot. One of my graduate school languages was French, and on an autumn afternoon, as I read a course assignment, I was struck by the difference between the look and the pronunciation of the name of the author I was reading: Rimbaud. An hour later, my wife came home from buying groceries. She mentioned that she'd bought some apples of a type that she'd never heard about before: Rambo. A French author's name and the name of an apple collided, and I recognized the sound of force.

While Rambo represented the disaffected, I needed a contrasting character to represent the establishment. Another news report, this time in print, aroused my indignation. In a southwestern American town, a group of hitchhiking hippies had been picked up by the local police, stripped, hosed, and shaved—not just their beards but their hair. The hippies had then been given back their clothes and driven to a desert road, where they were abandoned to walk to the next town, thirty miles away. I remembered the harassment that my own recently grown mustache and long hair had caused me. "Why don't you get a haircut? What the hell are you, a man or a woman?" I wondered what Rambo's reaction would be if, after risking his life in the service of his country, he were subjected to the insults that those hippies had received.

In my novel, the establishment's representative became a police chief, Wilfred Teasle. Wary of stereotypes, I wanted him to be as complex as the action would allow. I made Teasle old enough to be Rambo's father. That created a generation gap, with the added dimension that Teasle wishes he had a son. Next, I decided that Teasle would be a Korean War hero, his Distinguished Service Cross second only to Rambo's Congressional Medal of Honor. There were many other facets to Teasle's character, and in each case, the intention was to make him as motivated and sympathetic as Rambo, because the viewpoints that divided America came from deep, well-meant convictions.

To emphasize their polarity, I structured the novel so that a scene from Rambo's perspective would be followed by one from Teasle's, the subsequent scene from Rambo's, the next scene again from Teasle's. That tactic, I hoped, would make the reader identify with each character and at the same time feel ambivalent about them. Who was the hero, who the villain, or were *both* men heroes, *both* men villains? The final confrontation between Rambo and Teasle would show that in this microcosmic version of the Vietnam War and American attitudes about it, escalating force results in disaster. Nobody wins.

Due to the rigors of graduate school, I didn't complete *First Blood* until after I'd graduated from Penn State in 1970 and taught at the University of Iowa for a year. Following the book's publication in 1972, it was translated into twenty-one languages and eventually became the basis for a well-known film.

The latter was a decade in the making. I had sold the film rights to Columbia Pictures in 1972. One year later, Columbia sold the rights to Warner Bros. Then Warner Bros. sold...Well, for ten years after its publication, the story passed through three movie companies, eighteen screenplays, and such directors as Richard Brooks, Martin Ritt, Sydney Pollack, and John Frankenheimer. Meanwhile Paul Newman, Al Pacino, Steve McQueen,

Clint Eastwood, Robert De Niro, Nick Nolte, and Michael Douglas were all considered to play Rambo. The novel became a Hollywood legend. How could so much money and so much talent be spent on an enterprise that somehow couldn't get off the page?

Part of the reason was the mood of the seventies. America's involvement in Vietnam had ended badly, and feelings about the war were bitter. The few films that referred to Vietnam (*Coming Home*, for example) reflected that attitude. Then came the eighties. Ronald Reagan was president. He promised to make America feel optimistic again. The defeat in Vietnam seemed far behind.

At that point, Andrew Vajna and Mario Kassar, two film distributors who'd been successful in the Orient, decided to become producers. Seeking a project, they happened upon *First Blood* and decided that with modification the story would play well in America. More important, their experience in foreign film markets told them that the movie, if it emphasized action, would attract large audiences around the world.

In the process, some changes were made from my novel. The film's locale was shifted from Kentucky to the Pacific Northwest (to avoid harsh winter weather; ironically, the production was shut down by a blizzard). Rambo acquired the first name John ("When Johnny comes marching home"). Also he was made less lethal than in my novel. In the film, Rambo throws a rock at a helicopter, causing a demented sharpshooter to fall to his death. Later, Rambo bumps a stolen truck against a pursuing police car filled with gun-blazing deputies; they crash into a car at the side of the road. Neither incident is in the novel. That's the total body count in the film. The police chief—now a stereotypical redneck—is badly wounded but lives. But in my novel the casualties are virtually uncountable. *My* intent was to transpose the

Vietnam war to America. In contrast, the *film's* intent was to make the audience cheer for the underdog.

The most important change between my novel and the film almost didn't occur. I had been determined that there be no winners, and so both the police chief and Rambo die. In the novel, Sam Trautman (I thought of him as a continuation of the allegory, as "Uncle Sam"; the Special Forces officer who trained Rambo, who made Rambo what he is) blows the top of his former student's head off with a shotgun. A variation—in which Rambo commits suicide—was filmed. But test audiences found that conclusion too depressing. The film crew returned to Canada to stage a new ending, and Rambo lived. Thus, inadvertently, it was possible to do sequels prompted by the film's success.

The first sequel, 1985's *Rambo (First Blood Part II)*, was an international box-office sensation. An action film, it was intended as an entertainment. But because it dealt with a highly charged political issue (whether or not there were American prisoners of war in Vietnam), it was also extremely controversial (as was the second sequel, 1988's *Rambo III*, which dealt with the Soviet invasion of Afghanistan). President Reagan didn't seem to mind the controversy, however. One evening, during a televised press conference, he said that he had seen a Rambo movie the night before and now he knew what to do the next time there was a terrorist hostage crisis. Unfortunately, many people equated the Rambo movies with America's military policy, to the point that while I was on a book tour in Britain in 1986, I read with dismay the London *Times* headline: "U.S. Rambo Jets Bomb Libya."

I wasn't involved with the films. However, I did write a novelization for each of the sequels in an effort to supply the characterization that they omitted. I felt that it was important to remind readers of what the novel's Rambo had been about. In the seventies and early eighties, the book had been taught in high schools and universities across the country. For years, I had received numerous letters from teachers telling me how strongly students had responded to the novel and its issues. But by the mid-eighties, the controversy generated by the films had caused teachers to shy away from the book. It was no longer included on reading assignments. The letters stopped. Not that I object to the movies. Their level of action is nowhere as extreme as current examples of the genre. Politics aside, they're a lot like westerns or Tarzan films (although in retrospect I think *Rambo III* was *too much* like an old movie). At the same time, I think it's ironic that a novel about political polarization in America (for and against the Vietnam war) was the basis for films that resulted in similar polarization (for and against Ronald Reagan) a decade after the novel was written.

Sometimes I compare the Rambo books and movies to trains that are similar but headed in different directions. Sometimes I think of Rambo as a son who grew up and out of his father's control. Sometimes I read or hear Rambo's name in a newspaper, in a magazine, on the radio, on television—in reference to politicians, financiers, athletes, whomever—used as a noun, an adjective, a verb, whatever—and it takes me a moment before I remind myself that if not for the *CBS Evening News*, if not for Rimbaud, my wife, and the name of an apple, if not for Philip Klass and my determination to be a fiction writer, a recent edition of the *Oxford English Dictionary* wouldn't have cited this novel as the source for the creation of a word.

Rambo. Complicated, troubled, haunted, too often misunderstood. If you've heard about him but haven't met him before, he's about to surprise you.

David Morrell
Santa Fe, 2000

PART ONE

1

His name was Rambo, and he was just some nothing kid for all anybody knew, standing by the pump of a gas station at the outskirts of Madison, Kentucky. He had a long heavy beard, and his hair was hanging down over his ears to his neck, and he had his hand out trying to thumb a ride from a car that was stopped at the pump. To see him there, leaning on one hip, a Coke bottle in his hand and a rolled-up sleeping bag near his boots on the tar pavement, you could never have guessed that on Tuesday, a day later, most of the police in Basalt County would be hunting him down. Certainly you could not have guessed that by Thursday he would be running from the Kentucky National Guard and the police of six counties and a good many private citizens who liked to shoot. But then from just seeing him there ragged and dusty by the pump of the gas station, you could never have figured the kind of kid Rambo was, or what was about to make it all begin.

Rambo knew there was going to be trouble, though. Big trouble, if somebody didn't watch out. The car he was trying to thumb a ride with nearly ran him over when it left the pump. The station attendant crammed a charge slip and a book of trade stamps into his pocket and grinned at the tire marks on the hot tar close to Rambo's feet. Then the police car pulled out of traffic toward him and he recognized the start of the pattern again and stiffened. "No, by God. Not this time. This time I won't be pushed."

The cruiser was marked CHIEF OF POLICE, MADISON. It stopped next to Rambo, its radio antenna swaying, and the policeman inside leaned across the front seat, opening the passenger door. He stared at the mud-crusted boots, the rumpled jeans ripped at the cuffs and patched on one thigh, the blue sweat shirt speckled with what looked like dry blood, the buckskin jacket. He lingered over the beard and the long hair. No, that's not what was bothering him. It was something else, and he couldn't quite put his finger on it. "Well then, hop in," he said.

But Rambo did not move.

"I said hop in," the man repeated. "Must be awful hot out there in that jacket."

But Rambo just sipped his Coke, glanced up and down the street at the cars passing, looked down at the policeman in the cruiser, and stayed where he was.

"Something wrong with your hearing?" the policeman said. "Get in here before you make me sore."

Rambo studied him just as he himself had been studied: short and chunky behind the wheel, wrinkles around his eyes and shallow pockmarks in his cheeks that gave them a grain like weathered board.

"Don't stare at me," the policeman said.

But Rambo kept on studying him: the gray uniform, top button of his shirt open, tie loose, the front of his shirt soaked dark with sweat. Rambo looked but could not see what kind his handgun was. The policeman had it holstered to the left, away from the passenger side.

"I'm telling you," the policeman said. "I don't like being stared at."

"Who does?"

Rambo glanced around once more, then picked up his sleeping bag. As he got into the cruiser, he set the bag between himself and the policeman.

"Been waiting long?" the policeman asked.

"An hour. Since I came."

"You could have waited a lot longer than that. People around here don't generally stop for a hitchhiker. Especially if he looks like you. It's against the law."

"Looking like me?"

"Don't be smart. I mean hitchhiking's against the law. Too many people stop for a kid on the road, and next thing they're robbed or maybe dead. Close your door."

Rambo took a slow sip of Coke before he did what he was told. He looked over at the gas station attendant who was still at the pump grinning as the policeman pulled the cruiser into traffic and headed downtown.

"No need to worry," Rambo told the policeman. "I won't try to rob you."

"That's very funny. In case you missed the sign on the door, I'm the Chief of Police. Teasle. Wilfred Teasle. But then I don't guess there's much point in telling you my name."

He drove on through a main intersection where the light was turning orange. Far down both sides of the street were stores squeezed together—a drug store, a pool hall, a gun and tackle shop, dozens more. Over the top of them, far back on the horizon, mountains rose up, tall and green, touched here and there with red and yellow where the leaves had begun to die.

Rambo watched a cloud shadow slip across the mountains.

"Where you headed?" he heard Teasle ask.

"Does it matter?"

"No. Come to think of it, I don't guess there's much point in knowing that either. Just the same—where you headed?"

"Maybe Louisville."

"And maybe not."

"That's right."

"Where did you sleep? In the woods?"

"That's right."

"It's safe enough now, I suppose. The nights are getting colder, and the snakes like to hole up instead of going out to hunt. Still, one of these times you might find yourself with a bed partner who's just crazy about your body heat."

They passed a carwash, an A&P, a hamburger drive-in with a big Dr. Pepper sign in the window. "Just look at that eyesore drive-in," Teasle said. "They put that thing here on the main street, and ever since, all we've had is kids parked, beeping their horns, throwing crap on the sidewalk."

Rambo sipped his Coke.

"Somebody from town give you a ride in?" Teasle asked.

"I walked. I've been walking since after dawn."

"Sure am sorry to hear that. Least this ride will help some, won't it?"

Rambo did not answer. He knew what was coming. They drove over a bridge and a stream into the town square, an old stone courthouse at the right end, more shops squeezed together down both sides.

"Yeah, the police station is right up there by the courthouse," Teasle said. But he drove right on through the square and down the street until there were only houses, first neat and prosperous, then gray cracked wooden shacks with children playing in the dirt in front. He went up a rise in the road between two cliffs to a level where there were no houses at all, only fields of stunted corn turning brown in the sun. And just after a sign that read YOU ARE NOW LEAVING MADISON. DRIVE SAFELY, he pulled off the pavement onto the gravel shoulder.

"Take care," he said.

"And keep out of trouble," Rambo answered. "Isn't that how it goes?"

"That's good. You've been this route before. Now I don't need to waste time explaining how guys who look like you have this habit of being a disturbance." He lifted the sleeping bag from where Rambo had put it between them, set it on Rambo's lap, and leaned across Rambo to open the passenger door. "Take good care now."

Rambo got slowly out of the car. "I'll be seeing you," he said and flipped the door shut.

"No," Teasle answered through the open passenger window. "I guess you won't."

He drove the cruiser up the road, made a U-turn, and headed back toward town, sounding his car horn as he passed.

Rambo watched the cruiser disappear down the road between the two cliffs. He sipped the last of his Coke, tossed the bottle in a ditch, and with his sleeping bag slung by its rope around his shoulder, he started back to town.

2

The air was sticky with frying grease. Rambo watched the old lady behind the counter peer out the bottom of her bifocal glasses at his clothes and hair and beard.

"Two hamburgers and a Coke," he told her.

"Make that to go," he heard from behind.

He looked at the reflection in the mirror behind the counter and saw Teasle braced in the front doorway, holding the screen door open, letting it slam shut with a whack. "And make that a rush job, will you, Merle?" Teasle said. "This kid's in a powerful hurry."

Only a few customers were in the place, sitting at the counter and in some of the booths. Rambo watched their reflection in the mirror as they quit chewing and looked over at him. But then Teasle leaned against the jukebox by the door, and it seemed like nothing serious was going to happen, so they went back to work on their food.

The old lady behind the counter had her white head cocked to one side, puzzled.

"Oh yeah, Merle, and while you're fixing that stuff, how about a fast coffee," Teasle said.

"Whatever you like, Wilfred," she said, still puzzled, and went to pour the coffee.

That left Rambo looking at the mirror at Teasle looking at him. Teasle had an American Legion pin opposite his badge on his shirt. I wonder which war, Rambo thought. You're just a bit young for the second one.

He swung round on his stool and faced him. "Korea?" he said, pointing at the pin.

"That's right," Teasle said flatly.

And they went on watching each other.

Rambo shifted his eyes down to Teasle's left side and the handgun he wore. It was a surprise, not the standard police revolver but a semi-automatic pistol, and from the big handle Rambo decided it was a Browning 9 millimeter. He had used a Browning once himself. The handle was big because it held a clip of thirteen bullets instead of the seven or eight that most pistols held. You couldn't slam a man flat on his back with one shot from it, but you could sure hurt him bad, and two more would finish him, and you still had ten more shots for anybody else around. Rambo had to admit that Teasle carried it awfully well, too. Teasle was five foot six, maybe seven, and for a smallish man that big pistol ought to have hung awkward, but it didn't. You have to be pretty large to get a grip on that big handle though, Rambo thought. And then he looked at Teasle's hands, amazed at the size of them.

"I warned you about that staring," Teasle said. Leaning against the jukebox, he unstuck his wet shirt from his chest. Left-handed, he took a cigarette from a pack in his shirt pocket, lit it, snapping the wood match he had used in half, then snickered, shaking his head in amusement as he walked over to the counter and smiled strangely down at Rambo on the stool. "Well, you sure put one over on me, didn't you?" he said.

"I wasn't trying to."

"Of course not. Of course you weren't. But you sure put one over on me just the same, didn't you?"

The old lady set Teasle's coffee down and faced Rambo. "How do you want your burgers? Plain or dragged through the garden?"

"What?"

"Plain or with fixings?"

"With lots of onion."

"Whatever you like." She went off to fry the hamburgers.

"Yeah, you really did," Teasle said to him and smiled strangely again. "You really put one over." He frowned at the dirty cotton bulging from a rip in the stool next to Rambo and sat reluctantly. "I mean, you act like you're smart. And you talk like you're smart, so I naturally assumed you got the idea. But then you come dragging back here and fool me, and that's enough to make a man wonder if maybe you're not smart at all. Is there something wrong with you? Is that what it is?"

"I'm hungry."

"Well, that just doesn't interest me at all," Teasle said, drawing on his cigarette. It had no filter and after he exhaled, he picked off bits of tobacco that were stuck to his lips and tongue. "A fellow like you, he ought to have brains to carry a lunch with him. You know, for when he has some emergency, like *you* have *now*."

He lifted the cream pitcher to pour into his coffee, but then he noticed the bottom of the pitcher, and his mouth went sour at the yellow curds that were clinging there. "You need a job?" he asked quietly.

"No."

"Then you already got a job."

"No, I don't have a job either. I don't want a job."

"That's called being a vagrant."

"Call it whatever the hell you want."

Teasle's hand slammed like a shot on the counter. "You watch your mouth!"

Everyone in the place jerked his head toward Teasle. He looked around at them, and smiled as if he had said something funny, and leaned close to the counter to sip his coffee. "That'll give them something to talk about." He smiled and took another draw on his cigarette, picking more specks of tobacco off his tongue. The joke was over. "Listen, I don't get it. That rig of yours, the clothes and hair and all. Didn't you know when you came back down the main street out there you'd stand out like you weren't wearing any clothes at all? My crew radioed in about you five minutes after you got back."

"What took them so long?"

"The mouth," Teasle said. "I warned you."

He looked like he was ready to say more, but then the old lady brought Rambo a half-full paper bag and said, "Buck thirty-one."

"For what? For that little bit?"

"You said you wanted the fixings."

"Just pay her," Teasle said.

She held on to the bag until Rambo gave her the money.

"O.K., let's go," Teasle said.

"Where?"

"Where I take you." He emptied his cup in four quick swallows and put down a quarter. "Thanks, Merle." Everybody looked at the two of them as they walked to the door.

"Almost forgot," Teasle said. "Hey, Merle, one more thing. How about cleaning the bottom on that cream pitcher."

3

The cruiser was directly outside. "Get in," Teasle said, tugging at his sweaty shirt. "Damn, for the first of October it sure is hot. I don't know how you tolerate wearing that hot jacket."

"I don't sweat."

Teasle looked at him. "Sure you don't." He dropped his cigarette down a manhole grate by the curb, and they got into the cruiser. Rambo watched the traffic and the people going past. In the bright sun after the dark lunch counter, his eyes hurt. One man walking by the cruiser waved to Teasle, and Teasle waved back, then pulled away from the curb into a break in traffic. He was driving fast this time.

They went down past a hardware store and a used car lot and old men smoking cigars on benches and women pushing children in strollers.

"Look at those women," Teasle said. "A hot day like this and they don't have the sense to keep their kids indoors."

Rambo did not bother looking. He just closed his eyes and leaned back. When he opened them, the cruiser was speeding up the road between the two cliffs, up onto the level where the

stunted corn drooped in the fields, past the YOU ARE NOW
LEAVING MADISON sign. Teasle stopped the car abruptly on
the gravel shoulder and turned to him.

"Now get it clear," he said. "I don't want a kid who looks like
you and doesn't have a job in my town. First thing I know, a
bunch of your friends will show up, mooching food, maybe stealing, maybe pushing drugs. As it is, I've half a notion to lock you
up for the inconvenience you've caused me. But the way I see
it, a kid like you, he's entitled to a mistake. It's like your judgment's not as developed as an older man's and I have to make
allowances. But you come back again and I'll fix you so you won't
know whether your asshole's bored, bunched, or pecked out by
crows. Is that plain enough for you to understand? Is that clear?"

Rambo grabbed hold of the lunch sack and his sleeping bag
and got out of the car.

"I asked you a question," Teasle said out the open passenger
door. "*I want to know if you heard me tell you not to come back.*"

"I heard you," Rambo said, flipping the door shut.

"Then dammit, do what you hear you're told!"

Teasle stomped on the gas pedal and the cruiser lurched off
the road shoulder, gravel flying, onto the smooth hot pavement.
He made a severe U-turn, tires squealing, and sped back toward
town. This time he did not sound his car horn going past.

Rambo watched the cruiser get smaller and disappear down
the hill between the two cliffs, and when he could no longer see it,
he glanced around at the fields of corn and the mountains in the
distance and the white sun in the stark sky. He eased down into
the ditch, stretching out in the long, dust-covered grass to open
his paper sack.

A sonofabitch of a hamburger. He had asked for lots of onion
and got one crushed string of it. The tomato slice was thin and yel-

low. The bun was greasy, the meat full of pork gristle. Chewing reluctantly, he pried the top off the plastic cup of Coke and washed his mouth and swallowed. Everything went down in a sweet cruddy lump. The thing to do, he decided, was to save enough Coke for both hamburgers so he would not have to taste them.

When he was done, he put the cup and the two pieces of wax paper from the hamburgers into the bag and lit a match, setting fire to it all. He held on, studying the spread of the flames, calculating how close the fire would get to his hand before he would have to let go. The fire stung his fingers and singed the hair on the back of his hand before he dropped the bag onto the grass and let it burn to ashes. Then he crushed the ashes with his boot and, careful they were out, he scattered them. Christ, he thought. Six months back from the war and still he had the urge to destroy what was left of what he had eaten so he would not leave a trace of where he had been.

He shook his head. Thinking about the war had been a mistake. Instantly he was reminded of his other habits from the war: trouble getting to sleep, waking with the slightest noise, needing to sleep in the open, the hole where they had kept him prisoner fresh in his mind.

"You'd better think of something else," he said out loud and then realized he was talking to himself. "What's it going to be? Which way?" He looked where the road stretched into town, where it stretched away from town, and then he was decided. He grabbed the rope on his sleeping bag, slung it around his shoulder and started hiking into Madison again.

At the bottom of the hill into town, trees lined the road, half-green, half-red, the red leaves always on the branches that hung over the road. From exhaust fumes, he thought. Exhaust fumes kill them early.

Dead animals lay here and there along the roadside, likely hit by cars, bloated and speckled with flies in the sun. First a cat, tiger-striped—looked like it had been a nice cat too—next a cocker spaniel, then a rabbit, then a squirrel. That was another thing the war had given him. He noticed dead things more. Not in horror. Just in curiosity of how they had come to end.

He walked past them down the right side of the road, thumb out for a ride. His clothes were filmed yellow with dust, his long hair and beard were matted dirty, and all the people driving by took a look at him, and nobody stopped. So why don't you clean up your act? he thought. Shave and get a haircut. Fix up your clothes. You'll get your rides that way. *Because. A razor's just one more thing to slow you down, and haircuts waste money you can spend on food, and where would you shave anyhow; you can't sleep in the woods and come out looking like some kind of prince.* Then why walk around like this, sleeping in the woods? And with that, his mind moved in a circle and he was back to the war. Think about something else, he told himself. Why not turn around and go? Why come back to this town? It's nothing special. *Because. I have a right to decide for myself whether I'll stay in it or not. I won't have somebody decide that for me.*

But this cop is friendlier than the rest were. More reasonable. Why bug him? Do what he says.

Just because somebody smiles when he hands me a bag of shit, that doesn't mean I have to take it. I don't give a damn how friendly he is. It's what he does that matters.

But you do look a little rough, as if you might cause trouble. He has a point.

So do I. In fifteen goddamn towns this has happened to me. This is the last. I won't be fucking shoved anymore.

Why not explain that to him, clean yourself up a bit? Or do you want this trouble that's coming? You're hungry for some action, is that it? So you can show him your stuff?

I don't have to explain myself to him or anybody else. After what I've been through, I have a right without explanation.

At least tell him about your medal, what it cost you.

Too late to stop his mind from completing the circle. Once again he returned to the war.

4

Teasle was waiting for him. As soon as he drove past the kid, he had glanced up at his rearview mirror, and there the kid had been, reflected small and clear. But the kid was not moving. He was just standing there at the side of the road where he had last been, watching the cruiser, just standing there, getting smaller, watching the cruiser.

Well, what's the holdup, kid? Teasle had thought. Go on, clear out.

But the kid had not. He had just kept standing there, getting smaller in the mirror, looking toward the cruiser. And then the road into town had sloped sharply down between the cliffs, and Teasle could not see him reflected anymore.

My God, you're planning to come back again, he had suddenly realized, shaking his head and laughing once. You're honestly planning to come back.

He turned right onto a side street and drove a quarter-way up a row of gray clapboard houses. He swung into a gravel driveway and backed out and parked so the cruiser was aimed toward the main road he had just left. Then he slumped behind the steering wheel, lighting a cigarette.

The look on the kid's face. He was honest-to-God planning to come back. Teasle could not get over it.

From where he was parked, he could see everything that passed on the main road. The traffic wasn't much, it never was on Monday afternoons: the kid couldn't walk along the far sidewalk and be hidden by the passing cars.

So Teasle watched. The street he was on met the main road in a T. There were cars and trucks going both ways on the main road, a sidewalk on the far side, beyond that the stream which ran along the road and beyond that the old Madison Dance Palace. It had been condemned last month. Teasle remembered when he was in high school how he had worked there Friday and Saturday nights parking cars. Hoagy Carmichael had almost played there once, but the owners hadn't been able to promise him enough money.

Where's the kid?

Maybe he isn't coming. Maybe he really left.

I saw that look on his face. He's coming all right.

Teasle took a deep drag on his cigarette and glanced up at the green-brown mountains lumped close on the horizon. There was a sudden cool wind that smelled of crisp leaves and then it was gone.

"Teasle to station," he said into the microphone of his car radio. "Has the mail come in yet?"

As always, Shingleton, the day radioman, was quick to answer, his voice crackling from static. "Sure has, Chief. I already checked it for you. Nothing from your wife, I'm afraid."

"What about from a lawyer? Or maybe something from California that she didn't put her name on the outside."

"I already checked that too, Chief. Sorry. Nothing."

"Anything important I ought to know about?"

"Just a set of traffic lights that shorted out, but I got the works department over there fixing it."

"If that's all then, I'll be a few minutes yet coming back."

This kid was a nuisance, waiting for him. He wanted to get back to the station and phone her. She was gone three weeks now and she had promised to write at the most by today and here she had not. He did not care anymore about keeping his own promise to her not to call, he was going to phone anyway. Maybe she had thought it over and changed her mind.

But he doubted it.

He lit another cigarette and glanced to the side. There were neighbor women out on porches looking to see what he was up to. That was the end, he decided. He flipped the cigarette out the cruiser window, switched the ignition and drove down to the main road to find out where the hell the kid was.

Nowhere in sight.

Sure. He's gone and left and that look was just to make me think he was coming back.

So he headed toward the station to phone, and three blocks later when all at once he saw the kid up on the left sidewalk, leaning against a wire fence over the stream, he slammed on his brakes so hard in surprise that the car following crashed into the rear end of the cruiser.

The guy who had hit him was sitting shocked behind the wheel, his hand over his mouth. Teasle opened the cruiser door and stared at the guy a second before he walked over to where the kid was leaning against the wire fence.

"How did you get into town without me seeing you?"

"Magic."

"Get in the car."

"I don't think so."

"You think a little more."

There were cars lined up behind the car that had struck the

cruiser. The driver was now standing in the middle of the road, peering at the smashed taillight, shaking his head. Teasle's open door angled into the opposite lane, slowing traffic. Drivers blared their horns; customers and clerks came sticking their heads out of shops across the street.

"You listen," Teasle said. "I'm going to clear that mess of traffic. The time I'm through, you be in that cruiser."

They eyed each other. The next thing, Teasle was over to the guy who had hit the cruiser. The guy was still shaking his head at the damage.

"Driver's license, insurance card, ownership papers," Teasle told him. "Please." He went and shut the cruiser door.

"But I didn't have a chance to stop."

"You were following too close."

"But you slammed on your brakes too fast."

"It doesn't matter. The law says the car in back is always wrong. You were following too close for an emergency."

"But—"

"I'm not about to argue with you," Teasle told him. "Please give me your driver's license, insurance card and ownership papers." He looked over at the kid, and of course the kid was gone.

5

Rambo stayed out walking in the open to make it clear that he was not trying to hide. Teasle could give up the game at this point and leave him alone; if he did not, well then it was Teasle who wanted the trouble, not himself.

He walked along the left-hand sidewalk, looking down at the stream wide and fast in the sun. Across the stream was the bright yellow, freshly sandblasted wall of a building with balconies over the water and a sign high on top MADISON HISTORIC HOTEL. Rambo tried to figure what was historic about a building that looked as if it had just been put up last year.

In the center of town, he turned left onto a big orange bridge, sliding a hand along the smooth warm paint on the metal rail until he was half across. He stopped to peer down at the water. The afternoon was glaring hot, the water fast and cool-looking.

Next to him, welded to the rail, was a machine with a glass top full of gumballs. He took a penny from his jeans and reached to put it in the slot and held it back in time. He had been wrong. The machine was not full of gumballs. It was full of grainy balls of fish food. There was a small metal plate stamped onto the machine.

FEED THE FISH, it read. 10 CENTS. PROCEEDS BENEFIT
BASALT COUNTY YOUTH CORPS. BUSY YOUTH
MAKE HAPPY YOUTH.

Sure they do, Rambo thought. And the early bird gets the
shaft.

He peered down at the water again. It was not long before he
heard somebody walk up behind him. He did not bother to see
who it was.

"Get in the car."

Rambo concentrated on the water, "Will you look at all the fish
down there," he said. "Must be a couple of thousand. What's the
name of that big gold one? It can't be a real gold fish. Not that
big."

"Palomino trout," he heard behind him. "Get in the car."

Rambo peered further down at the water. "Must be a new
strain. I never heard of it."

"Hey, boy, I'm talking to you. Look at me."

But Rambo did not. "I used to go fishing quite a bit," he said,
peering down. "When I was young. But now most streams are
fished out or polluted. Does the town stock this one? Is that why
there's so many fish down there?"

That was why all right. The town had stocked the stream for as
long as Teasle could remember. His father often used to bring him
down and watch the workmen from the state fish hatchery stock
it. The workmen would carry pails from a truck down the slope
to the stream, set them in the water and ease the pails over to let
the fish slide out, the length of a man's hand and sleek and sometimes rainbow colored.

"Jesus, *look* at me!" Teasle said.

Rambo felt a hand grab on his sleeve. He tugged loose. "Hands off," he said, peering down at the water. Then he felt the hand grabbing at him again and this time he swung around. "I'm telling you!" he said. "Hands off!"

Teasle shrugged. "All right, play it tough if you want. That doesn't bother me none." He unhooked the handcuffs from his gun belt. "Let's have your wrists."

Rambo kept them at his sides. "I mean it. Let me be."

Teasle laughed. "You mean it?" he said and laughed. "You mean it? You don't seem to understand I mean it too. Sooner or later you're getting in that cruiser. Only question is, how much force I have to use before you do it." He rested his left hand on his pistol and smiled. "It's such a little thing, getting in the cruiser is. What do you say we don't lose our perspective?"

People walking by looked curious at them.

"You would draw that thing," Rambo said, watching Teasle's hand on the pistol. "At first I thought you were different. But now I see I've met crazy ones like you before."

"Then you're one up on me," Teasle said. "Because I've *never* met anything quite like *you* before." He stopped smiling and closed his big hand around the grip of his gun. "Move."

And that was it, Rambo decided. One of them was going to have to back down, or else Teasle was going to get hurt. Bad. He watched Teasle's hand on the holstered pistol, and he thought, You bloody stupid cop, before you pull that gun, I could snap off both your arms and legs at the joints. I could smash your Adam's apple to sauce and heave you over the rail. Then the fish would really have something to feed on.

But not for this, he suddenly told himself, not for this. Just thinking about what he could do to Teasle he managed to satisfy his anger and control himself. It was a control he had not been capable of before, and thinking about his control made him feel better too. Six months ago when he finished convalescing in the hospital, he had been unable to keep hold of himself. In a bar in Philadelphia some guy had kept pushing ahead of him to see the go-go girl take off her pants, and he had broken the guy's nose for him. A month later, in Pittsburgh, he had slit the throat of a kid who pulled a knife on him when he was sleeping one night by a lake in a park. The kid had brought a friend who tried to run, and Rambo had hunted him all through the park until he finally caught him trying to start his convertible.

No, not for this, he told himself. You're all right now.

It was his turn to smile. "O.K., let's have another ride," he said to Teasle. "But I don't know what the point is. I'm only going to walk back into town again."

6

The police station was in an old schoolhouse. And red yet, Rambo thought as Teasle drove into the parking lot at the side. He almost asked Teasle if painting the schoolhouse red was somebody's idea of a joke, but he knew that none of this was a joke, and he wondered if he should try talking himself out of it all.

You don't even like this place. It doesn't even interest you. If Teasle hadn't picked you up, you would have gone straight through on your own.

That doesn't make a difference.

The cement steps leading up to the front door of the station looked new to him, the shiny aluminum door was certainly new, and inside there was a bright white room that took up the width of the building and half the length and smelled of turpentine. The room was checkered with desks, only two of which had anybody at them, a policeman typing, and another policeman talking into the two-way radio that was along the right back wall. They both stopped when they saw him, and he waited for it to come.

"Now that's a sorry sight," the man by the typewriter said.

It never failed to come. "Sure," Rambo told him. "And now

you're supposed to say, What am I, a girl or a boy. And after that you're supposed to say, If I'm too poor to get a bath and a haircut, you'll take up a collection for me."

"It's not his looks I mind," Teasle said. "It's his mouth. Shingleton, have you anything new I ought to know about?" he asked the man by the radio.

The man sat tall and solid. He had an almost perfectly rectangular face, neat sideburns down to slightly below his ears. "Stolen car," he said.

"Who's handling it?"

"Ward."

"That'll be fine," Teasle said and turned to Rambo. "Come on then. Let's get this over."

They went across the room and down a corridor to the rear of the building. Footsteps and voices were coming out open doors on both sides, office workers in most of the rooms, policemen in the rest. The corridor was glossy white, and the turpentine smelled worse, and down at the end there was a scaffold under a dirty green part of the ceiling that had been left unpainted. Rambo read the sign that was taped to the scaffold: OUT OF WHITE PAINT BUT WE GOT MORE COMING IN TOMORROW AND WE GOT THE BLUE PAINT YOU WANT TO COVER THE RED OUTSIDE.

Then Teasle opened the door into an office at the very end of the hall, and Rambo held back a moment.

Are you absolutely sure you want to go through with this? he asked himself. It's still not too late to try and talk your way out.

Out of what? I haven't done anything wrong.

"Well, come on, get in there," Teasle said. "This is what you've been working for."

It had been a mistake not to go in there right away. Holding back at the door looked like he was afraid, and he did not want that. But now if he went inside after Teasle had ordered him, it would look like he was obeying, and he did not want that either. He went in before Teasle had another chance to order him.

The office ceiling came down close to his head, and he felt so closed in that he wanted to stoop, but he did not allow himself. The floor had a rug that was green and worn, like grass that had been trimmed too close to the earth. On the left behind a desk, there was a case of handguns. He centered on a .44 magnum and remembered it from Special Forces training camp: the most powerful handgun made, able to shoot through four inches of wood or bring down an elephant, but with a kick so great that he himself had always disliked using it.

"Sit down on the bench, boy," Teasle said. "Let's have your name."

"Just call me boy," Rambo said. The bench was along the right wall. He leaned his sleeping bag against it and sat down extremely straight and rigid.

"It's none of it funny anymore, kid. Let's have your name."

"I'm known as kid too. You can call me that too if you want."

"You're right I will," Teasle said. "I'm at the point where I'm ready to call you any damn thing I feel like."

7

The kid was more damn nuisance than he could tolerate. All he wanted was to have him out of the office so he could phone. It was four-thirty now, and figuring the time shift, it was, what, three-thirty, two-thirty, one-thirty in California. Maybe she would not be in at her sister's now. Maybe she was out having lunch with somebody. Who, he wondered. Where. That was why he was spending so much time with the kid—because he was impatient to call. You did not let your troubles interfere with your job. You kept your life at home where it belonged. If your problems made you start to rush through something, then you forced yourself to slow and do it extra well.

In this case, maybe the rule was paying off. The kid did not want to give his name, and the only reason people did not give a name was that they had something to hide and were afraid of being checked out in the fugitive files. Maybe this was more than just a kid who would not listen.

Well, he would take it slow and find out. He sat on the corner of his desk, opposite the kid on the bench, and calmly lit a cigarette. "Would you like a smoke?" he asked the kid.

"I don't smoke."

Teasle nodded and leisurely drew on the cigarette. "How be we try this again. What's your name?"

"None of your business."

Dear God, Teasle thought. In spite of himself he pushed away from the desk and took a few steps toward the kid. Slowly though, he told himself. Make it calm. "You didn't say that. I can't believe I actually heard that."

"You heard me all right. My name is my business. You haven't given me a reason to make it yours."

"I'm the Chief of Police you're talking to."

"That's not a good enough reason."

"It's the best damn reason in the world," he said, then waited for the heat to drain from his face. Quietly, "Let me have your wallet."

"I don't carry one."

"Let me have your I.D. cards."

"I don't carry them either."

"No driver's license, no social security card, no draft card, no birth certificate, no—"

"That's right," the kid cut him off.

"Don't pull that with me. Get out your I.D. cards."

Now the kid was not even bothering to look at him. He was turned toward the guncase, pointing at the medal above the line of shooting trophies. "The Distinguished Service Cross. Really gave them hell in Korea, did you?"

"O.K.," Teasle said. "On your feet."

It was the second highest medal he could get, ranking above the bronze star, silver star, Purple Heart, Distinguished Flying Medal, and Distinguished Service Medal. Only the Congressional Medal of Honor ranked above it. *To Marine Corps Master Sergeant Wilfred Lo-*

gan Teasle. For conspicuous and valiant leadership in the face of over-whelming enemy fire, his citation read. *The Choisin Reservoir Campaign. December 6, 1950.* That was when he was twenty, and he was not about to let any kid who didn't look much older mock it.

"Get on your feet. I'm sick of telling you everything twice. Get on your feet and pull out your pockets."

The kid shrugged and took his time standing. He went from one pocket of his jeans to the other, pulling them out, and there was nothing.

"You didn't pull out the pockets in your jacket," Teasle said.

"By God, you're right." When he pulled them, he came out with two dollars and twenty-three cents plus a book of matches.

"Why the matches?" Teasle said. "You told me you don't smoke."

"I need to start fires to cook on."

"But you don't have any job or money. Where do you get the food to cook?"

"What do you expect me to say? That I steal it?"

Teasle looked at the kid's sleeping bag against the side of the bench, guessing where the I.D. cards were. He untied it and threw it out unrolled on the floor. There was a clean shirt and a tooth brush. When he started feeling through the shirt, the kid said, "Hey, I spent a lot of time ironing that shirt. Be careful not to wrinkle it." And Teasle was suddenly very tired of him.

He pressed the intercom on his desk. "Shingleton, you had a look at this kid when he came through. I want you to radio his description to the state police. Say I'd like him identified the quickest they can. While you're at it, check if he matches any description we have in the files. He has no job and no money, but he sure looks well fed. I want to know why."

"So you're determined to push this thing," the kid said.

"That's wrong. I'm not the one who's pushing."

8

The Justice of the Peace had an air conditioner. It hummed a bit and rattled every so often and made the office so cold that Rambo had to shiver. The man behind the desk was bundled in an over-sized blue sweater. His name was Dobzyn, the sign on the door said. He was chewing tobacco, and as soon as he took a look at Rambo coming in, he stopped chewing.

"Well, I'll be," he said and rolled his swivel chair squeaking back from the desk. "When you phoned, Will, you should have told me that the circus was in town."

Always it came, some remark. Always. This whole business was getting out of hand, and he knew that he had better give in soon, that they could make a lot of trouble for him if he did not. But here the crap was coming his way again, they would not let up, and Jesus, he was just not going to take it.

"Listen, son," Dobzyn was saying. "I really have to ask you a question." His face was very round. When he spoke, he slipped his chewing tobacco against one cheek, and that side of his face bulged out. "I see kids on the TV demonstrating and rioting and all, and——"

"I'm no demonstrator."

"What I have to know, doesn't that hair get itchy down the back of your neck?"

Always they asked the same. "It did at first."

Dobzyn scratched his eyebrow and thought about that answer. "Yeah, I suppose you can get used to just about anything if you put your mind to it. But what about the beard? Doesn't that get itchy in this heat?"

"Sometimes."

"Then what possessed you to let it grow?"

"I have a rash on my face and I'm not supposed to shave."

"Like I have a pain in my rear-end and I'm not supposed to wipe it," Teasle said by the door.

"Now wait a second, Will. It may be he's telling the truth."

Rambo could not resist. "I'm not."

"Then what did you say all that for?"

"I get tired of people asking me why I grew the beard."

"Why *did* you grow the beard?"

"I have a rash on my face and I'm not supposed to shave."

Dobzyn looked like he had been slapped in the face. The air conditioner whirred and rattled. "Well, well," he said quietly, extending the words. "I guess I walked into that one. Didn't I, Will? The laugh's on me." He tried a brief chuckle. "I walked right into it. I surely did. My, yes." He chewed on his tobacco. "Just what's the charge, Will?"

"There's two of them. Vagrancy and resisting arrest. But those are just to hold him while I find out if he's wanted anywhere. My guess is theft someplace."

"We'll take up the vagrancy first. You guilty, son?"

Rambo said he wasn't.

"Do you have a job? Do you have more than ten dollars?"

Rambo said he didn't.

"Then there's no way around it, son. You're a vagrant. That'll cost you five days in jail or fifty dollars fine. Which will it be?"

"I just told you I don't have ten, so where the hell would I get fifty?"

"This is a court of law," Dobzyn said, leaning suddenly forward in his chair. "I will not tolerate abusive language in my court. One more outburst and I'll charge you with contempt." He was a moment before he settled back in his chair and started to chew again, thinking. "Even as it is, I don't see how I can keep your attitude out of mind when I'm sentencing you. Like this matter of resisting arrest."

"Not guilty."

"I haven't asked you yet. Wait until I ask you. What's the story on this resisting arrest, Will?"

"I picked him up for hitchhiking and did him a favor and gave him a lift to outside town. Figured it would be best for everybody if he kept right on moving." Teasle leaned one hip on the creaky rail that separated the office from the waiting-space near the door. "But he came back."

"I had a right."

"So I drove him out of town again and he came back again and when I told him to get in the cruiser, he refused. I finally had to threaten force before he'd listen."

"You think I got in the car because I was afraid of you?"

"He won't tell me his name."

"Why should I?"

"Claims he has no I.D. cards."

"Why the hell do I need any?"

"Listen I can't sit here all night while you two have it out with each other," Dobzyn said. "My wife is sick, and I was supposed to be home to cook dinner for the kids at five. I'm late already. Thirty days in jail or two hundred dollars fine. What'll it be, son?"

"Two hundred? Christ, I just told you I don't have more than ten."

"Then it's thirty-*five* days in jail," Dobzyn said and rose out of his chair, unbuttoning his sweater. "I was about to cancel the five days for vagrancy, but your attitude is intolerable. I have to go. I'm late."

The air conditioner began to rattle more than it was humming, and Rambo could not tell if he was shivering from cold or rage. "Hey, Dobzyn," he said, catching him as he went by. *"I'm still waiting for you to ask me if I'm guilty of resisting arrest."*

9

The doors on both sides of the corridor were closed now. He passed the painters' scaffold near the end of the hall, heading for Teasle's office.

"No, this time you go this way," Teasle said. He pointed to the last door on the right, a door with bars in a little window at the top, and reached with a key to unlock it before he saw that the door was already open a quarter-inch. Shaking his head disgustedly at that, he pushed the door the rest of the way open and motioned Rambo through to a stairwell with an iron bannister and cement steps going down and fluorescent lights in the ceiling. As soon as Rambo was in, Teasle came through behind him, locking the door, and they walked down, their footsteps scraping on the cement stairs, echoing.

Rambo heard the spray before he reached the basement. The cement floor was wet and reflected the fluorescent lights, and down at the far end a thin policeman was hosing the floor of a cell, water running out between the bars and down a drain. When he saw Teasle and Rambo, he screwed the nozzle tight; the water flared out in a wide arc and abruptly stopped.

Teasle's voice echoed. "Galt. Why is that upstairs door unlocked again?"

"Did I...? We don't have any more prisoners. The last one just
woke up, and I let him go."

"It doesn't matter if we have prisoners or not. If you get in
the habit of leaving it open when we're empty, then you might
start forgetting to lock it when there's somebody down here. So I
want the door locked regardless. I don't like to say this—it may
be tough getting used to a new job and a new routine, but if you
don't soon learn to be careful, I might have to look for somebody
else."

Rambo was as cold as he had been in Dobzyn's office, shivering. The lights in the ceiling were too close to his head; even so,
the place seemed dark. Iron and cement. Christ, he should never
have let Teasle bring him down. Walking across from the courthouse, he should have broken Teasle and escaped. Anything, even
being on the run, was better than thirty-five days down here.

What the hell else did you expect? he told himself. You asked
for this, didn't you? You wouldn't back off.

Damn right I wouldn't. And I still won't. Just because I'll be
locked up, doesn't mean I'm finished. I'll fight this as far as it goes.
By the time he's ready to let me out, he'll be glad to be rid of me.

Sure you'll fight. Sure. What a laugh. Take a look at yourself.
Already you're shaking. Already you know what this place re-
minds you of. Two days in that cramped cell and you'll be pissing
down your pantlegs.

"You've got to understand I can't stay in there." He could not
stop himself. "The wet. I can't stand being closed in where it's
wet." The hole, he was thinking, his scalp alive. The bamboo
grate over the top. Water seeping through the dirt, the walls
crumbling, the inches of slimy muck he had to try sleeping on.

Tell him, for God's sake.

Screw, you mean beg him.

Sure, now when it was too late, now the kid was coming around and trying to talk himself out of this. Teasle could not get over the needlessness of it all, how the kid had actually tried his damndest to work himself down here. "Just be thankful it *is* wet," he told the kid. "That we hose everything down. We get weekend drunks in here, and come Mondays when we kick them out, they've been sick up the walls and all over the place."

He glanced at the cells, and the water on the floor made them look clean, sparkling. "You may be careless with that door upstairs, Galt," he told him. "But you sure did a job on those cells. Do me a favor will you, go up and get some bedding and an outfit for this kid? You," he told the kid, "I guess the middle cell is fine. Go in, take off your boots, your pants, your jacket. Leave on your socks, your underwear, your sweatshirt. Take off any jewelry, any chain around your neck, any watch—. Galt, what are you looking at?"

"Nothing."

"What about the gear I sent you for?"

"I was just looking. I'll get it." He hurried up the stairs.

"Aren't you going to tell him again to lock the door?" the kid said.

"No need."

Teasle listened to the rattle of the door being unlocked. He waited, then heard Galt lock the door after him. "Start with the boots," he told the kid.

So what else did he expect? The kid took off his jacket.

"There you go again. I told you start with the boots."

"The floor is wet."

"And I told you get in there."

"I'm not going in there any sooner than I have to." He folded his jacket, squinted at the water on the floor, and set the jacket on the stairs. He put his boots beside it, took off his jeans, folded them and put them on top of the jacket.

"What's that big scar above your left knee?" Teasle said. "What happened?"

The kid did not answer.

"It looks like a bullet scar," Teasle said. "Where did you get it?"

"My socks are wet on this floor."

"Take them off then."

Teasle had to step back to keep from being hit by them.

"Now take off your sweatshirt," he said.

"What for? Don't tell me you're still looking for my I.D. cards."

"Let's just say I like a thorough search, that I want to see if you've anything hidden under your arms."

"Like what? Dope? Grass?"

"Who knows? It's happened."

"Well not me. I gave up that stuff a long time ago. Hell, it's against the law."

"Very funny. Just take off your sweatshirt."

For once the kid did what he was told. As slow as he could, of course. His stomach muscles showed tight, and there were three straight scars across his chest.

"Where did *they* come from?" Teasle said surprised. "Knife scars. What the hell have you been up to anyway?"

The kid squinted at the lights and did not answer. He had a large triangular patch of black hair on his chest. Two of the scars cut through it.

"Hold up your arms and turn around," Teasle said.

"That isn't necessary."

"If there was a quicker way to search you, I would sure have found it. Turn around."

There were dozens of small jagged scars across the kid's back.

"Jesus, what's going on here?" Teasle said. "Those are lash marks. Who's been lashing you?"

The kid still did not answer.

"That's going to be some interesting report the state police sends back on you."

He hesitated: now came the part he hated.

"All right, pull down your shorts."

The kid looked at him. And looked at him.

"Don't give me any bashful looks," he said, disliking this. "Everybody has to go through this, and everybody is still a virgin when I'm finished. Just pull the shorts down. That's enough. Stop right there at your knees. I don't want to see anymore of you than I have to. Hold yourself up down there. I want to see if there's anything hidden. Not two hands. One. Just your fingertips."

Keeping a distance, Teasle stooped and peered at the kid's groin from several angles. The testes were bunched up close under. Now came the worst part of all. He would have told somebody like Galt to do it, but he did not like passing on dirty jobs. "Turn around and bend over."

The kid really looked at him. "Get your jollies off somebody else. I won't put up with anymore of this."

"Yes you will. Aside from what you might have hid up it, I'm not interested in your rear end whatsoever. Just do what you're told. Now reach back and spread your cheeks. Come on, it's not a sight I enjoy. There. You know, when I worked in Louisville, I once had a prisoner with a three-inch knife in a leather case shoved up himself. It always beat me how he could sit down."

Upstairs Galt was unlocking the door and opening it.

"O.K., you're clean," Teasle said to the kid. "You can pull up your shorts."

Teasle listened for Galt to close and lock the upstairs door, and then Galt came scraping his shoes down the cement steps. He was carrying a pair of faded denim coveralls, a thin mattress, a rubberized sheet, a gray blanket. He looked at the kid standing there in his shorts, and he said to Teasle, "Ward just called in about that stolen car. He found it in the stone quarry north of here."

"Tell him to stay put and tell Shingleton to call the state police for a fingerprint crew."

"Shingleton already called them."

Galt went into the cell, and the kid started to follow, his bare feet making a slapping noise in the water on the floor.

"Not yet," Teasle told him.

"Well make up your mind. First you want me in there. Now you don't want me in there. I wish you knew what you wanted."

"What I want is for you to go down to that shower at the end. And I want you to take off your shorts and wash yourself good before you put on the clean uniform. Be sure to wash that hair of yours. I want it clean before I have to touch it."

"What do you mean touch it?"

"I have to cut it."

"What are you talking about? You're not cutting my hair. You're not going anywhere near my head with any scissors."

"I told you everybody has to go through this. Everybody from car thieves to drunks gets searched like you, and takes a shower, and gets any long hair cut. The mattress we're giving you is clean, and we want it back clean without any ticks or fleas from where you've been sleeping in sheds and fields and God knows where."

"You're not cutting it."

"With a little encouragement I could arrange for you to spend another thirty-five days here. You wanted in damn bad enough. Now you're going through with the rest of it. Why don't you just give in and make things easy for the two of us? Galt, why don't you go up and get the scissors, shaving cream, and razor?"

"I'll only agree to the shower," the kid said.

"That'll be fine for now. One thing at a time."

As the kid walked slowly down to the shower stall, Teasle looked again at the lash marks on his back. It was almost six o'clock. The state police would be reporting soon.

Thinking about the time, he counted back to three o'clock in California, unsure now whether to call. If she had changed her mind, she would already have been in touch with him. So if he did phone, he would only be putting pressure on and driving her farther away.

All the same, he had to try. Maybe later when he was done with the kid, he would call and just talk without mentioning the divorce.

Who are you fooling? The first thing you'll ask her is whether she's changed her mind.

Inside the stall the kid turned on the spray.

10

The hole was ten feet deep, barely wide enough for him to sit with his legs outstretched. In the evenings they sometimes came with flashlights to peer down at him through the bamboo grate. Shortly after each dawn they removed the grate and hoisted him up to do their chores. It was the same jungle camp they had tortured him in, the same thatched huts and rich green mountains. For a reason he did not at first understand, they had treated his wounds while he was unconscious: the slashes in his chest where the officer had repeatedly punctured him with a slender knife and drawn the blade across, grating against his ribs; the lacerations in his back where the officer had crept up behind, suddenly lashing. Lashing. His leg was badly infected, but when they had opened fire on his unit and captured him, no bone had been hit, only thigh muscle, and eventually he was able to limp around.

Now they did not question him anymore, did not threaten him, did not even talk to him. They always made gestures to show him his work: dumping slops, digging latrines, building cookfires. He guessed their silence toward him was punishment for pretending not to understand their language. Still, at night in his hole, he heard their conversations dimly and from the scraps of words he was satisfied that even while unconscious he had not told them what they wanted to know. After the ambush and his capture, the rest of his unit must have gone on to its objective, because now he heard about the exploded factories and how this camp was one of many in the mountains watching for other American guerrillas.

Soon they had him doing more chores, heavier ones, feeding him less, making him work longer, sleep less. He came to understand. Too much time had gone by for him to know where his team would be. Since he could not give them information, they had fixed his wounds so they could play with him some more and find out how much work he could take before it killed him. Well, he would show them a long wait for that. There was not much they could do to him that his instructors had not already put him through. Special Forces school and the five miles they made him run before breakfast, the ten miles of running *after* breakfast, heaving up the meal as he ran but careful not to break ranks because the penalty was ten extra miles for anyone who broke ranks to be sick. Climbing high towers, shouting his roster number to the jumpmaster, leaping, legs together, feet braced, elbows tucked in, yelling "One thousand, two thousand, three thousand, four thousand" as he dropped, stomach rising to his throat, spring-harness jerking him up just before the ground. Thirty pushups for every lapse in the routine, plus a pushup shouted "For the Airborne!" Another thirty pushups if the shout was weak, plus another one "For the Airborne!" In the mess hall, on the toilet, everywhere, the officers waited, abruptly yelling "Hit it," and he would have to snap down in a jumping pose, shouting "One thousand, two thousand, three thousand, four thousand," snapping to attention till dismissed, then shouting "Clear, sir," running off shouting "Airborne! Airborne! Airborne!" Day-jumps into forests. Night-jumps into swamps, to live there for a week, his only equipment a knife. Classes in weapons, explosives, surveillance, interrogation, hand-to-hand combat. A field of cattle, he and the other students holding knives. Bowels and stomachs strewn across the field, animals still alive and screeching. Hollowed carcasses and the order to crawl in, to wrap the carcass around him, to wash himself in blood.

That was the point of becoming a Green Beret. He could take anything. But each day in the jungle camp he grew weaker, and at last he was afraid that his body could not keep on. More work, more heavy work, less food, less sleep. What he saw went gray and blurred; he stumbled, moaning, talking to himself. After three days without food, they tossed a snake flopping into his hole to squirm in the dirt, and they watched as he twisted off its head and ate the body raw. He only managed to keep a little of it down. Not until later—a few minutes, a few days, the time was all the same—did he wonder if the snake was poisonous or not. That and the bugs he found in his hole and the chunks of garbage they occasionally threw down at him, that was all that gave him life the next few days—or weeks, he could not tell. Hauling a dead tree through the jungle back to camp, he was permitted to pick fruit and eat it, and by nightfall he had dysentery. He lay in a stupor in his hole, mired in his excrement, hearing them talk about his foolishness.

But he had not been foolish. In his delirium his mind seemed better than it had been since his capture, and the dysentery was intentional. He had eaten just enough to catch it mildly so the next day when they hauled him up he could pretend his cramps were more severe than they were actually, so he could collapse while dragging the dead trees back to camp. Maybe they would not make him work for a while then. Maybe his guard would leave him in the jungle and go for help to carry him to camp, and by the time the guard returned, he would have been able to escape.

But then he realized that his mind was not better at all. He had eaten too much fruit, and the cramps were worse than he expected, and once he could no longer work, the guard would likely shoot him, and even if he did escape, how long could he last, how far could he get, starved and half-dead and diarrheic? He could not remember if he realized all this before or after. Everything became confused, and suddenly he was on his own, crashing through the jungle, collapsing into a stream. The next thing he knew, he was crawling through ferns up a slope, standing at the top, falling onto level grass, standing again and straining to get across the level, then crawling up another slope, at the top no longer able to stand, only to crawl. The mountain tribes, he was thinking. Get to a tribe, was all he could think.

Somebody was making him drink. The soldiers had caught him he was sure, and he fought to break away, but somebody was holding him down and making him swallow. It wasn't soldiers, it couldn't be: they let him break away, stumbling through the jungle. Sometimes he thought he was back in his hole, only dreaming he was loose. Other times he thought he was still dropping from the plane with the rest of his team, his chute not opening, the mountains looming up. He woke sprawled beneath some bushes, he discovered he was running, he found himself flat out on a rock. When the sun began to set, he took a bearing from it and headed south. Then he was afraid that he had mixed up time again, that he had lain unconscious through the night, confusing sunrise with sunset and taking the wrong direction, north instead of south. He stared and the sun kept going down and he relaxed. Then it was night and when he couldn't see anymore he collapsed.

He came to in the morning, braced between boughs high in a tree. When or how he had dragged himself up he could not recall, but he would have been dead if he hadn't: a man alone, unconscious, would not have survived the night animals that hunted the jungle. He stayed in the tree all day, twisting branches here and there to give himself better cover, sleeping, slowly eating the dried meat and the rice cakes that he was surprised to find tied to his neck in a sack made of the rags he wore. The people who had held him down and made him swallow, they must have been villagers, this food had to be theirs. He saved the last of it for night when he climbed down the tree and, taking his direction from the setting sun, continued heading south. But why had they helped him? Was it because of the way he looked that they had decided to give him a chance?

He fled only by night after that, using the stars as his compass, eating roots, bark, the cress in streams. Often in the dark he heard soldiers close by and lay still in the undergrowth until the sounds were gone. Often his delirium went away and then returned more confused than ever, making him imagine the snap of an automatic rifle slide pulled back, making him roll into the brush before he recognized that the snap was only from a branch that he himself had snapped.

In two weeks the rain started, coming down forever. Mud. Wood rot. Showers streaming down so thick that he could hardly breathe. He kept on, dazed by the pelt of the rain, infuriated by the suck of the mud, by the wet bushes clinging to him. He could not tell which way was south anymore—the night clouds would break and he would take a bearing from a star, but then the clouds would close up and he'd have to travel blind, and when the clouds once more opened, he'd discover he had lost direction. One morning he found he had wandered in a circle, and after that he travelled only in the day. He had to go slower, more carefully, to keep from being spotted. When clouds obscured the sun, he aimed toward far-off landmarks, a mountain peak or a towering tree. And each day, every day, the rains came.

He fell out of the forest, staggering across a field, and somebody shot at him. He stumbled to the ground, crawling back to the trees. Another shot. People running through the grass. "I told you identify yourself," a man was saying. "If it weren't I saw you didn't have a weapon, I'd have killed you. Stand the hell up and identify yourself."

Americans. He started laughing. He could not stop laughing. They held him in the hospital for a month before his hysteria left him. His drop into the north had been at the start of December, and it was now the start of May they told him. How long he had been a prisoner he didn't know. How long he had been on the run he didn't know. But between then and now he had covered the distance between his drop area and this American base in the south, three hundred and ninety miles. And what had started him laughing was that he must have been in American territory for days, some of the soldiers he had heard in the night and hid from must have been Americans.

11

He put off going back out there as long as he could. He knew he would not be able to stand it when Teasle came touching the scissors to his head and cutting. The spray of water on him, he glanced out the shower, and Galt was suddenly at the bottom of the stairs, holding the scissors and a can of shaving cream and a straight razor. His stomach tightened. He watched frantically as Teasle pointed at a desk and chair by the bottom of the stairs, saying something to Galt that came muffled through the noise of the spray. Galt brought the chair around in front of the desk, took some newspapers from inside the desk and spread them under the chair. He was not long doing it at all. Directly Teasle came toward him in the stall, close enough for him to hear.

"Turn off the water," Teasle said.

Rambo pretended not to hear.

Teasle came farther down. "Turn off the water," he repeated.

Rambo went on washing his arms and chest. The soap was a big yellow cake that smelled strongly of disinfectant. He switched to soaping his legs. It was the third time he had soaped them. Teasle nodded and walked out of sight to the left of the

stall where there must have been a shut-off valve because in
a second the water quit spraying. Rambo's legs and shoulders
tightened, water dripping from him onto the hollow metal bottom of the stall, and then Teasle was in sight again, holding a
towel.

"There's no sense in putting this off," Teasle said. "You'll just
catch cold."

Rambo had no choice. He stepped out slowly. He knew that
if he didn't Teasle would reach in for him, and he didn't want
Teasle touching him. He dried himself repeatedly with the towel.
In the cold the towel made prickle marks on his arms. His testicles
felt exposed.

"Dry yourself anymore and you'll wear out the towel," Teasle
said.

He went on drying himself. Teasle reached to guide him toward the chair, and Rambo side-stepped, keeping Teasle and Galt
in front of him as he backed over to the chair. Without a pause
everything built up in quick sequence.

First Teasle touched the scissors to the side of his head, snipping, and Rambo tried, but could not stop himself from flinching.

"Hold still," Teasle said. "You'll jerk against the scissors and
maybe hurt yourself."

Next Teasle snipped off a large clump of hair, and Rambo's left
ear was cool and unprotected in the damp basement air. "You've
got more up here than I guessed," Teasle said and dropped the
clump onto the newspaper spread out on the floor. "Your head's
going to weigh a lot less in a minute." The newspaper was turning
gray, soaking up water.

Then Teasle snipped off more, and Rambo had to flinch again.
Teasle stepped back of him, and Rambo tensed from not being
able to see what was going on behind. He swung his head to see,

and Teasle pressed him forward. Rambo slipped his head from under the hand.

But Teasle snipped the scissors to his head again, and Rambo flinched again, and hair caught in the swivel of the scissors, yanking sharply at his scalp. He could not bear it anymore. He surged from the chair and spun around to Teasle.

"Get away."

"Sit down in that chair."

"You're not cutting anymore. You want my hair cut, you get a barber down here."

"It's after six. There aren't any barbers working now. You're not putting on that uniform until your hair is cut."

"Then I'll stay like this."

"You'll sit on the chair. Galt, go up and bring Shingleton. I've made as many allowances as I can. We'll cut his hair so fast it'll be like we used sheep shears."

Galt looked happy to get away. Rambo listened to him unlock the door at the top of the stairs, the rattle echoing down. It was all happening even faster now. He did not want to hurt anyone, but he knew that was coming, he could feel his anger spreading out of control. Instantly a man was rushing down the stairs, Galt half a flight behind. Shingleton. He seemed huge now that he was standing, his head up near the bright lights in the ceiling. The bones above his eyes and around the bottom of his face stuck out in the glare. He looked at Rambo, and Rambo felt twice as naked.

"Trouble?" Shingleton said to Teasle. "I hear you have trouble."

"No, but *he* does," Teasle said. "You and Galt sit him on the chair."

Shingleton came right over. Galt hesitated, then he came over too.

"I don't know what this is all about," Shingleton said to

Rambo. "But I'm reasonable. I'll give you a choice. Do you walk, or do I carry you?"

"I think you'd better not touch me." He was determined to keep control. There would be just the next five minutes and the continual touch of the scissors, and then it would be over, he would be all right.

He started toward the chair, his feet slick in the water, and behind him Shingleton said, "Good God, where did you get all the scars on your back?"

"In the war." That was a weakness. He should not have answered.

"Oh sure. Sure you did. In which army?"

Rambo almost killed him right then.

But Teasle took another snip at his hair and startled him. There were clumps of long hair scattered across the gray wet newspaper, some of them tangled around Rambo's bare feet. He expected Teasle to go on snipping at his head. He braced himself for it. But then Teasle brought the scissors too close to his right eye, cutting his beard, and Rambo instinctively dipped his head to the left.

"Hold still," Teasle said. "Shingleton, you and Galt hold him steady."

Shingleton pulled his head up straight, and Rambo slammed his arm away. Teasle snipped again at his beard, catching it in the scissors, pinching his cheek.

"Christ." He squirmed. They were too close. They were crowding him so he wanted to scream.

"This could go on all night," Teasle said. "Galt, go get the shaving cream and the razor off the desk."

Rambo squirmed. "You're not shaving me. You're not coming near me with that razor."

Then Galt was there handing it to Teasle, and Rambo watched the long blade flash in the lights, and remembered the enemy officer slicing his chest, and that was the end. He broke, grabbing the razor and standing, pushing them away. He fought the impulse to attack. Not here. Not in the goddamned police station. All he wanted was the razor away from them. But Galt was white-faced, eyes on the razor, and he was fumbling for his gun.

"No, Galt!" Teasle shouted. "No guns!"

But Galt continued fumbling for his gun, and awkwardly he had it out. He must really have been new on the job: he looked as though he could not believe he was actually raising the gun, his hand shaking, squeezing on the trigger, and Rambo slashed the razor straight across his stomach. Galt peered stupidly down at the neat deep slash across his belly, blood soaking his shirt and pouring down his pants, organs bulging out like a pumped-up inner tube through a slit in a tire. He took a finger and tried poking the organs back in, but they kept bulging out, blood soaking his pants and running out his cuffs onto the floor as he made a funny little noise in his throat and toppled across the chair, upsetting it.

Rambo was already charging up the stairs. He had looked at Teasle and Shingleton, and the one was over by the cells, the other by the wall, and he knew they were too far apart for him to slash both of them before at least one had time to pull his handgun and fire. Even as he rounded the landing halfway up the stairs, the first shot came from behind him, whacking into the landing's concrete wall.

The top half of the stairs was at an angle the reverse of the lower half, so he was out of their sight now, over their heads, pounding up toward the door to the main hall. He heard shouts below him and then running on the first half of the stairs The door. He had forgotten about the door. Teasle had warned Galt about making sure to lock it. He rushed up, praying that Galt had been in too big a hurry when he came back with Shingleton, hearing "Stop!" down behind him and a gun being cocked as he wrenched the handle and pulled at the door and sweet Jesus, it came open. He was just ducking around the corner when two shots cracked into the bright white wall across from him. He heaved on the painters' scaffold, and the thing came crashing down in front of the door, planks and paint cans and steel poles piling together, barring the way.

"What's going on?" somebody said in the hall behind him, and he turned to a policeman standing surprised, staring at Rambo naked, reaching for his gun. Four quick steps and Rambo chopped the flat edge of his hand across the bridge of the guy's nose and caught the gun dropping from the guy's hand as he fell. Somebody from downstairs was pushing at the wreck of the scaffold. Rambo fired twice, hearing Teasle cry out, hoping the shots would hold back Teasle long enough for him to reach the front door.

He made it there, firing once again at the scaffold before he burst outside naked into the hot glare of the evening sun. An old woman on the sidewalk screamed; a man slowed his car and stared. Rambo leapt down the front steps onto the sidewalk, past the old woman screaming, toward a man in work clothes going by on a motorcycle. The man made the mistake of slowing down to look, because by the time he decided to speed up, Rambo had got to him and lunged him off the cycle. The man hit the street headfirst, his yellow crash helmet scraping across the pavement. Rambo swung onto the cycle, his bare hips on the hot black seat, and the cycle roared off, with him firing his last three bullets at Teasle who had just rushed out the front door of the station and then ducked back in when he saw Rambo aiming. Rambo raced the cycle down past the courthouse, weaving, zigzagging to throw off Teasle's aim. Ahead people were standing on a corner, looking, and he hoped the risk of hitting them would keep Teasle from shooting. He heard shouts behind him, shouts ahead of him from the people on the corner. One man came running off the corner to stop him, but Rambo kicked him away and then he was whipping left around the corner, and for now he was safe and he really got the cycle going.

12

Six bullets, Teasle counted. The kid's gun was empty. He charged outside squinting in the sun just in time to see the kid disappearing round the corner. Shingleton had his gun aimed; Teasle yanked it down.

"Christ, don't you see all those people?"

"I could've had him!"

"You could've had more than him!" He ran back in the station, swinging open the front door, three bullet holes in the aluminum screen. "Get in here! Check Galt and Preston! Phone a doctor!" He was running across the room to the two-way radio, astonished that Shingleton had tried firing. The guy was so efficient in the office, always second-guessing; now, with no routine for this kind of trouble, he was stupidly acting on impulse.

The screen door whacked shut as Shingleton rushed in and down the hall; Teasle jabbed at a switch on the radio, talking fast into the microphone. His hands were shaking; his bowels felt full of loose hot waste. "Ward! Where the hell are you, Ward?" he called into the radio, but Ward wasn't answering, and then at last

Teasle had him, telling him what happened, figuring his tactics. "He knows Center Road will take him out of town! He's headed west in that direction! Cut him off!"

Shingleton came rushing around the hall corner into the front room, over to Teasle. "Galt. He's dead. God, his guts are hanging out," he blurted as he came. He swallowed, trying to catch his breath. "Preston's alive. I don't know for how long. *He's got blood coming out his eyes.*"

"Snap up! Phone an ambulance! A doctor!" Teasle jabbed another switch on the radio. His hands wouldn't stop shaking. His bowels felt warmer, looser. "State police," he called quickly into the microphone. "Madison to state police. Emergency." They didn't answer. He called louder.

"I'm not deaf, Madison," a man's voice crackled. "What's your trouble?"

"Jailbreak. One officer dead," he told him hurriedly, hating to waste time reporting what had happened. Requesting roadblocks. The voice was instantly alert.

Shingleton put down the phone. Teasle hadn't even heard him dial. "The ambulance is on its way."

"Phone me Orval Kellerman." Teasle jabbed another switch, calling another cruiser, ordering it after the kid.

Shingleton had already dialed again. Thank God he was all right now. "Kellerman's outside. I've got his wife. She won't let me talk to him."

Teasle took the phone. "Mrs. Kellerman, it's Wilfred. I need Orval in a hurry."

"Wilfred?" Her voice was thin and brittle. "What a surprise, Wilfred. We haven't heard from you in so long." Why didn't she speak faster? "We were meaning to come around and tell you how sorry we were about Anna leaving?"

He had to cut her off. "Mrs. Kellerman, I've got to speak to Orval. It's important."

"Dear, I'm awfully sorry. He's outside working with the dogs, and you know I can't disturb him when he's working with the dogs."

"You've got to ask him to the phone. *Please*. Believe me, it's important."

He heard her breathing. "All right I'll ask him, but I can't promise he'll come in. You know how he is when he's working the dogs."

He heard her set the phone down, and quickly he lit a cigarette. Fifteen years he had been a policeman and he had never lost a prisoner and he had never had a partner killed. He wanted to smash the kid's face against cement.

"What did he have to do it for?" he said to Shingleton. "It's fucking crazy. He comes around looking for trouble, and in one afternoon he goes from vagrancy to murder. Hey, are you all right? Sit down and put your head between your knees."

"I've never seen a man slashed before. Galt. I had lunch with him for crissake."

"Doesn't matter how many times you see it. I must have watched fifty guys bayonetted in Korea, and I never kept from feeling sick. One man I knew from Louisville, twenty years on the force. He went to check out a knifing in a bar one night, and there was so much blood mixed in with the beer on the floor he had a heart attack and died trying to make it back to the cruiser."

He heard somebody picking up the phone on the other end. Please let it be Orval.

"So what is it, Will? This better be as important as you say."

It *was* him. Orval had been his father's best friend, and the three of them used to go out hunting together every Saturday of the season. Then, after Teasle's father had been killed, Orval had become a second father to him. He was retired now, but he was in better shape than men half as young, and he had the best-trained pack of hounds in the county.

"Orval, we just had a jailbreak here. I don't have time to explain, but it's a kid we're after, and he's killed one of my men, and I don't think he'll stay on the roads with the state police after him. I'm positive he'll head for the mountains, and I'm hoping like hell that you're in the mood to give those dogs of yours the run of their lives."

13

Rambo roared the bike down Center Road. Wind was stinging his face and chest, his eyes were watering in the wind, and he was afraid he would have to slow to see what was ahead. Cars were stopping abruptly, drivers staring out their windows at him naked on the cycle. People all along the street were turning at him, pointing. A siren started far behind him. He revved the cycle up to sixty, racing through a red light, barely able to swerve in time to miss a big oil truck lumbering across the intersection. Another siren started far to his left. There was no way a cycle could outrun police cars. But a cycle could go where police cars couldn't: the mountains.

The street dipped sharply and then rose long uphill, and Rambo sped up it, hearing the sirens. The one on his left had swung over to join the one behind him. He hit the top of the hill so fast that the cycle left the pavement, jolting back down, forcing him to slow and catch his balance. Then he was racing again.

He passed the YOU ARE NOW LEAVING MADISON sign, passed the ditch where he had eaten his hamburgers that afternoon. The fields of brown corn swept off on both sides, and the sirens were closer, and the mountains were off to the right. He swerved that way onto a dirt road, almost spilling when he turned sharply to miss a dairy truck. The driver leaned out his window, shouting at him.

Now he was throwing up dust behind him, holding his speed at fifty to keep from sliding on the loose gravel. The sirens were behind him to the right, then directly behind him. They were coming too fast. If he stayed on this dirt road, he would never lose them in time to get to the mountains; he had to leave this road for someplace they could not go. He dodged to the left through an open gate down a narrow wagon road, its ruts deep and yellow in the ground. The corn remained on both sides, the mountains were still off to the right, and he was searching for a way to get over to them. The sirens louder, he reached the end of the corn-fields, turning right onto a field of wilted grass, the cycle heaving on the uneven ground, dipping and rising, whipping through the grass. But the police cars would still be able to chase him this way, and then he heard their sirens louder yet, directly behind him again.

A stout wooden fence ahead. He sped closer, frantic from the sirens, seeing cattle. What must have been a hundred. They were in this field, but they were moving out ahead of him, ambling through an open gate in the fence and up a slope toward trees. The roar of his cycle started them galloping before he got to them, Jersey brown, bellowing, heaving three abreast through the open gate and up the slope, their milk sacks swinging full. They loomed larger the closer he came behind them, scattering, hooves thundering as he pushed through the gate with the last of them and raced up the slope. It was steep, and he had to lean forward to keep the front wheel from tipping up. Past one tree, then another, the mountains close, and then he was off the slope, speeding onto level ground. He leapt the bike over a narrow stream, almost upsetting on the other bank. But the mountains were wonderfully close now, and he steadied the bike and revved the throttle to its limit. Ahead a line of trees, then thick forest, rocks, underbrush. At last he saw what he was looking for—a draw between two slopes up into the rocky hills—and he steered that way as the sirens began dying close behind him.

That meant the cruisers had stopped. The police would be jumping out now, aiming at him. He concentrated on the draw. A crack of a gun, bullet zipping past his head, whunking into a tree. He bore fast into scattered trees, zigzagging toward the draw. Another crack of a gun, but the bullet nowhere close, and then he was into thick forest, out of sight up into the draw. Thirty feet ahead a tangle of rocks and upturned trees blocked his path, and he slid off the cycle, letting it roll crashing into the rocks. He scrambled up the dense slope, sharp branches digging everywhere into him. There would be more police after him. A lot more. Soon. At least he would have a little time to climb high into the mountains before they came. He would head for Mexico. He would hole up in Mexico in a little coast town and swim every day in the sea. But he had better not ever see that sonofabitch Teasle again. He had promised himself that he was through hurting people, and now that sonofabitch had made him kill once more, and if Teasle kept pushing, Rambo was determined to give back a fight Teasle would wish to God he had never started.

PART TWO

1

Teasle did not have much time; he needed to get his men organized and into the woods before the state police. He swerved the cruiser off the wagon road onto the grassland, racing over the tracks the two police cars and the kid's motorcycle had made in the grass, toward the wood fence at the end of the field, toward the open gate. Next to him, Shingleton had his hands braced against the dashboard, the cruiser heaving and lurching across the field, potholes so deep that the car's heavy frame was crashing down past its springs onto the axles.

"The gate's too narrow," Shingleton warned him. "You'll never get through."

"The others did."

He braked suddenly, slowing through the gate, an inch to spare on his side, then speeding up the steep slope toward the two police cars that were parked a quarter-way from the top. They must have stalled there: when he reached them, the slope angled so high that his motor started missing. He wrenched the gearshift into first and floored the accelerator, feeling the rear wheels dig into the grass, the cruiser rocketing toward the summit.

The deputy Ward was up on the level, waiting, tinted red from the swollen sun that was already glaring halfway down the mountains to the left. His shoulders sloped forward, and he walked with his stomach a little forward, his gun belt high on his waist. He was over to the car before Teasle had it stopped.

"This way," he said, pointing toward the draw inside the line of trees. "Be careful of the stream. Lester already fell in."

Crickets were sounding by the stream. Teasle was just out of the car when he heard a motor down near the wagon road. He looked quickly, hoping it wasn't the state police.

"Orval."

An old Volkswagen van, it, too, flooded with red from the sun, was rumbling across the grassland at the bottom. It stopped at the base, not built to make the climb his own car had, and Orval got out, tall and thin, a policeman with him. Teasle became afraid the dogs were not in the van; he could not hear them yelping. He knew Orval had them trained so well that they only barked when they were supposed to. But he could not help worrying that they were silent now because Orval had not brought them.

Orval and the policeman were hurrying up the slope. The policeman was twenty-six, the youngest on Teasle's staff, his gunbelt the reverse of Ward's, slung low like an old-time gunfighter's. Orval passed him running up, his long legs stretching. The top of his head was shiny bald, white hair on both sides. He had on his glasses and a green nylon jacket, green denim pants, high-laced field boots.

The state police, Teasle thought again and glanced down at the wagon road, making sure they were not on their way. He glanced back at Orval, closer now. Before, he had only been able to see the thin, dark, weathered face, but now he saw the deep rivers and furrows in it, and the flabby skin down the front of his neck, and he was shocked by how much older the man looked since he had last seen him three months ago. Orval wasn't acting any older though. He was still managing to get up that slope, hardly winded, well before the young deputy.

"The dogs," Teasle called. "Did you bring the dogs?"

"Sure, but I don't see the use of sending that deputy to help rush them into the van," Orval answered at the top, slowing. "Look at that sun. It'll be dark in an hour."

"Don't you think I know it."

"I believe you do," Orval said. "I didn't mean to try and tell you anything."

Teasle wished he had kept quiet. He could not afford to let it start again. This was too important. Orval was always treating him like he was still thirteen, telling him everything to do and how to do it, just as he had when Teasle lived with him as a boy. Teasle would be cleaning a gun or preparing a special cartridge load, and right away Orval would step in, giving his advice, taking over, and Teasle hated it, told him to butt out, that he could do things himself, often argued with him. He understood why he did not like advice: there were teachers he sometimes met who could not stop lecturing once they were out of class, and he was a little like them, so used to giving orders that he could not accept someone telling him what to do. He did not always refuse advice. If it was good, he often took it. But he could not let that be a habit; to do his job properly he had to rely on himself alone. If Orval had only on occasion tried to tell him what to do, he would not have minded. But not every time they were together. And now they had almost started at each other again, and Teasle was going to have to keep himself quiet. Orval was the one man he needed right now, and Orval was just stubborn enough to take his dogs back home if they got into another argument.

Teasle did his best to smile. "Hey, Orval, that's just me sounding miserable again. Don't pay attention. I'm glad to see you." He reached to shake hands with him. It had been Orval who taught him how to shake hands when he was a boy. Long and firm, Orval had said. Make your handshake as good as your word. Long and firm. Now, as their hands met, Teasle felt his throat constrict. In spite of everything, he loved this old man, and he could not adjust to the new wrinkles in his face, the white hair at the sides of his head that had become thinner and wispy like spider strands.

Their handshake was awkward. Teasle had deliberately not seen Orval in three months, ever since he had walked yelling out of Orval's house because a simple remark he had made had turned into a long argument over which way to strap on a holster, pointed forward or back. Soon after, he had been embarrassed about leaving the house like that, and he was embarrassed now, trying to act natural and look Orval straight in the face, doing a poor job of it. "Orval—about last time—I'm sorry. I mean it. Thanks for coming so quick when I need you."

Orval just grinned; he was beautiful. "Didn't I tell you never to talk to a man when you're shaking hands with him? Look him straight in the eyes. Don't jabber at him. I still think a holster should be pointed backward." He winked at the other men. His voice was low and resonant. "What about this kid? Where's he gone to?"

"Over here," Ward said. He directed them across two loose rocks in the stream, over to the line of trees and up into the draw. It was gray and cool under the trees as they hiked up to where the cycle lay on its side over the fallen branches of a dead tree. The crickets were not sounding anymore. Then Teasle and the rest stopped walking through the grass, and the crickets started again.

Orval nodded at the blockade of rocks and upturned trees across the draw, at the underbrush on both sides. "Yeah you can see where he scrambled up through the bushes on the right side."

As if his voice were a signal, something big up there rustled in the brush, and guessing there was a chance it was the kid, Teasle stepped back, instinctively drawing his pistol.

"Nobody around," a man said up there, pebbles and loose dirt sliding, and it was Lester coming down off balance through the bushes. He was soaking wet from where he had fallen in the stream. His eyes usually bulged somewhat, and when he saw Teasle's gun, they enlarged even more. "Hey now, it's only me. I was only checking if the kid might still be close by."

Orval scratched under his chin. "I wish you hadn't done that. You've maybe confused the scent. Will, do you have something from the kid to give my dogs a smell of?"

"In the trunk of the car. Underwear, pants, boots."

"All we need then are food and a night's sleep. We get this organized right and we can start by sunup."

"No. Tonight."

"How's that?"

"We're starting now."

"Didn't you just hear me say it'll be dark in an hour? There'll be no moon tonight. This big a gang, we'll separate and lose each other in the dark."

Teasle had been expecting this; he had been certain that Orval would want to hold off until morning. That was the practical way. There was just one thing wrong with the practical way: he could not wait that long.

"Moon or not, we still have to go after him now," he told Orval. "We've chased him out of our jurisdiction, and the only way to keep after him is if we stay in pursuit. Once I wait till morning I have to turn the job over to the state police."

"Then give it to them. It's a dirty job anyhow."

"No."

"What difference does it make? The state police will be out here in no time anyway—just as soon as the guy who owns this land calls them about all these cars driving across his fields. You'll have to turn this over to them no matter what."

"Not if I'm in these woods before they get here."

It would have been better for him to try convincing Orval without his men next to him listening. If he did not press Orval, then he would come off less to his men, but if he pressed too much, Orval would just throw up his hands and go home.

What Orval said next did not help any. "No, Will, I'm sorry to have to disappoint you. I'll do a lot of things for you—but those hills are tough to get through even in the day, and I won't take my dogs up there at night to run them blind just because you want this show all to yourself."

"I'm not asking you to run them blind. All I'm asking is that you bring your dogs in with me, and the minute you think it's gone too dark, we'll stop and camp. That's all it takes for me to stay in pursuit. Come on, we've camped out before, you and I. It'll be like when Dad was around."

Orval let out a deep breath and looked around at the forest. It was darker, cooler. "Don't you see how crazy this is? We don't have equipment to hunt him. We don't have rifles or food or—"

"Shingleton can stay behind to get whatever we need. We'll give him one of your dogs so in the morning he can track us to where we camped. I have enough deputies to keep charge of town so four of them can come in with Shingleton tomorrow. I have a friend at the county airport who says he'll lend his helicopter and fly us anything more we need and fly ahead to see if he can spot the kid. The only thing that can hold us up now is you. I'm asking you. Will you help?"

Orval was looking down at his feet, scuffling one boot back and forth in the dirt.

"I don't have much time, Orval. If we get up in there soon enough, the state police will have to let me stay in control. They'll back me up and have cruisers watching the main roads down out of the hills and leave us to chase him across the high ground. But I'm telling you, I might just as well forget about catching him if you don't chip in your dogs."

Orval glanced up and slowly reached into his jacket for a tobacco pouch and cigarette paper. He was mulling it over as he carefully rolled a cigarette, and Teasle knew not to rush him. Finally, just before Orval struck a match: "Could be, if I understood. What did this kid do to you, Will?"

"He sliced one deputy nearly in half and beat another maybe blind."

"Yeah, Will," Orval said and struck the match, cupping it to light his cigarette. "But you didn't answer me. What did this kid do to you?"

2

The country was high and wild, thickly wooded, slashed by ravines and draws and pocked with hollows. Just like the North Carolina hills in which he had been trained. Much like the hills he had escaped through in the war. His kind of land and his kind of fight and nobody had better push too close or he would push back—hard. Fighting to beat the fading light, he ran as far and as fast as he could, always up. His naked body was filmed with blood from the branches jabbing into him; his bare feet were gashed and bloody from the sharp sticks lying across his trail, from the rocky slopes and cliff walls. He came up a rise where the skeleton of a power pylon straddled the top and a swath had been cut down through the trees to stop the electric tension wires from tangling in the treetops. The clear section was gravel and boulders and scrub brush, and he scrambled painfully up, high tension wires overhead. He needed to reach the tallest vantage point he could before it got dark; he needed to see what was on the other side of the rise and figure which way to go.

At the top beneath the pylon, the air was bright and clear, and hurrying up into it he was touched by the last of the setting sun far to the left. He paused, letting the faint warm light soak into him, luxuriating in the soft feel of the ground here beneath his feet. The next peak across from him was bright in the sun as well, but its slope was gray, and the hollow at its base was already dark. That was where he headed, away from the soft ground at the top, down more gravel and boulders, toward the hollow. If he did not find what he wanted there, he would have to angle up to the left toward a stream he had sighted, and then he would have to follow the stream. It would be easier going that way along the bank, and what he was looking for would almost surely be near a stream. He came charging down the gravel toward the hollow, slipping, falling, sweat burning salty into his cuts. The hollow was no good when he got there, a swamp straight across, bog and murky water. But at least the earth was soft again, and he rounded the swamp to the left until he reached the stream that fed it, then started up along the stream, no longer running, just walking fast now. He had travelled almost five miles he could tell, and the distance had tired him: he still was not as fit as he had been before he was captured in the war, he still had not got over his weeks in the hospital. All the same, he remembered every trick of getting along, and if he could not run much farther without trouble, he had done five miles very well.

The stream twisted and turned, and he followed it. Soon there would be dogs after him he knew, but he did not bother wading in the stream to try to throw them off his scent. That would only slow him down, and since he would have to come out of the water sometime on one bank or the other, the man working the dogs would merely split the pack along both banks until they picked up the scent again, and he himself would just have wasted time.

It went dark faster than he expected. Climbing uphill he was catching the last gray light, and then the forest and underbrush merged into shadow. Soon only the biggest of trees and boulders were distinguishable in outline, and then it was black. There was the sound of the stream trickling over bedrocks and the sound of crickets and nightbirds and animals at home in the dark, and he started calling. For sure nobody he was looking for would let him know they were around if all he did was keep following the stream and holler for somebody. He had to make himself sound interesting. He had to make them want to see just who the hell this was. He called out in Vietnamese, in the little French he had learned in high school. He mocked a southern accent, a western one. He strung out long lists of the vilest obscenities he could conjure.

The stream dipped into a brief hollow on the side of the slope. Nobody there. The stream climbed and dipped into another hollow and climbed and dipped, and still nobody, and still he called. If he did not soon find someone, he would be so far up the hillside that the stream would maybe reach its source and he would have no bearing to follow. Which happened. His sweat chilling in the night air, he came to where the stream turned into a little marsh and a spring that he could hear bubbling up.

So much for that. He called once more, letting his obscene words echo up and down the darkened hill, waited, then set off upward. If he kept going straight up slopes and down, he figured eventually to reach another stream and follow it. He was thirty feet past the spring when the two flashlights opened bright on him from left and right, and he stopped absolutely still.

Under any other circumstances he would have leapt free from the glare of the flashlights and crawled off into the darkness. It was worth a man's life to wander around these hills at night, poking where he had no business—how many men had been shot in the head for what he was about, dumped in a shallow grave to let the night animals dig them up.

The flashlights blazed directly on him, one on his face, the other on his naked body. He still did not move, just stood there, head up, staring calmly ahead between the lights as if he belonged there and did this every night of his life. Insects were flying aglitter in and out of the flashlight beams. A bird took off fluttering out of a tree.

"Yeah, best you drop that gun and razor," an old man said on the right, his throat raspy.

Rambo breathed easier: they weren't going to kill him, at least not right away, he had made them curious enough. Just the same, keeping the handgun and the razor had been a gamble. Once these people had seen them, they might have felt threatened and shot him. But he could not let himself walk these woods at night without something to fight with if he had to.

"Yes sir," Rambo said evenly and let the gun and razor plop onto the ground. "No need to worry. The gun's not loaded."

"Course it isn't."

With an old man on the right, the one on the left would be young, Rambo thought. Father and son maybe. Or uncle and nephew. That was how these outfits were run, always in the family, an old man to give the orders and one or more juniors to do the work. Rambo could feel these two behind their flashlights sizing him up. The old man was keeping quiet now, and Rambo was not about to say anything more until he was asked to. An intruder, he had just better keep his mouth shut.

"Yeah, all that filth and crud you been hollering," the old man said. "You been calling us, or who you been calling cocksuckers?"

"Pa, ask him what he's walking around buck-naked with his

doings dangling for," the one on the left said. He sounded much younger than Rambo had expected.

"You shut up," the old man ordered the boy. "I told you not a peep from you."

Rambo heard a gun being cocked where the old man was. "Wait a minute," he said fast. "I'm alone. I need help. Don't shoot till you hear me out."

The old man did not answer.

"I mean it. I'm not here for trouble. It doesn't make any difference if I know that you're not two men, that one of you is just a boy. I won't try hurting anybody just because I know that."

It was a wild guess. Sure the old man might only have lost his curiosity and decided to shoot. But Rambo was guessing that naked and bloody, he looked dangerous to the old man, that the old man was not taking any chances now that Rambo knew they were just one man and a boy.

"I'm on the run from the police. They took my clothes. I killed one of them. I've been calling to get someone to help me."

"Yeah, you need help," the old man said. "Question is, from who?"

"They'll bring dogs after me. They'll find the still if we don't work to stop them."

Now was the touchy part. If they were going to kill him, now was the time.

"Still?" the old man said. "Who told you there's a still up here? You think I got a still up here?"

"We're pitch dark in a hollow near a spring. What else would bring you here? You must have it damn well covered. Even knowing it's here, I can't make out the flames from your furnace."

"You expect if I knew a still was around I'd be wasting time with you instead of hustling over to it? Hell, I'm a coon hunter."

"With no dogs? We don't have time for this. We have to fix things before those real dogs get here tomorrow."

The old man was swearing to himself.

"You're in a mess all right," Rambo said. "I'm sorry about getting you into it, but I don't have any choice. I need food and clothes and a rifle, and I'm not letting you out of this until I get them."

"Let's just shoot him, Pa," the boy said on the left. "He's going to pull some trick."

The old man did not answer, and Rambo kept quiet too. He had to give the old man time to think. If he tried to rush this business, the old man might feel cornered and shoot.

On his left Rambo heard the boy cocking a gun.

"You lower that shotgun, Matthew," the old man said.

"But he's pulling some trick. Don't you see it? Don't you see he's some government man likely?"

"I'll see that shotgun wrapped around your ears if you don't lower it like I said." The old man chuckled then. "Government man. Bushwah. Look at him, where the hell would he hide his badge?"

"Better listen to your dad," Rambo said. "He understands the bind. If you kill me, those police who find me in the morning will want to know who did it. They'll set the dogs on *your* trail next. It won't matter where you bury me or how you try to hide the scent; they'll—"

"Quicklime," the boy said smartly.

"Sure quicklime will help to cover my scent. But the smell of it will be all over you, and they'll set the dogs tracking *that*."

He paused, peering at each flashlight, giving them time to think.

"The trouble is, if you don't give me food and clothes and a rifle, then I'm not leaving here until I find that still of yours, and in the morning the police will follow my track through there. It won't matter if you take the thing apart tonight and hide it. I'll come after you to where the parts are hid."

"We'd wait for dawn to take it apart," the old man said. "You can't afford to stay here that long."

"With bare feet I can't go much farther anyway. No. Believe me. The way I am, they have a good chance of bringing me down, and I might just as well take the two of you down with me."

After a moment the old man was swearing again.

"But if you help me, if you give me what I need, then I'll swing around away from here, and the police won't come anywhere close to your still."

That was the simplest Rambo could make it. The idea sounded convincing to him. If they wanted to protect their outfit, they would have to help. Of course they might get angry at how he was forcing them and take a chance on killing him. Or they might be an inbred family, not intelligent enough to see the logic he was using.

It was colder, and Rambo couldn't stop himself from shivering. Now that everybody was silent, the crickets seemed extra loud.

Finally the old man spoke. "Matthew. I suppose you better run up to the house and bring back what he says." His voice was not very happy.

"And bring a can of kerosene," Rambo said. "Since you're helping, let's make sure you don't get hurt for it. I'll douse the clothes with the kerosene and let them dry before I put them on. The kerosene won't stop the dogs from trailing me, but it will keep them from picking up your scent on the clothes and following it to see who helped me."

The boy's flashlight beam glared steady on Rambo. "I'll do what my pa says, not you."

"Go on do what he wants," the old man said. "I don't like him either, but he sure knows what the hell he's got us into."

The boy's flashlight beam remained steady on Rambo a moment longer, as though the boy were deciding if he would go, or maybe saving face. Then the beam swung off Rambo into the bushes and the light clicked off and Rambo heard him set out brushing through the undergrowth. He had probably come and gone from home to this spring and back again so many times that he could do it with his eyes shut, let alone without a light.

"Thanks," Rambo told the old man whose light remained shining on his face. Then the light went out. "Thanks for that too," Rambo said, the image of the light remaining on his eyes a few seconds, slowly fading.

"Just helping the batteries."

Rambo heard him start to come forward through the underbrush. "Better not come closer," he said to the old man. "We don't want to mix your scent with mine."

"I wasn't about to. There's a log here I wanted to sit on is all."

The old man lit a match and touched it to the bowl of a pipe. The match did not stay lit very long, but as the old man puffed on his pipe and the flame from the match got high and low, Rambo saw a tousled head of hair and a gristled face and the top half of a red-checkered shirt with suspenders over the shoulders.

"Do you have any of your stuff with you?" Rambo asked.

"Maybe."

"It's cold like this. I wouldn't mind a swallow."

The old man waited, then switched on his flashlight and heaved over a jug so that Rambo could see in the light to catch it. The jug weighed like a bowling ball, and in his surprise Rambo almost dropped it. The old man chuckled. Rambo pried out the cork, wet and squeaking, and in spite of the jug's weight he drank with one hand the way he knew the old man would respect, shoving a forefinger through the hook at the top, balancing the jug on the crook of his elbow. It tasted like two hundred proof, golden-strong and burning his tongue and throat, flooding hot every inch down to his stomach. He almost choked. When he lowered the jug, his eyes were watering.

"A little strong?" the old man asked.

"A little," Rambo said, having trouble getting his voice to work. "What is it?"

"Corn mash. But it's a little strong though, ain't it?"

"Yeah, I'd say it's a little strong," Rambo repeated, his voice giving him more trouble.

The old man laughed. "Yeah, it's a little strong all right."

Rambo lifted the jug and drank again, gagging on the hot thick liquor, and the old man laughed one more quick burst.

3

The first songs of the morning birds wakened Teasle in the dark, and he lay there on the ground by the fire, huddled in the blanket he had brought from the cruiser, peering up at the late stars beyond the treetops. It had been years since he slept out in the woods. Over *twenty* years, he realized, counting back to 1950. Not the end of 1950: sleeping in frozen foxholes in Korea hardly qualified. Hell no, the last time he had really camped out was that spring when he got his draft notice and decided to enlist in the Marines, and he and Orval hiked into the hills for the first weekend it was warm enough. Now he was stiff from sleeping on the rough ground, his clothes were damp from where the dew had soaked through the blanket, and even near the fire, he was bone-cold. But he had not felt this alive in years, excited to be in action again, eager to chase after the kid. There was no point though in rousing everybody until Shingleton came back with the supplies and the rest of the men, and for now, the only one awake, he loved being alone this way, so different from the nights he had been spending alone since Anna had left. He wrapped himself tighter in the blanket.

Then the smell reached him, and he looked, and Orval was sitting at the end of the fire, dragging on a thin self-rolled cigarette, the smoke drifting toward Teasle in the cool early breeze.

"I didn't know you were awake," Teasle whispered, not to disturb the others. "How long?"

"Before you."

"But I've been awake over an hour."

"I know it. I don't sleep much anymore. Not because I can't. I just begrudge the time spent."

Clutching his blanket, Teasle shifted close to Orval and lit a cigarette off the glow of a stick from the fire. The flames were flicking low, and when Teasle churned the stick back into them, they rose warm, crackling. He had been right when he told Orval this would be like old times, although he had not believed it then, needing Orval to come along and disliking himself for using that kind of emotional argument on the man. But the feel of gathering firewood, tossing away stones and twigs to make the ground less rough, spreading his blanket, he had forgotten how solid and good that all was.

"So she left," Orval said.

Teasle did not want to talk about it. She was the one who had left, not the other way around, and that made it look as though he was in the wrong. Maybe he was. But she was too. Still he could not bring himself to put blame on her just so Orval might not think poorly of him. He tried to explain it neutrally. "She might come back. She's thinking about that. I haven't let on much, but for a while there, we were arguing quite a bit."

"You're not an easy man to get along with."

"Well, Christ, neither are you."

"But I've lived with the same woman forty years, and as far as I can guess, Bea hasn't thought much about leaving. I know people must be asking you this a lot now, but considering what you and I are, I believe I have a right. What were the arguments about?"

He almost did not answer. Talking about very personal things always embarrassed him, especially this which he had not yet reasoned out—who was right, whether he was justified. "Kids," he said, and then since he had begun, he went on. "I asked her for at least one. I don't care, boy or girl. It's just that I'd like someone to be to me like I was to you. I—I don't know how to explain it. I even feel stupid talking about it."

"Don't you tell me that's stupid, buddy. Not when I tried so long to have a kid of my own."

Teasle looked at him.

"Oh, you're like my own," Orval said. "*Like* my own. But I can't help wondering what sort of kid Bea and I would have made. If we had been able."

It hurt—as if all these years he had been no more to Orval than the once needy child of a dead best friend. He could not accept that; it was more self-doubt from Anna leaving, and now that he was talking about her, he had to get it in the open, finished.

"Last Christmas," he said, "before we came to dinner at your place, we went over to Shingleton's for a drink, and watching his two kids, the look on their faces with their presents, I thought, maybe it would be good to have one. It certainly surprised me that at my age I wanted one, and it sure as hell surprised *her*. We talked about it, and she kept saying no, and after a while I suppose I made too big a thing of it. What happened, it's like she weighed me against the trouble she thought a baby would be. And left. The crazy thing is, as much as I can't sleep for wishing her to come back, in a way I'm glad she went, I'm on my own again, no more arguments, free to do what I want when I want, come home late without calling to explain I'm sorry to miss dinner, go out if I feel like it, screw around. Sometimes I even think the worst part about her leaving is how much the divorce will cost me. And at the same time I can't tell you how much I need her back with me."

His breath came out in frost. The birds were gathered loudly. He watched Orval drag on the last of his cigarette close to his fingers, their joints gnarled and yellow from nicotine.

"And what about who we're after?" Orval said. "Are you taking it all out on him?"

"No."

"You sure?"

"You know I am. I don't act tougher than I have to. You know as well as I do that a town stays safe because of the little things kept in control. You can't do anything to prevent something big like a holdup or a murder. If somebody wants to do them bad enough, he will. But it's the little things that make a town what it is, that you can watch to make it safe. If I had just grinned and took what the kid was handing me, fairly soon I might have got used to the idea and let other kids hand it to me, and in a little while I would have been letting other things go by. It's me I was concerned about as much as the kid. I can't allow myself to loosen up. I can't keep order one time and not another."

"You're still awfully eager to chase after him, even though your part of the job is ended. This is state police business now."

"But it's my man he killed and it's my responsibility to bring him in. I want all my force to know I'll stop at nothing to get at anybody who hurts them."

Orval looked at the pinched butt of the cigarette he was holding and nodded, flicking it into the fire.

The shadows were lifting, trees and bushes distinct. It was the false dawn, and before long the light would appear to dim again, and then the sun would show and everything would be clear. They could have been up and starting now, Teasle thought. Where was Shingleton with the men and supplies? He should have been back a half hour ago. Maybe something had gone wrong in town. Maybe the state police were stopping him from coming in. Teasle churned a stick in the low fire, raising flames. Where *was* he?

Then he heard the first bark from the dog far off in the woods, and it stirred the dogs that were leashed to the tree nearest Orval. There were five of them here, and they had been awake, stomachs flat out on the ground, eyes intent on Orval. Now they were up, excited, barking in answer. "Shush," Orval said, and they looked at him and went quiet. Their withers were trembling.

Ward, Lester and the young deputy fidgeted in their sleep. They were down close to the other side of the fire, hugging their blankets. "Uh," Ward said.

"In a minute," Lester said asleep.

The dog barked far off again, though sounding a little closer, and the dogs by Orval cocked their ears, barking excitedly in return.

"Shush," Orval said stronger. "Get down."

Instead they jerked their heads toward another bark far off, their nostrils quivering.

"Get down," Orval demanded, and slowly one by one they obeyed.

Ward squirmed on his side in the blanket, knees up near his chest. "What's wrong? What's happening?"

"Just time to get up," Teasle said.

"What?" Lester said and squirmed. "God, it's cold."

"Time to get up."

"In a minute."

"That's about how long they'll take to get here."

People were crashing through the underbrush out there, breaking closer. Teasle lit another cigarette, his mouth and throat dry, and felt the energy building in him. It might be the state police, he all of a sudden realized, and stood hurriedly, drawing on his cigarette, straining to see into the forest in the direction of the crackling underbrush.

"God, it's cold," Lester said. "I hope Shingleton's bringing hot food."

Teasle hoped it was just Shingleton and the deputies out there and not the state police. Abruptly five men were in sight, rushing between trees and through the bushes in the pale cold light, but Teasle could not make out what color their uniforms were. They were talking to each other, one man tripped and swore, but Teasle could not identify the voices. If they were state police, he was trying to figure some way of keeping in charge.

Then they were close, hurrying out of the trees up this brief rise, and Teasle saw Shingleton stumbling after the dog that was straining on its leash, and he saw it was his own men behind, never so glad to see them before. They were carrying bulged-out burlap sacks, and rifles, and rope, and Shingleton had a field radio slung over his shoulder, the dog lurching him into camp.

"Hot food," Lester was up asking him. "Did you bring hot food?"

Shingleton apparently did not hear. He was out of breath, handing the dog over to Orval. Lester turned in a rush to the deputies. "Did you bring hot food?"

"Ham and egg sandwiches," a deputy said, chest heaving. "Thermos of coffee."

Lester reached for the sack the deputy carried.

"Not in there," the deputy told him. "Mitch. Behind me."

Mitch was grinning, opening his sack, handing out wax-paper-wrapped sandwiches, and everybody grabbed, eating.

"You covered one hell of a distance last night in the dark," Shingleton told Teasle, catching his breath, leaning against a tree. "I figured to find you in less than half an hour, and here it took me twice that."

"We couldn't move as fast as them last night, remember," Mitch said. "We had more to carry."

"They covered one hell of a distance just the same."

Teasle could not decide whether Shingleton was making excuses for being late, or whether he was really admiring.

Teasle bit into a sandwich, greasy and barely warm, but Christ, it was good. He took a paper cup that Mitch had poured full of steaming coffee; he blew on it and sipped, burning his upper lip and the roof of his mouth and his tongue, feeling the cold mulch of the egg and ham hot in his mouth. "What's going on back there?"

Shingleton laughed. "The state police had a fit over what you pulled." He stopped to chew into a sandwich. "Like you said, I waited in that field last night, and they showed up ten minutes after you climbed into the woods. They were sweet Jesus mad over you taking advantage of the little daylight you had left so you could chase after the kid and stay in the game. It surprised me they figured it out so fast what you were up to."

"But what's happened back there?"

Shingleton grinned proudly and bit another mouthful off the sandwich. "I spent half the night at the station with them, and finally they agreed to play along with you. They're going to block the roads down out of the hills and stay out of here. It took some amount of convincing to get them not to come in, I'll tell you."

"Thanks." He knew Shingleton was waiting for that.

Shingleton nodded, chewing. "What finally clinched things was I said you knew the kid better than they did and you'd know best what he might do."

"Any word from them who he is or what else he might be wanted for?"

"They're working on it. They said keep reporting on this radio. The first sign of trouble they say they're coming in with everything they've got."

"There won't be trouble. Somebody kick Balford there awake," he said, pointing to the young deputy snuggled in his blanket by the fire. "That guy will sleep through anything."

Orval patted the dog Shingleton had given him; he brought it over to lick Balford's face, and the young deputy whipped up, angrily wiping saliva from his mouth. "What the hell's going on?"

The men laughed, and in the middle stopped surprised. There was the drone of a motor. It was too far off for Teasle to guess what kind it was, but it was roaring more distinct all the time, and then deep and thunderous the helicopter loomed into view over the treetops, circling huge, sunlight glinting.

"What the—" Lester started.

"How'd it know where we were?"

The dogs got barking. Above the din of the motor, the blades shrieked through the air.

"Something new the state police gave me," Shingleton said, bringing out what looked like a dull gray cigarette case. "It gives off a radio signal. They said they want to know where you are at all times and made me carry it and gave the other half to the guy you asked to lend his helicopter."

Teasle bolted down the last of his sandwich. "Who's our deputy up there with him?"

"Lang."

"Does your radio connect up there?"

"You bet it does."

The radio was where Shingleton had set it in the low crook of a tree. Teasle flipped a switch on the control panel, and peering up at where the helicopter circled close, sunlight glinting off the shrieking blades, he said loud into the microphone, "Lang. Portis. All set up there?"

"Whenever you are, Chief." The voice was flat and scratchy. It sounded like it came from miles away.

Teasle could barely hear it in the roar from the motor. He glanced around at his men. Orval was hurriedly gathering the paper cups and wax paper from the sandwiches, tossing them on the fire. The others were strapping on equipment, slinging on rifles. The cups and paper in ashes, Orval was kicking dirt on the flames. "All right then," Teasle said. "Let's move it."

He had trouble hooking the microphone back onto the radio he was so excited.

4

All the morning as he ran and walked and ran and walked, he heard a motor droning miles off and occasional muffled gunshots and a deep male voice murmuring through a loudspeaker. Then the motor was a few peaks over and he recognized the sound of the helicopters in the war and he started moving faster.

He had been dressed now for almost twelve hours, but after his climb naked into the hills in the cold night air, he was still enjoying the warm rough feel of clothes. He wore heavy old shoes that the son had brought around midnight to the hollow by the spring. At first the shoes had been too large, but he had stuffed leaves into the toes and that had made the shoes tight so his feet would not slide up and down inside and give him blisters. Even then, the leather was sharp and stiff against his bare feet, and he wished the son had remembered to bring socks. Maybe the son had forgotten them on purpose. The pants, though, were too tight, and guessing the son had brought them on purpose also, he had to laugh. Shoes too large, pants too tight, it was a good joke on him.

These looked like they were onetime dress pants that had been ripped in the seat and patched and now were work pants, light-colored, with dark oil and grease stains. The shirt was white cotton, frayed at the cuffs and buttonholes and collar, and to go over top and keep him warm in the nights, the old man had even handed over his thick red-squared wool shirt. That had surprised him, the old man turning so friendly and generous toward the last. Maybe the whiskey had been what did it. After he and the old man had eaten the carrots and cold fried chicken the son had brought, they had heaved the jug of whiskey back and forth repeatedly, the son included, and finally the old man had gone as far as giving up his rifle plus a handkerchief tied full of cartridges.

"Had to hole up once in the hills a couple days myself," the old man had said. "Long time ago. When I wasn't much older than my boy." He had not said why, and Rambo had been careful not to ask. "Wasn't even a chance to go home and grab my rifle. Sure could've used it on them. You get out of this, you send me money for that rifle. I want your word. Not that it's the money I care about. The stuff I make, God knows I can afford another. But you get through this, I'd like to know how you made it, and I figure on the rifle reminding you to let me know. She's a good one." And she was: a .30-30 lever action, the power to whack a bullet through a man a half-mile away as if close through a block of cheese. The old man had a thick pad of leather on the end of the stock to ease the recoil. He had a speck of luminous paint on the sight at the tip of the barrel to help aiming at night.

Then Rambo had done what he promised, backtracking down the stream away from where the old man might have his boiler and coils and jugs; soon he had pushed west, still planning eventually to turn south for Mexico. He did not fool himself that reaching there would be easy. Since he was not about to risk giving himself away by stealing a car, he would have to travel for months on foot through the back country, living off the land. All

the same, he could not think of any place closer where he would
be safe, and far as the border was, at least for the time being it
gave him some direction. When he had gone a few miles, forced
to move slow because of the dark, he slept in a tree, wakened
with the sun and breakfasted on more carrots and chicken that
he had saved from the old man to take with him. Now the sun
high and glaring, he was miles off, rushing through trees up a
long wide draw. The shouts were louder, the voice from the loudspeaker more defined, and he knew before long the helicopter
would be checking this draw along with the rest. He broke from
the woods to run across an open reach of grass and fern, and one
quarter across he heard the flapping roar almost onto him and
swung in panicked search of cover. Alone in the grass, its trunk
shattered by what must have been lightning, the fallen pine tree
was all there was, no time to charge back to the woods. He ran
and dove beneath its thick smothering branches, scraping his back
as he sprawled under, and then, staring through the pine needles,
he saw the thing appear down the draw. It grew magnified. Its
landing props were close to skimming the topmost branches of
the forest.

"This is the police," the man's voice boomed from the chopper's
loudspeaker. "You don't have a chance, give up. Anyone in these
woods. A dangerous fugitive may be near you. Show yourselves.
Wave if you've seen one young man alone." The voice stopped,
then started awkwardly, as if the words were being read from a
card. "This is the police. You don't have a chance, give up. Anyone in these woods. A dangerous fugitive may be near you."

And on it went, and then it stopped and started again, and
Rambo lay beneath the branches perfectly still, knowing the maze
of needles hid him from the land, not sure he was covered from
the air, watching the chopper sweep over the trees toward the

grass. It was near enough for him to see up into the Plexiglas-fronted cockpit. There were two men staring out the open windows on each side, a civilian pilot and a policeman, his uniform the gray of Teasle's men, and out his window he was aiming a high-powered rifle with a telescopic sight. Ca-rack! the shot echoed, aimed at a tangle of rock and bush at the edge of the forest the chopper had just flown over.

God, Teasle really wanted him bad, telling his man to shoot at likely hiding places, unafraid of hitting anyone innocent because most people would obey the announcement and come out to show themselves. From Teasle's point of view, why not? As far as Teasle was concerned, he was a cop-killer and could not be allowed to get away, had to be made an example so nobody else would think to kill a cop. Even so, Teasle was too good a policeman to condone gunning him down without first giving him a chance to give up. That was why the announcement, and the idea of shooting at spots where he might hide was probably to scare him out more than to hit him. But the odds were too great that he might be hit anyhow, so it did not matter if the shots were to scare him or not.

Ca-rack! at another clump of brush at the edge of the trees, and now they were flying over the grass and they would be on top of him in seconds, almost certain to fire. He aimed his rifle through the branches, centering on the gunman's face as he flew nearer, ready to blast him to hell the instant he lowered his eyes to the gunsight. He did not want to kill anymore, but he had no alternative. Worse, if he did shoot this man, then the pilot would duck down to the floor of the chopper out of his aim and fly away damn fast to radio for help, and everybody would know where he was. Unless he stopped the pilot by exploding the helicopter gas tanks, which he knew was foolish to think about. For sure he could hit them. But explode them? It was

only in dreams that a man without phosphorus-tipped ammunition ever managed that trick.

He lay rigid waiting, his heartbeat sickening, as the helicopter
roared onto him. Immediately the gunman dipped his face to the
telescope on his rifle, and he himself was just squeezing the trigger when he saw what the gunman was after, and thanking Christ
he had seen in time, eased off. Fifty yards to the left there was
a wall of boulders and brush near a pool of water. He had almost hidden there when he first heard the chopper coming up
the draw, but it had been too far to reach. Now the chopper was
swooping toward it—Ca-rack!—and he could not believe it, he
thought his eyes were playing tricks on him. The bushes were
moving. He blinked, and the bushes heaved, and then he knew it
was not his eyes, as the bushes burst wide apart and a great, huge-
antlered, massive-shouldered deer stumbled up clambering over
the boulders. It fell, it rose up, leaping across the grassland toward
the woods on the other side, the helicopter after it. There was a
stream of deep rich blood glistening down the deer's left hip, but
that did not seem to matter, not the way it was charging in those
magnificent long bounding strides toward the trees, the helicopter
after it. His heart pounded wildly.

It would not stop pounding. They would be back. The deer
was just a toy. As soon as it leapt into the trees out of sight, they
would be back. Since there had been something hidden in those
bushes by the pool, then there might be something underneath
this fallen tree. He had to get out fast.

But he had to wait until the chopper's tail was pointed toward
him, the men watching straight ahead at the deer they were chasing. He strained waiting, and finally he could wait no more,
rolling out from under the branches, racing where the grass was
shortest and would not leave a trail. He was nearing the bushes

and rocks. Too soon the noise of the helicopter changed, roaring higher. The deer had made it to the woods. The chopper was circling back. Frantic, he ran stooped toward the cover of the boulders, tumbling under the bushes, bracing himself to shoot if they had seen him make his run.

Ca-rack! Ca-rack! the first shot as the chopper came upon the fallen pine tree, the second as it hovered over, lingering, slowly pivoting to continue up the draw. Leaving him. "This is the police," the voice was booming again. "You don't have a chance, give up. Anyone in these woods. A dangerous fugitive may be near you. Show yourselves. Wave if you've seen one young man alone." A mouthful of undigested carrots and chicken bolted sourly up from his stomach, and he spat it on the grass, the bitterness soaking into his tongue. This was the narrow end of the draw. Cliffs on both sides closed in farther up, and weak from having vomited, he watched through the bushes as the chopper swept over the trees that way and then rose up, skirted the top of a cliff, and settled into the next draw, its roar slowly dying away, the voice from the loudspeaker going muffled.

He could not stand, his legs were trembling too much. Because he was trembling, he trembled even more: the helicopter should not have frightened him so. In the war he had been through action far worse than this, and had come out of it badly shaken, but never so extreme that he could not make his body work. His skin was clammy, and he needed to drink, but the pool among the bushes was green and stagnant, and it would make him sicker than he was.

You've been away from fighting too long, that's all, he told himself. You're out of condition is all. You'll get used to it in a while.

Sure, he thought. That has to be the answer.

Gripping a boulder, he forced himself to stand, slowly, and head above the bushes, he turned to see if anyone was near. Satisfied, he leaned against the boulder, his legs yet unsteady, and brushed pine needles from the firing mechanism of his rifle. Regardless of anything, he had to keep his weapon in repair. The smell of the kerosene he had doused on his clothes was gone, in its place the faint acrid smell of turpentine that the pine tree had left on him. It mixed with the bitterness in his mouth, and he thought he might be sick again.

At first he was not sure he heard correctly: a wind blew up and dispersed the sound. Then the air was still and he definitely heard them, the first dim echoes of dogs barking behind him down at the wide end of the draw. A new tremor swept through his legs. He swung to his right where the grass sloped up to rocks and scattered trees and after that a cliff, and bracing his leg muscles, he ran.

5

The kid did not have much headstart, Teasle was figuring, as he and his men pressed forward through the trees and underbrush after the dogs. The kid had broken out of jail at six-thirty, it had got dark at eight-thirty, and he could not have gone far in these hills at night, an hour, possibly two all told. He would have started with the sun, the same as themselves, so that made him altogether just four hours ahead. But other things considered, he was probably only two, and maybe even less: he was naked and that would slow him down; he didn't know this country, so he would now and then head up steep gullies and into hollows that did not have an exit, and that would lose him more time coming out to find another way. Plus he had no food, and that would tire him, slow him more, narrow the distance.

"Less than two hours ahead of us for certain," Orval said, running. "He can't be more than one. Look at these dogs. His scent is so fresh they don't even have to nose the ground."

Orval was in front of Teasle and the others, racing with the dogs, his arm taut like an extension of their master leash he held, and Teasle was climbing, scrambling through bushes, trying to keep up with him. In a way, it was funny, a seventy-two-year-old man setting the pace, running them all into the ground. But then Orval jogged five miles each morning, smoked only four cigarettes a day and never drank, while he himself smoked a pack and a half of cigarettes, drank beer by the six-pack and had not exercised in years. It was something just to be able to keep pace with Orval as much as he was. He was breathing so deeply and rapidly that his lungs were burning, he had the stab of shinsplints in his legs, but at least he was not running as awkwardly as at the start. He had been a boxer in the Marines, and they had taught him how to run to train. His body was long out of practice though, and he was having to learn over again a smooth quick comfortable stride, leaning a little forward, letting the pull of his body force his legs to push him on so he would not fall. Gradually he was getting it, running faster, easier, his pain diminishing, a pleasure of exertion swelling up inside him.

He had last felt like this five years ago, when he came back from Louisville as Madison's new police chief. The town had not changed much, yet it had all looked different. The old brick house he had grown up in, the tree in his backyard where his father had rigged a swing, the gravestones of his parents—in the years he had been away, his memory of them had gone flat and colorless as in black and white photographs. But now they had length and depth, and they were green and brown and red, and the tombstones purple marble. He had not believed seeing the graves again would depress his return that greatly. The baby girl, a fetus really, in a plastic bag by his mother's feet in her coffin. Both bodies long since corrupted into dust. All because she was a Catholic. The fetus had been poisoning her, the Church had refused an abortion, so of course she had obeyed and died and the baby with her. That had been when he was ten, and he had not understood why his father had stopped going to church after that. His father, trying to be a mother as well then, showing him about guns and fish, how to darn his own socks and cook for himself, how to clean house and wash clothes, making him independent, almost as if the man had foreseen his gunshot death in the woods three years later. Then Orval to raise him, then Korea, and Louisville, and then at age thirty-five, he was home again.

Except that it was no more home, just the place where he had grown up, and that first day back, touring the once familiar places only made him realize that he had already lived close to half his life. He was sorry he had come, almost phoned Louisville to see if he could return to work there. Finally just before it closed, he went to the real estate office, and that night he and an agent set out to look at places for sale or rent. But all the houses and apartments he saw were still being lived in, and he could not see himself alone in any of them. The agent gave him a book of listings with photographs to study before he slept, and flipping through it in his small hotel room, he came upon the place he needed: a summer camphouse in the hills near town, with a stream in front, a wooden bridge, and a thick slope of trees in back. The windows were smashed; the roof sagged and the front porch was collapsed; the paint was chipped and peeling; the shutters were split and dangling.

The next morning it was his, and in the days and nights and weeks to come, he was never busier. From eight to five he organized his force, interviewing the men already on the job, firing those who did not want to go nights to the shooting range or the state police night school, hiring men who did not mind extra duty, throwing out obsolete equipment and buying new, streamlining the cluttered operation that his predecessor had left when he died on the front steps of a heart attack. Then from five until he dropped to sleep, he worked on the house, roofing it, putting new glass in the windows and caulking them, building a new porch, painting it all rust color to blend with the green of the trees. The bad wood that he stripped from the roof and the porch he used for a fire in the yard every night, and he sat by it, cooking, eating chili con carne, steak and baked potatoes, or hamburgers. Food had never tasted better, nor had he slept sounder or his body felt greater, the calluses on his hands making him proud, the stiffness in his legs and arms turning to strength and smooth-moving ease. For three months he was like that, and then the job on the house was done, and for a time he found small things to fix, but then there were nights with nothing to do, and he went out for a beer or else he stayed longer at the shooting range or else he went home to watch television and drink beer. Then he got married and now that was ended, and racing through the trees out into the grass, breath rasping, sweat stinging, he felt so good that he wondered why he had ever stopped taking care of himself.

The dogs were yelping ahead, and Orval's long legs were stretching to stay with them. The deputies were trying to keep up with Teasle, and he was straining to keep up with Orval, and there was a moment as he raced across the grass, the sun bright and hot on him, his arms and legs in swift steady rhythm, when he felt he could go on forever. Abruptly Orval surged farther ahead, and Teasle could not match his speed anymore. His legs grew heavy. The good feeling drained from him.

"Slow down, Orval!"

But Orval stayed right on going with the dogs.

6

When he reached the line of trees and rocks he had to slow, placing his shoes carefully so he would not slip on the rocks and maybe break a leg. At the base of the cliff he hurried along, seeking an easy way to the top, and found a crack in the cliff that went in three feet and rose straight to the top, and climbed. Near the top the jutting stones that he had used for handholds were wide apart, and he had to claw and boost himself, but then the climbing got better again until shortly he was out of the crack onto level stone.

The yapping from the dogs echoed loudly on top. He crouched to see if the helicopter was nearby. It was not—he could not even hear it—and there was no sign of anybody watching him from a neighboring height or from below. He slipped into bushes and trees near the cliff edge and crept swiftly to his right toward an outcrop with a long view of the draw, and there he lay, watching the alternate strips of grass and woods. A mile down the draw he saw that men were racing from trees across a wide clear space toward more trees. In the distance the men were small and hard to distinguish; he counted what he thought were ten. He could not make out the dogs at all, but they sounded like quite a lot. It wasn't their number that bothered him, though. What did was that they had obviously found his scent and were tracking him fast. Fifteen minutes and they would be where he was now. Teasle should not have been able to catch up to him this fast. Teasle should have been hours behind. There had to be somebody, maybe Teasle, maybe one of his men, who knew the country and knew from his general direction the shortcuts to head him off.

He ran back to the niche up through the cliff: there was no way Teasle was going to have the easy climb he himself had. He set his rifle on a grassy mound where no dirt would get into it, and began pushing at a boulder that was near the cliff. The boulder was large and heavy, but once he had it rolling somewhat, the shift of its weight helped him to push. Soon he had it where he wanted, completely blocking off the top of the crack, one side extending over the cliff edge. A man coming at the boulder from below would not be able to get around or over it. He would have to shove it out of the way before he could get on top, but braced from below, he would not have the leverage to move it. He would need several men helping him, but the crack was too narrow for several men to fit at once. Teasle would be a while figuring out how to clear the boulder away, and by then he himself would be long gone.

He hoped. Glancing down at the draw, he was amazed that while he positioned the boulder, the posse had been traveling so fast they were already at the pool and bushes where he had hidden. The men in miniature down there stopped looking at the bushes to watch the dogs sniffing the ground, barking in circles. Something must have confused the scent. The wounded deer, he realized. When he had dove into the bushes, some of the deer blood had smeared on to him, and now the dogs were trying to decide which track to follow, his or the deer's. They chose damn fast. The second they sprang yelping on his path toward the cliff, he turned and grabbed his rifle and ran through more bushes and trees, inland. Where the undergrowth was very thick, he swung and pushed through backward, and then ran forward again until once more he had to push through backward. His effort shoving the boulder over to the niche in the cliff had lathered his face and chest with sweat that stung and bit, and now more sweat poured out as he struggled through a wall of nettles, scraping his knuckles raw, filming them with blood.

Then in a second he was free. He came breaking out of the dark wood into the bright sunlight on a slope of rock and shale, and paused quickly to catch his breath, and slid cautiously down to the edge. There was a cliff and a wide forest at the bottom, leaves red and orange and brown. The cliff was too sheer for him to climb down.

So now there was a cliff before him and behind him, which meant he could go only two other routes. If he went to the east, he would be moving back toward the wide end of the draw. But Teasle likely had groups searching the highlands on both sides of the draw, in case he doubled back. That gave him just one other course, to the west, in the direction the helicopter had taken, and he ran that way until he came upon another drop and found that he had trapped himself.

Christ. The dogs were barking louder, and he clenched his rifle, cursing himself for having ignored one of the most basic rules he had ever learned. Always choose a route that won't trap you. Never run where you might cut yourself off. Christ. Had his mind gone soft along with his body from lying in all those hospital beds? He should never have climbed up that cliff back there.

He deserved to be caught. He deserved the shit that Teasle would do to him if he *let* himself be caught.

The dogs were barking even closer. Sweat smarting his face, he touched a hand to it and felt the sharp rough stubble of his beard, and brought down the hand sticky with blood from where the bushes and nettles had slashed and ripped him. The blood made him furious with himself. He had thought that running away from Teasle would be fairly simple and routine, that after what he had been through in the war, he could handle anything. Now he was telling himself to think again. The way he had been shaking from the helicopter should have warned him, he knew, but still he had been so confident he could outrun Teasle that he had gone and cornered himself, and now he would be damn lucky to get out of this with just the blood that was already on him. There was only one thing yet that he could do. He rushed along the top of the new cliff, staring down checking the height, stopping where the cliff seemed lowest. Two hundred feet.

All right, he told himself. It's your mistake, you pay for it.

Let's see just how good you really are.

He slipped the rifle snugly between his belt and his pants, shifting it around so it went straight down his side, the butt near his armpit, the barrel by his knee. Certain that it would not work loose and fall to smash on the rocks far below, he lay flat on his stomach, eased himself over the edge, and hung by his hands, his feet dangling. Toeholds, he could not find any toeholds.

The dogs began yelping hysterically as if they had reached the blocked-off niche in the cliff.

7

To use its pulley and winch for clearing the boulder, to check the bluff in case he was still up there, for whatever reason, Teasle must have radioed for it almost immediately. Rambo was ten body-lengths down the cliff when he heard it again, droning far off, gathering volume. He had taken what he judged was nearly a minute for every body-length down this far, each fissure and outcrop he grabbed on to hard to find, each toehold having to be tested, settling down, resting his weight on it little by little, breathing with relief when it stayed firm. Often he had dangled as he had at the top, shoes flailing against the rockface, scrabbling for support. His holds had been so far apart that climbing back up to avoid being seen by the helicopter would be as difficult as climbing down had been. Even then, he would probably not get up before the helicopter passed over him, so there was no point in trying, he might just as well keep climbing down, hoping the chopper would not spot him.

The rocks below distorted huge, attracting him, as though he were leaning closer and closer into their image in a magnifying glass, and he tried to pretend this was merely like an exercise at jump school. It was not though, and as he listened to the dogs, the helicopter droning near, he quickened his descent, hanging to the limit of his reach, taking less care to test his footholds, sweat dribbling itchy down his cheeks, accumulating tremulously on his lips and chin. Before, when he had heard the chopper as he ran across the field of grass toward the cover of the fallen pine tree, the sound of its approach had been like a solid force that was pushing him. But here, now, restricted, slow in spite of his haste, he felt its growing roar as a slippery thing that was inching up from the small of his back, heavier the higher it came. When the thing leeched up to the base of his skull, he glanced over toward the sky behind him and clung motionless to the wall, the helicopter enlarging rapidly over the trees, bearing toward this cliff. His outside wool shirt was red against the gray of stone; he prayed the gunman would somehow fail to see it.

But he knew that the gunman would *have* to see it.

His fingers were dug bleeding into a slit in the cliff. The toes of his shoes were pressed hard onto an inch-wide ledge; his throat shuddered involuntarily as one shoe slipped off the ledge. The close whack of the bullet into the cliff by his right shoulder dazed him, and so startled that he almost lost his grip, shaking his head to clear it, he began groping frantically down.

He managed only three more toeholds and then there were no more. Ca-rang! the second bullet ricocheted off the rock, striking higher, nearer to his head, startling him as much as the first one, and he knew he was as good as dead. The vibration of the chopper was all that had saved him from being hit so far: it was throwing off the gunman's aim, and the pilot was bringing on the chopper fast, which made the vibration worse, but it would not be long before the pilot understood and held the chopper steady. His arms and legs trembling from the strain, he grasped down for a handhold and then another and then let down his feet, taking a chance, dangling again, scraping the cliff with his shoes for something, anything, to step onto.

But there wasn't anything. He hung by his bleeding fingers, and the helicopter swooped toward him like some grotesque dragonfly, and sweet Jesus, keep that damn thing moving, don't let it hang still so he can get a decent shot. Ca-rang! Chips of stone and molten bullet ripped burning into the side of his face. He peered at the rocks a hundred feet below. Sweat stinging his eyes, he barely made out a lush fir tree that rose up toward him, its top branches maybe ten feet under him. Or fifteen, or twenty: he had no chance to figure.

The helicopter looming huge, wind from the rotors rushing over him, he aimed his body at the top of the tree and let loose his pulpy fingers and dropped. His stomach gushed up, his throat expanded in the sudden emptiness, and it was so long, so endless before he slammed past the first branches, plummeted through the clutching boughs, cracked to a stop against a stout limb.

Absolutely numb.

He could not breathe. He gasped, and pain flooded his body; his chest throbbed sharply, and his back, and he was certain he had been shot.

But he hadn't, and the din of the chopper above the tree and the slash of a bullet through the branches got him moving. He was high in the tree. His rifle was still between his belt and his pants, but the impact when he hit had rammed it violently against his side, half-paralyzing him. In agony, forcing his arm to bend, he clutched the gun and tugged, but it would not come. Above, the helicopter was circling, returning for another shot, and he was tugging at the gun, wrenching it free, the release so strong that the branch he was on started swaying. He slipped off balance, scraping his thigh along sharp bark, desperately hooking his arm around the branch above him. It made a crack; he quit breathing. If it broke, it would send him falling outward past the ends of the boughs down onto the rocks deep below. The branch made one more crack before it held firm, and he breathed again.

But the sound from the chopper was different now. Constant. Steady. The pilot was getting the idea, keeping it still. Rambo didn't know if they could see him in the tree or not, but that didn't matter much—the area at the top of the tree was so small that if the gunman sprayed it with bullets he was sure to be hit. He didn't have time to switch to a stronger branch; the next bullet might finish him. Hurried, desperate, he pushed away needles and light boughs and sought where the helicopter hung there whipping in the air.

Across from him. A house distance high. And craning his head out the open cockpit window was the gunman. Rambo saw his round, big-nosed face quite clearly as the man prepared to fire once more; a glance was all Rambo needed. In one smooth instinctive motion, he raised his gun barrel to the branch above him, steadied it there, and aimed out along it at the center of the round face, at the tip of the big nose.

A gentle squeeze on the trigger. Bull's eye.

Inside the cockpit the gunman clutched his sunken face. He was dead before he had a chance to open his mouth and scream. There was a moment when the pilot went on holding the helicopter steady like nothing had happened, and then at once Rambo saw through the glass front of the cockpit how it registered on the man that there were bits of bone and hair and brain everywhere, that the top of his partner's head was gone. Rambo saw him gape down in horror at the blood that was spattered across his shirt and pants. The man's eyes went wide; his mouth convulsed. The next thing he was fumbling with his seat belt, clutching his throttle stick crazily as he dove to the cockpit floor.

Rambo was trying to get a shot at him from the tree. He could not see the pilot, but he had a fair idea where the man would be huddled on the floor, and he was just aiming at that part of the floor when the helicopter veered sharply up the cliff. Its top section cleared the ridge nicely, but the angle of the chopper was so steep that the rear section caught on the edge of the cliff. In the roar of the motor, he thought he heard a metallic crack when the rear section struck: he could not be certain. The helicopter seemed interminably suspended there, and then with an abrupt flip over backward, it plunged down directly against the cliff wall, screeching, cracking, blades bending and breaking as the explosion came, a deafening ball of fire and zing of metal that flashed up past the tree and died. The outer branches of the tree burst into flame. A stench rose up of gasoline and burning flesh.

Straight-off Rambo was on the move, scrambling down the tree. The branches were too thick. He had to circle the trunk to find where he could squeeze down. The dogs were barking louder, fiercer now, as if they were past the barricade up onto the ridge. That boulder should have taken longer to clear away; he couldn't understand how Teasle and the posse had climbed up so fast. He held tightly to his rifle, scraping down past the branches, through the pointed needles pricking at his hands and face. His chest was throbbing from his drop into the tree—it hurt like some ribs were cracked or broken, but he couldn't let that bother him. The dogs were yelping closer; he had to climb down faster, twisting, sliding. His outside wool shirt caught on a branch and he ripped it loose. Faster. Those sonofabitch dogs. He had to go faster.

Near the bottom he reached thick black smoke that choked his

lungs, and saw indistinctly through it the twisted wreck of the helicopter burning and crackling. Twenty feet from the bottom he
could not climb down any farther: there were no more branches.
He couldn't spread his arms around the trunk and shinny down:
it was too wide. Jump. No other way. The dogs yelping up on
top, he checked the rocks and boulders underneath him and chose
a spot where dirt and silt and dry brown needles were gathered
in a pocket between the rocks, and without realizing, smiled—
this sort of thing was what he had been trained to do—the weeks
of leaping from towers at parachute school. Holding his rifle, he
grabbed the last bough with his free hand and eased down hanging and dropped. And struck the ground perfectly. His knees
buckled just right and he slumped and rolled just right and came
to his feet as properly as he had done a thousand times before.
It wasn't until he left the choking smoke around the shelter of
the tree and scurried over the rocks that the pain in his chest got
worse. Much worse. And the smile disappeared. Christ, I'm going
to lose.

He charged over the rocks down a slope toward the forest, legs
pounding, chest heaving painfully. There was grass ahead, and
then he was out of the rocks and into the grass, racing toward
the trees, and then he heard the dogs insanely loud on top behind
him. They had to be where he tried climbing down the cliff; the
posse would be shooting at him anytime now. Out in the open
like this, he didn't have a chance, he needed to get to the trees,
dodging, ducking his head, using every trick he knew to make
himself an awkward target, tensing himself to take the first bullet
that would blow his back and chest apart as he burst through the
bushes and scrub into the woods, pushing farther on, stumbling
over vines and roots until he tripped and fell and stayed flat, gasping on the damp, sweet-smelling forest floor.

They hadn't shot. He couldn't understand it. He lay there gasping, filling his lungs to capacity and exhaling and breathing deeply again, ignoring the pain in his chest each time he swelled it. Why hadn't they shot? And then he knew: because they had never been on top of the cliff in the first place. They were still getting there. They had only sounded like they were on top. His stomach retched, but this time nothing came up, and he flopped onto his back, staring past the autumn-colored leaves toward the deep sky. What was the matter with him? He had never misjudged like that before.

Mexico. The image of a warm, wave-lapped beach flashed inside his mind. Get moving. Have to start moving. He struggled to his feet and was just trudging farther into the forest when he heard men shouting behind him, dogs barking, and the posse was undoubtedly on top of the cliff now. He stopped and listened, and still gasping for breath, he turned back the way he had come.

Not the exact same path. The grass into the forest had been long, and he knew he had left a track through it that would be quite plain from on top of the cliff; the posse would be studying that part of the forest where he had entered, and as he came back, he might make some sign that would show them where he was. So he headed to the left, approaching a part of the forest's edge where they would have no reason to expect him. When the trees began to thin out, he sank low and crawled to the edge, and crouching behind some brush he saw something beautiful: a hundred yards off, clear as could be on top of the cliff, were the men and the dogs. They were all running toward where he had climbed down, the dogs barking, one man behind the dogs hanging on to a master leash, the rest of the men rushing up behind, all stopping now and staring down at the smoke and fire of the helicopter. They were the closest Rambo had seen them since the hunt began, the sun stark on them, making them seem very close, strangely magnified. Six dogs, he counted, and ten men, nine in the gray police uniform of Teasle's men and one in a green jacket and pants, that one holding the dogs' master leash. The dogs were sniffing at where he had climbed over the edge, circling to check if the scent went anywhere else, returning to the edge and barking in frustration. The man in green was older than the rest and taller; he was soothing the dogs, patting them, talking to them gently in words that came across to him muffled. Some of the policemen were sitting, others standing to look down at the blazing helicopter or else point toward the forest where he had entered.

But he wasn't interested in those, only in the one pacing back and forth, slapping his hand against his thigh. Teasle. There was no missing that short chunk of a body, that puffed-out chest, that low head that darted side to side like a fighting rooster. Sure. Like a cock. That's what you are, Teasle. A cock.

The joke made him smile. It was shadowed where he lay under the bush, and resting was luxurious. He lined up Teasle in his rifle sights just as Teasle spoke to the man in green. Wouldn't Teasle be surprised to find that in the middle of a word a bullet had gone in and out of his throat. What a joke that would be. He became so fascinated he almost pulled the trigger.

It would have been a mistake. He wanted to kill him all right: after his scare being caught between the helicopter and the posse, he didn't care what he had to do to get away, and now that he thought about the two men he had killed in the helicopter, he realized he wasn't bothered as he had been after he killed Galt. He was getting used to death again.

But there was a question of priorities. The cliff wouldn't stop Teasle; it would just put him behind an hour or so. And killing Teasle wouldn't necessarily stop the posse; they would still have the hounds to keep them tracking fast. The hounds. They weren't vicious like the German Shepherds he had seen in the war, but just the same they were natural hunters, and if they ever caught him, they might even attack instead of merely cornering him as hounds were schooled to do. So he had to shoot them first. After that he would shoot Teasle. Or the man in green, if he showed before Teasle. The way the man handled the dogs, Rambo was sure he knew a lot about tracking, and with both him and Teasle dead, the others likely wouldn't know what to do, they'd have to drift back home.

For sure they didn't seem to know much about this kind of fighting. They were standing or sitting in plain view up there, and he sniffed in disgust. The man in green was having trouble getting the dogs quiet; they were bunched together, tangled, in each other's way. The man separated the master leash and handed over three dogs to a deputy. Rambo lay beneath the cool underbrush and aimed at the three that the man in green had kept and shot two of them just like that. He would have hit the third dog with his next shot if the man in green had not yanked it back from the edge. The policemen were shouting, jumping low out of sight. The other set of dogs was acting wild, howling, straining to get away from the deputy who held them. Rambo quickly shot one. Another shied and slipped off the cliff, and the deputy holding the leash tried to pull it back instead of letting go, lost his balance and dragging the last of his dogs with him, he went over the side too. He wailed once just before he thumped on the rocks far below.

8

There was an instant when they lay flat paralyzed, the sun glaring on them, no wind, nothing. The instant stretched on and on. Then in a scramble Shingleton aimed down at the forest, shooting along its edge. He had four shots off when another man joined him, and then another, and then except for Teasle and Orval, everyone was laying down a heavy line of fire, the gun reports rattling off together, as if a bandoleer of ammunition had been thrown into a furnace and the heated cartridges were exploding in a steady roll.

"That's enough," Teasle ordered.

But nobody obeyed. They were spread flat along the ridge, behind rocks and mounds of earth, shooting as fast as their rifles would allow. Crack, crack, crack, their trigger hands in constant motion, ejecting old shells, chambering fresh ones, not really aiming as they yanked off their bullets, the recoils jolting them. Crack, crack, crack. And Teasle was sprawled in a furrow of rock, shouting. "That's enough I told you! Stop I said!"

But they kept right on, strafing the line of trees and scrub, homing in where another's bullet had churned the leaves and made it seem that someone was there moving. A few were reloading and starting again. Most had already done so. Rifles of different make: Winchester, Springfield, Remington, Marlin, Savage. Different calibers: .270, .300, .30–06, .30–30. Bolts and levers and different-sized magazines holding six rounds or seven or nine, empty cartridges strewn around and more coming all the time. Orval was holding steady his one last dog, shouting "Stop it!" And Teasle was rising from the furrow, crouching as if to pounce, the veins in his neck bulging as he yelled, "Dammit, stop I said! The next man pulls a trigger loses two days' pay!"

That struck them. Some had not yet reloaded the second time. The rest somehow checked themselves, tense, rifles at their shoulders, fingers poised over triggers, eager to resume. Then a cloud shut out the sun and they were all right. They sucked in air and swallowed and lowered their rifles sluggishly.

A breeze came up, gently brushing the dry leaves in the forest up behind them. "Christ," Shingleton said. His cheeks were pale and taut like the skin on a drum.

Ward relaxed off his elbows onto his stomach and licked at the corners of his mouth. "Christ is right," he said.

"Never so scared," somebody was mumbling over and over. Teasle looked and it was the young deputy.

"What's that smell?" Lester said.

"Never so scared."

"Him. It's coming from him."

"My pants. I—"

"Leave him alone," Teasle said.

The cloud that had shut out the sun passed smoothly on, and the bright glare retouched him, and glancing over at where the sun was low in the valley, Teasle watched another cloud approaching, a bigger one, and behind it, not far off, the sky was rumpled with them, black and puffy. He unstuck his sweaty shirt from his chest and then leaving it alone because it stuck right back to his skin, he hoped it might rain. At least that would cool things off.

Next to him he heard Lester talking about the young deputy: "I know he can't help it, but Christ what a smell."

"Never so scared."

"Leave him alone," Teasle said, still looking at the clouds.

"Any bets we hit that kid just now?" Mitch said.

"Anybody hurt? Everybody O.K.?" Ward said.

"Yeah sure," Lester said. "Everybody's fine."

Teasle looked sharply at him. "Guess again. There's only nine of us. Jeremy went over the side."

"And three of my dogs went over with him. And two others are shot," Orval said. His voice was all in one tone, like from a machine, and the strangeness of it made everybody turn to him. "Five. Five of them gone." His face was the gray of powdered cement.

"Orval. I'm sorry," Teasle said.

"You damn well should be. This was your damn foolish idea in the first place. You just couldn't wait and let the state police take over."

The last dog was trembling on its haunches, whining. "There now. There now," Orval told it, gently stroking its back as he squinted through his glasses at the two dead dogs along the edge of the cliff. "We'll get even, don't you worry. If he's still alive down there, we'll get even." He shifted his squint toward Teasle, and his voice went louder. "You just couldn't wait for the goddamn state police to take over, could you?"

The men looked at Teasle for an answer. He moved his mouth, but no words came out.

"What's that?" Orval said. "Jesus, if you've got something to say, then say it clear like a man."

"I said nobody forced you to come. You've had a hell of a good time showing us what a tough old shit you are, running ahead of everybody, quick climbing up that break in the cliff to move the boulder and prove how smart you are. It's your own fault the dogs were hit. You know so much, you should have kept them back from the edge."

Orval shook with anger, and Teasle wished he had not said that. He stared down at the ground. It was not right of him to mock Orval's need to outdo everyone. He had been grateful enough when Orval realized how to free the boulder, climbing up to tie one end of a rope around it, telling the others to haul on the other end of the rope while he used a thick bough to lever at the boulder. It had come hurtling over the top in a rumble and crash and splintering of rock that they had all just managed to stumble back from. "All right, listen, Orval," he said, calm now. "I'm sorry. They were fine dogs. Believe me, I'm sorry."

There was a sudden movement next to him. Shingleton was sighting his rifle, firing down at a clump of brush.

"Shingleton, I told you to stop."

"I saw something move."

"Two days' pay that cost you, Shingleton. Your wife's going to be mad as hell."

"But I saw something move I tell you."

"Don't tell me what you think you saw. You're shooting excited like you wanted to back at the station when the kid broke out. Just listen. That goes for all of you. Listen. You hit nowhere close to that kid. The time you took returning his fire, he could have crapped and buried it and *still* got away."

"Come on, Will, two days' pay?" Shingleton said. "You can't mean that."

"I'm not finished. All of you, look at all the shells you wasted. Half your ammunition's gone."

They scanned the empty cartridges lying all around them in the dirt, looking surprised at how many there were.

"What'll you do when you run into him again? Use up the rest of your shells and then throw rocks at him?"

"The state police can fly us more," Lester said.

"And won't you feel great when they come in here, laughing at how you wasted all your shells."

He pointed once more at the empty cartridges, and for the first time he noticed that one group of shells was very different from the rest. The men had to lower their eyes in embarrassment as he scooped up the shells. "These aren't even fired. One of you dummies pumped out all his bullets without even pulling the trigger."

It was obvious to him what had happened. Buck fever. The first day of hunting season a man could get so excited when he saw his target that he stupidly pumped out all his shells without first pulling the trigger, completely mystified why he wasn't hitting what he was aiming at. Teasle couldn't let it pass, he had to make an issue of it. "Come on, who did it? Who's the baby? Give me your gun, I'll give you one that shoots caps."

The number on the cartridges was .300. He was about to check whose rifle was that caliber when he saw Orval point toward the edge of the cliff—and then he heard the whimper. Not all the dogs the kid had shot were dead. One had been shocked unconscious by the force of the bullet, was now coming to, kicking, whimpering.

"Gutshot," Orval said disgustedly. He spat and stroked the dog he had been holding and gave its leash to Lester next to him.

"Hang on tight," he said. "You see how she's quivering. She smells that other dog's blood, and she's liable to go crazy." He spat again and stood, dust and sweat mixed on the green of his clothes.

"Wait now," Lester said. "You mean this one might get vicious?"

"Maybe. I doubt it. Most likely she'll try to break free and run off. Just hold tight."

"I don't like this one bit."

"Nobody asked you to like it."

He left Lester holding the leash and walked over to the wounded dog. It was on its side, kicking its legs, trying to roll over and stand, always sinking back on its side, whining miserably.

"Sure," Orval said. "Gut shot. That bastard gutshot her."

He wiped his sleeve across his mouth and squinted over at the dog that was untouched. It was tugging on its leash to get away from Lester.

"Mind you hang on tight to that one," Orval told him. "I have something to do that'll make her jump."

He bent down to inspect the wound in the dog's stomach, came up shaking his head disgustedly at the glistening rolls of intestine, and without a pause he shot the dog behind the ear. "A God damn terrible shame," he muttered, watching the body contort spastically and then settle. His face had changed from gray to red, wrinkled worse than ever. "So what's to wait for?" he said quietly to Teasle. "Let's go butcher that kid."

He took one step away from the dog and staggered violently off balance, dropping his rifle, clutching queerly at his spine, the report from the gun in the woods below echoing as he whipped forward and hit the ground hard with his face and chest. The shock of landing split his glasses apart on his nose. And this time nobody returned fire. "Down!" Teasle was shouting. "Everybody down!" They dove flat on the ground. The last dog broke free from Lester and bounded over to where Orval lay, and it flipped around shot too. And pressed low in the furrow, fists clenched, Teasle was vowing to track the kid forever, grab him, mutilate him. He would never let up. No more because of Galt, because he could not let somebody who had killed one of his men get away. Personal now. For himself. Father, foster father. Both shot. The insane anger of when his real father had been killed, wanting to strangle the kid until his throat was crushed, his eyes popping. You bastard. You fucking sonofabitch. It was only as he went through in his mind how to climb off this cliff and get his hands on the kid that he suddenly understood how big a mistake he had made. He had not been chasing the kid. It was the other way around. He had been letting the kid lead them into an ambush.

And Jesus what an ambush. With the nearest town thirty miles over hard country, with the helicopter crashed and the dogs dead, the kid could pick everybody off whenever he felt like it. Because the land didn't go straight back behind them. Because eight feet back from the edge of the cliff the land sloped up. To pull back they would have to run uphill in open sight while the kid blasted away at them from the woods below, and where in hell did he get his rifle and how in hell did he know enough to work an ambush like this.

That moment, where the clouds were looming black in the sky, it thundered loud.

9

Orval. Teasle couldn't stop looking at him. The old man was spread out quietly on his face by the edge of the cliff, and Teasle could hardly breathe. *Because of me. Just this once in his life he got careless, and I didn't warn him to stay down.* He began crawling toward him, to cradle him.

"The kid'll swing around," Lester said hoarsely.

Too hoarsely, Teasle thought. Reluctant he turned, worried about his men. They were only seven now, tightfaced, fingering their rifles, looking next to useless. All except Shingleton.

"I'm telling you the kid will swing around," Lester said. The knee was ripped out of his pants. "He'll swing up there behind us."

The men jerked to stare up at the rise behind them as if they expected the kid to be there already.

"He's going to come all right," the young deputy said. There was a brown liquid stain seeping through the seat of his gray pants, and the men had shifted away from him. "Dear God, I want out of here. Get me out of here."

"Go on then," Teasle said. "Run up the slope. See how far you get before he shoots you."

The deputy swallowed.

"What are you waiting for?" Teasle said. "Go on. Run up the slope."

"No," the deputy said. "I won't."

"Then stop it."

"But we have to get up there," Lester said. "Before he beats us to it. If we wait too long, he'll make it up there and we'll never get off this ledge."

The dark clouds hulking closer lit up with lightning. It thundered again, long and loud.

"What's that? I heard something," Lester said. His knee was scraped red where it showed through the rip in his pants.

"The thunder," Shingleton said. "It's playing tricks."

"No. I heard it too," Mitch said.

"Listen."

"The kid."

It was like weak vomiting, like a man choking. Orval. He was starting to move, hunched up, knees and head keeping his stomach off the ground while he clutched his chest, holding himself together. He looked like a caterpillar raising its back for traction to inch forward. But he wasn't going anywhere. Back arched high, he stiffened and collapsed. There was blood dripping from his arms and he was drooling, coughing blood.

Teasle was stopped in disbelief. He had been sure Orval was dead. "Orval," he said. And then he was hurrying before he knew it. "Stay down," he had to remind himself, pressing low to the rocks, trying not to make himself the target Orval had. But Orval was too close to the edge, Teasle was sure he would be seen from the woods below. He took hold of Orval's shoulder and struggled to drag him back to the furrow. But Orval was too heavy, it was taking too long, any second the kid might shoot. He tugged at

Orval and pulled and dragged, and slowly Orval moved. But not quick enough. The stones were too jagged. Orval's clothes were catching on the sharp rocks near the edge of the cliff.

"Help me," Teasle shouted to the men behind him.

Orval coughed more blood.

"Somebody help me! Give me a hand!"

And then in a rush somebody was beside him, helping him, both dragging Orval back from the edge, and all at once they were safe. Teasle let out his breath in a gasp. He wiped sweat from his eyes and didn't need to look to see who had helped him: Shingleton.

And Shingleton was grinning, laughing, not loud, not hilarious, but laughing just the same. It was mostly all inside him. His chest was heaving and he was laughing. "We made it. He didn't shoot, we made it."

And sure it was funny, and Teasle started laughing too. Then Orval coughed more blood and Teasle saw the pain on Orval's face and nothing seemed funny after that.

He reached to unbutton Orval's bloody shirt.

"Take it easy, Orval. We'll have a look and fix you up."

He tried to open the shirt gently but the blood had stuck the cloth to the flesh, and finally he had to tug at the shirt to free it and Orval groaned.

The wound was not something Teasle wanted to look at very long. There was a rank gas coming out the open chest.

"How…bad?" Orval said, wincing.

"Don't you worry about it," Teasle said. "We'll fix you up." He was unbuttoning his own shirt as he spoke, slipping it off his shoulders."

"I asked you…how bad." Each word was a distinct pained whisper.

"You've seen enough things wounded, Orval. You know how bad it is as much as I do." He was rolling his sweaty shirt into a ball, setting it on the hole in Orval's chest. Immediately the shirt was soaking blood.

"I want to hear you tell me. I asked you—"

"All right, Orval, save your strength. Don't talk." His hands were sticky with blood as he buttoned Orval's shirt over the bundle he had put on the wound. "I won't lie to you and I know you don't want me to lie. There's a lot of blood and hard to see for sure but it's my guess he hit a lung."

"Oh my Jesus."

"Now I want you to stop talking and save your strength."

"Please. You can't leave me. Don't leave me."

"That's the last thing you have to worry about. We're taking you back, and we're going to do everything we can for you. But you have to do something for me too. You hear? You have to concentrate on holding your chest. I have my shirt inside yours and I want you to hold it close to where you're hit. We have to stop the bleeding. Can you hear me? Do you understand?"

Orval licked his lips and nodded weakly, and Teasle's mouth tasted full of dry dust. There wasn't a hope that a rolled-up shirt would stop the bleeding from a wound that size. His mouth stayed dusty and he felt streaks of sweat trickle down his bare back. The sun was long gone behind the clouds, but the heat was continuing to press on him, and he thought of water, realizing how thirsty Orval must be.

He knew he shouldn't give him any. He knew that from Korea. A man shot in the chest or stomach would vomit water he drank, and the wound would rip larger, and the pain would get worse. But Orval was licking at his lips, licking at his lips, and Teasle couldn't bear to watch his pain. I'll give him a little. A little won't hurt.

There was a canteen snapped to Orval's belt. He worked it loose, the canvas cover rough, and unscrewed the cap, pouring a little into Orval's mouth. Orval coughed, and the water bubbled out mixed with blood.

"Dear God," Teasle said. For a moment his mind was blank: he didn't know what to do next. Then he thought of the radio and swung over to it. "Teasle calling state police. State police. Emergency." He raised his voice. "*Emergency*."

The radio crackled with static from the clouds.

"Teasle calling state police. Emergency!"

He had been determined not to radio for help no matter what happened. Even when he saw the crashed and burning helicopter, he had not called. But Orval. Orval was going to die.

"*State police come in*."

The radio shrieked with lightning, and in the ebb a voice came through, indistinct and raspy. "State…here…ble."

Teasle couldn't waste time asking him to say it again. "I can't hear you," he said hurriedly. "Our helicopter has crashed. I have a wounded man here. I need another helicopter for him."

"…done."

"I can't hear you. I need another helicopter."

"…impossible.   An   electric   storm   moving   in. Every…grounded."

"But dammit he's going to die!"

The voice answered something, but Teasle couldn't make it out, and then the voice dissolved in static and when it came back it was in the middle of a sentence.

"I can't hear you!" Teasle shouted.

"…sure picked…guy to try and hunt…Green Beret…Medal of Honor."

"What? Say that again."

"Green Beret?" Lester said.

The voice was starting to repeat, broke up, never came back again. It started to rain, light drops speckling the dust and dirt, spotting Teasle's pants and soaking in, pelting cool on his bare back. The black clouds shadowed over. Lightning crackled and lit up the cliff like a spotlight, and as fast as the spotlight came on, it went off and the shadows returned, bringing with them shock-waves of exploding thunder.

"Medal of Honor?" Lester said to Teasle. "Is that what you brought us after? A war hero? A fucking Green Beret?"

"He didn't shoot!" Mitch said.

Teasle looked sharply at him, afraid he was out of control. But Mitch wasn't. He was excited, trying to tell them something, and Teasle knew what it was: he had already thought of it and decided it was no good.

"When you dragged Orval back," Mitch was saying, "he didn't shoot. He isn't down there anymore. He's swinging around behind us and now's our chance to move!"

"No," Teasle told him, rain pelting his face.

"But we've got a chance to…"

"*No*. He might be swinging around, but what if he isn't. What if he doesn't want just one target, and he's waiting down there for the whole lot of us to get careless and show ourselves."

Their faces went ashen. The clouds unloaded and the rain came down for real.

10

It came and it came. Lashing at them solidly. Teasle had never been in anything like it. The wind was whipping the rain at his eyes, driving it into his mouth.

"Storm, my ass. It's a goddamn cloudburst."

He was lying in the water. He didn't think it could get worse, and then the rain increased, and he was almost buried in the water. Lightning cracked bright like the sun, darkness instantly was everywhere, darkness that got blacker and blacker until it was like night, only the time was late afternoon, and rain lashing blind at his eyes, Teasle couldn't even see to the edge of the cliff. Thunder shook him. "What *is* this?"

He shielded his eyes. Orval was lying face up, mouth open in the rain. He'll drown, Teasle thought. His mouth'll fill up with water and he'll breathe it in and drown.

He squinted at his men stretched out in the water on the ledge, and realized that Orval wasn't the only one who might drown. Where they all lay was now the bed of a raging stream. There was swift water rushing down the rise behind them, surging over them, sweeping toward the edge of the cliff, and though he couldn't see the ledge, he knew what it looked like. It was the top of a waterfall: if the storm got any worse, they'd all be washed over the side.

And Orval would be the first to go.

He grabbed Orval's legs. "Shingleton! Help me!" he called, rain driving into his mouth.

Through his words it thundered loud.

"Grab his arms, Shingleton! We're clearing out!" The temperature had gone down rapidly. The rain was now shocking cold on his bare back as he remembered stories about men caught in flash floods in the mountains, about men washed down draws and thrown over cliffs and crushed and broken on the rocks below. "We have to clear out!"

"But the kid!" somebody yelled.

"He can't see us now! He can't see anything!"

"But the kid might be waiting for us up there!"

"We don't have time to worry about him! We have to get off this ledge before the storm gets worse! It'll sweep us over!"

Lightning flashed brilliantly. He shook his head at what he saw. The men. Their faces. In the lightning and rain, their faces changed to white skulls. As suddenly as they came, the skulls were gone, and he was blinking in darkness and the thunder hit him like a string of mortar explosions.

"I'm here!" Shingleton yelled, grabbing Orval's arms. "I've got him. Let's go!"

They heaved him out of the water, bearing toward the rise. The rain doubled, heavier, faster. It was streaking at them almost sideways, drenching them, pouring off them in a constant rush. Teasle slipped. He fell hard on his shoulder and dropped Orval into the swirling current. He struggled splashing to grab Orval, to keep Orval's head above water, then slipped again so his own head went under water and he breathed.

He breathed. The water he sucked up his nose choked his nasal passages and spewed out the two small holes at the back of the roof of his mouth, wrenching them wide. He was wild, frantic, coughing, now up out of the water. Somebody had him. Shingleton was pulling him.

"No! Orval! Grab Orval!"

They couldn't find him.

"He'll go over the side!"

"Here!" somebody yelled. Teasle blinked rain out of his eyes, trying to see who it was yelling. "Orval! I've got him!"

The water rose to Teasle's knees. He waded, legs churning to where the man held Orval's head out of the water. "The current had him!" the man said. It was Ward, and he was tugging at Orval, working to drag him toward the rise. "He was drifting toward the cliff! He bumped me going past!"

Then Shingleton was there, and they all lifted Orval from the water and staggered with him toward the slope. When they reached it, Teasle understood why the water was rising so fast. There was a trough in the hillside, and the streams on top were draining into it, flooding down upon them.

"We have to move farther along!" Teasle said. "We have to find an easier way up!"

The wind shifted and the rain lanced at their faces from the left. As one, they stumbled toward the right, the wind helping them along. But where were the rest of the men, Teasle wanted to know. Were they already climbing the slope? Were they still on the ledge? Why in hell weren't they pitching in to move Orval?

The water rose above his knees. He hoisted Orval higher and they staggered on, and then the wind shifted again: it was no longer pushing them the way they wanted to go, it was shoving them back the way they had come, and they were straining into the full force of the wind and the rain. Shingleton had his arms around Orval's shoulders, Teasle had the legs, Ward was cradling the back, and they slipped and stumbled through the rain until they came at last to where the rise seemed easiest. There was a flood gushing down this part of the slope too, but not as strong as back at the trough, and there were big rocks jutting up for handholds. If only he could see the top, Teasle thought. If only he could be sure the rocks were like that right up to the top.

They started climbing. Shingleton was first; he went up backward, stooping to hold Orval up by the shoulders. He wedged a foot behind a rock and backed up onto it, and then squinted to see another rock behind him and wedged a foot behind that one and backed up onto it as well. Teasle and Ward followed, bent over taking most of Orval's weight, letting Shingleton worry about where to put his feet so he could back up higher. The stream rushed harder down the slope, swashing against their legs.

But where were the others, Teasle wanted to know. Why in Christ weren't they helping? The rain was biting cold on his back. He was lifting Orval blindly, and he felt Shingleton ahead, backing up the slope, pulling Orval with him, and Teasle's arms were aching in their sockets, muscles twisting with Orval's weight. It was taking too long. They wouldn't be able to keep carrying him much longer he knew. They had to get to the top. And then Ward slipped and fell and Teasle almost lost his grip on Orval. They tumbled flat on the slope and slid down a few feet sucked by the current as they all scrambled to hang on to Orval.

They had him. They started working farther up the slope.

And that was as far as they got with him. Shingleton all at once yelled and came falling past Orval, slamming into Teasle's chest. They reeled backward, falling, and Teasle lost hold of Orval, and the next thing he knew he was flat on his back at the bottom of the slope, water swelling over him, rocks tumbling painfully against him.

"I couldn't help it!" Shingleton cried. "The rock slipped out from under me!"

"Orval! The current's got him!"

Teasle splashed toward the cliff edge. He wiped his arm across his eyes, blinking to see in the rain. He couldn't let himself go too near the edge—the current was too strong there. But God, he had to stop Orval.

He slowed, groping closer, wiping his eyes. Lightning flashed. And there, distinct, bright, was Orval's body flipping over the side. Then it was black again, and Teasle's stomach heaved. Hot tears mixed with the cold rain on his face, and he screamed until his throat seized shut, "God damn those bastards, I'll kill them for not helping!"

Shingleton loomed beside him. "Orval! Can you see him?"

Teasle shouldered past. He made it to the rise. "I'll kill them!"

He grabbed for a rock and drew himself up and thrust a foot against a rock and shoved himself up and clawed and dug for handholds through the water sucking past him. All at once he reached the top, bolting into the forest. The din up there was deafening. Wind was bending trees, and rain was shrieking through branches and close-by lightning cracked bright through a trunk with the sharp sound of an ax splitting a solid piece of timber.

The tree crashed down in front of him. He vaulted over it.

"Chief!" somebody called. "Over here, Chief!"

He couldn't see the face. He only saw the body huddled by a tree.

"Over here, Chief!" The man was waving his arm in wide gestures. Teasle charged over to him, grabbing his shirt front. It was Mitch.

"What are you doing?" Mitch said. "What's the matter with you?"

"He went over the side!" Teasle said. Drawing back his fist, he punched Mitch hard in the teeth, jolting him against a tree and into the mud.

"Christ," Mitch said. He shook his head, shook it again. He moaned and held his bloody mouth. "Christ, what's the matter with you?" he was crying. "Lester and the others ran! I stayed behind to stick with you!"

11

Teasle must have made it into the forest by now. Rambo was certain of it. The storm had been going on too long and heavy—Teasle and his men could not have held out on that open ledge. With the rain giving them cover so he could not see to shoot, they must have taken their chance to get up that slope and into the trees. That was all right. They would not be far. He had done a lot of this kind of work in the rain and he knew exactly how to hunt men down in it.

He came out of the bushes and trees, bearing through the rain toward the base of the cliff. In the confusion of the storm, he knew he could escape the other way, deep into the forest, if he wanted. Judging from the wide dense cloud cover, he could be hours and miles away before the storm cleared enough for Teasle to track him—so far away that Teasle would never be able to catch up to him again. It was possible that after the ambush and the rain Teasle might not even have the heart to chase after him, but that did not matter: for the moment he was determined not to run anymore, whether he was being chased or not. He had been lying sheltered under the bushes, watching the top of the cliff for another target, thinking about how Teasle had made him into a killer once more and had got him wanted for murder; growing angrier as he thought about all the months, two months at least, that he would have to run and hide run and hide before he reached Mexico; and for now, by God, he was going to turn the game and make Teasle run from *him*, show him what it felt like. That bastard was going to pay for this.

But you asked for some of it yourself. It wasn't only Teasle. You could have backed off.

For the sixteenth time for crissake? No way.

Even if it was for the hundredth time, so what? Backing off would have been better than this. Leave it alone. End it. Get away.

And let him do this to somebody else? Screw. He has to be stopped.

What? That's not why you're doing this? Admit you wanted all this to happen. You *asked* for it—so you could show him what you knew, surprise him when he found you were the wrong guy to try and handle. You *like* this.

I didn't ask for anything. But damn right I like it. That bastard is going to pay.

The land was dark; his clothes clung icy to his skin. Ahead, long slick grass was bent over in the driving rain, and he waded through, the grass slippery on his smooth wet pants. He came to the stones and rocks that led up toward the base of the cliff, and he stepped cautiously onto them. There were streams of water swirling between them and over them, and in the wind it would be easy to slip and fall and hurt his ribs some more. They were throbbing from when he had leapt off the cliff and crashed against the tree limb, and each time he breathed he felt something pressing sharply inside his right chest. It was like a big fishhook in there, or a jagged chunk of broken bottle. He would have to fix it. Soon.

Very soon.

There was a roar. He had heard it back in the trees and had guessed it was from the sound of the wind and rain. But now it was getting louder as he climbed up over the rocks toward the cliff, and he knew it wasn't the rain. The cliff came into gray view and he saw. A cataract. The cliff had become a waterfall, and a flood was cascading down, roaring onto the rocks, spraying mist high up into the rain. It wasn't safe to go any closer; he began working to the right. About a hundred yards along he knew would be the tree he had leapt into. And very near would be the body of the policeman who had fallen off the cliff with his dogs.

He didn't find the body anywhere around the tree. He was about to look in the wreckage of the helicopter when he realized that the waterfall would have swept the body down over the rocks to the long grass. He went down and the guy was right at the border, facedown in the water. The top of his head was struck flat and his arms and legs were sticking off at queer angles. Rambo wondered about the dogs, but he couldn't find them. The carcasses must have been washed farther into the long grass. He knelt quickly to search the body.

The guy's equipment belt—he needed it. He held his rifle so it wouldn't drop in the water, and with one hand he pulled the body over. The face wasn't too bad, he had seen worse in the war. He stopped looking at it and concentrated on unbuckling the belt and yanking it free. The effort set him wincing—his ribs cut inside his chest. Finally he had the belt loose, and he checked what was on it.

A canteen that was dented but not split open. He unscrewed the cap and drank and the canteen sloshed half-full. The water from it had a stale metallic taste.

A revolver snug in a holster. There was a leather flap snapped

over the handle: not much water would have got in. He unhol-
stered the gun, impressed by how well Teasle equipped his men.
It was a Colt Python: a thick four-inch barrel with a big sighting pin at the end. The plastic handle it was always sold with had
been replaced by a stout wooden grip designed not to be slippery
if it got wet. The sights near the hammer had also been changed.
Usually they were stationary, but these had been made adjustable
for long distance shooting.

He had not hoped for this fine a gun. It was chambered for a
.357 magnum cartridge, the second most powerful handgun load.
A man could kill a deer with it. A man could shoot clean through
a deer with it. He pushed the lever at the side and swung out the
bullet cylinder. There were five shells in it; the chamber underneath the firing pin was empty. Quickly he slipped the gun back
into the holster out of the rain and checked the cartridge pouch
and counted fifteen more shells. Then he buckled the gunbelt
around his waist and stooped, his ribs biting, to search the guy's
pockets. But there wasn't anything to take. Especially no food. He
had thought the guy at least might have some chocolate.

Stooped, his chest was hurting worse than ever. He had to fix
it. Now. He unbuckled the guy's trouser belt and straightened
painfully with it, unbuttoning his outer wool shirt and the white
cotton shirt under that. The rain slapped at his chest. He wound
the belt around his ribs and cinched it like a roll of strong tape
holding him tight. And the pain stopped cutting. It switched to a
swelling, aching pressure against the belt. Hard to breathe. Tight.

But at least the pain had stopped cutting.

He buttoned up and felt the cotton shirt soggy cold against
him. Teasle. Time to go after him. For a second he hesitated and
almost went away in the forest: chasing Teasle would cost him
time getting away, and if there was another posse in these hills, he

might run into them. But two hours wasn't much. That was only as long as he would take to catch him, and after that, under cover of the night, he would still have time to get away. It was worth two hours to teach that bastard.

All right then, which way after him? The niche in the cliff, he decided. If Teasle wanted to get down off the bluff in a hurry, he would likely go back there. With any luck he would be able to head Teasle off and meet him as he came down. He hurried to the right, following the border of grass. Very soon he stumbled across the second body.

It was the old man in green. But how had he tumbled off the cliff so that he ended up all the way over here? His equipment belt didn't have a handgun. It did have a hunting knife, and it had a pouch, and inside Rambo touched something—food. Sticks of meat. A handful. He bit, barely chewing, swallowing, biting off more. Sausage, sticks of smoked sausage, wet and crushed a little from the old man slamming onto the rocks, but it was food, and he was biting into it, chewing, swallowing quickly, forcing himself to slow and mulch it around to all parts of his mouth; then it was almost gone and he was tucking the last bits into his mouth and sucking his fingers; and then all that was left was the smoke taste and his tongue slightly burning from the hot peppers that had been in with the meat.

Sudden lightning and then thunder as if the earth had shuddered. He had better watch himself; he was getting too lucky. First the gun, the bullets, the canteen, and now the knife and the sausage. They had been so easy to get that he had better watch himself. He knew how these things worked and how they evened out. One minute you got lucky and the next—well, he would make damn sure he watched himself so all the luck stayed with him.

12

Teasle kneaded his fist, opening, closing it. The knuckles had gashed on Mitch's teeth, swelling now, but Mitch's lips were swelling twice as bad. In the thunder Mitch tried to stand; one knee gave out and he fell weeping against a tree.

"You shouldn't have hit him so hard," Shingleton said.

"Don't I know it," Teasle said.

"You're a trained boxer. You didn't need to hit him so hard."

"I said I know it. I shouldn't have hit him at all. Let's leave it."

"But look at him. He can't even stand. How's he going to travel?"

"Never mind that," Ward said. "We've got worse troubles. The rifles, the radio, they've washed over the cliff."

"We've still got our handguns."

"But they don't have any range," Teasle said. "Not against a rifle. As soon as it's light, the kid can pick us off a mile away."

"Unless he takes advantage of the storm to clear out," Ward said.

"No. We have to assume he'll come for us. We've been too careless already, and we have to start acting as if the worst will happen. Even if he doesn't come, we're still finished. No food or equipment. No organization. Dead tired. We'll be lucky if we can crawl by the time we get back to town."

He looked at where Mitch was sitting in the rain and mud, holding his mouth, groaning. "Help me with him," he said, lifting Mitch to his feet.

Mitch shoved him away. "I'm all right," he murmured through his missing teeth. "You've done enough. Don't come near me."

"Let *me* try," Ward said.

But Mitch pushed him away too. "I'm all right, I tell you." His lips were swollen purple. His head drooped and he covered his face with his hands. "Dammit, I'm all right."

"Sure you are," Ward said and caught him as he sagged to his knees.

"I—Jesus, my teeth."

"I know," Teasle said, and together, he and Ward braced Mitch up.

Shingleton looked at Teasle, shaking his head. "What a mess. Look at how dull his eyes are. And look at you. How are you going to make it through the night without a shirt? You'll freeze."

"Don't worry about it. Just watch out for Lester and them."

"By now they're long gone."

"Not in this storm. They won't be able to see to walk in a straight line. They'll be wandering around this bluff somewhere, and if we stumble into them, look out. Lester and that young deputy are so scared about the kid coming, they're liable to think we're him and start shooting. I've seen it happen like that before."

Snowstorms in Korea where a sentry shot his own man by mistake, he was thinking, no time to explain. Rainy nights in Louisville where two policemen got confused and shot each other.

His father. Something like that had happened to his father too—
but he could not let himself think about it, remember it.

"Let's go," he said abruptly. "We've got a lot of miles to cover
and we're not getting any stronger."

The rain pushing at their backs, they guided Mitch through
the trees. At first his legs dragged in the mud; then clumsily, sluggishly, he managed walking.

A war hero, Teasle thought, his back numb from the cold rain
streaming down. If the kid had said he was in the war.... But
who would have thought to believe him? Why hadn't the kid explained more?

Would that have made a difference? Would you have handled
him different from anybody else?

No. I couldn't.

Fine, then you just worry about what he knows to do to you
when he comes.

If he comes. Maybe you're wrong. Maybe he won't come.

He came back to town all those times, didn't he? And he'll
come this time, too. Oh, he'll come all right.

"Hey, you're trembling," Shingleton said.

"Just look out for Lester and them."

He could not keep from thinking about it. Legs stiff and hard
to move, holding Mitch up as he and the others trudged wearily
through the trees in the rain, he could not help remembering
what had happened to his father, that Saturday, the six other
men who had gone on the deer hunt. His father had wanted him
along, but three had said he was too young, and his father had not
liked the way they said it, but gave in: that Saturday was the first
day of the season, an argument would spoil it.

So the story had come back. How they took up positions along
a dried-up streambed that was marked with fresh deer tracks and

droppings. How his father swung around to the top where he made a racket to frighten a deer down the streambed where the men would see it going by and shoot. The rule: everybody was to stay in position so that nobody would be confused about where anybody else was. But one of them, on his first hunt, tired of waiting all day for a deer to go by, wandered off to see what he could find on his own, heard noise, saw movement in the brush, fired, and split Teasle's father's head very nearly in half. The body almost didn't lie in open state: the head was even more shattered than it first seemed. But the undertaker used a wig and everyone said the body looked perfectly alive. Orval had been on that hunt and now Orval was shot too, and as Teasle guided Mitch through the storm across the bluff, he was more and more afraid that he himself was going to die as well. He strained to see if Lester and the others were in the dark trees ahead. If they did lose direction and shoot scared, he knew it would be nobody's fault but his own. What were his men anyhow? Fifty-seven-hundred-dollar-a-year traffic police, small-town deputies trained to handle small-town crime, always hoping nothing serious would happen, always near help if they needed it; and here they were in the wildest mountains in Kentucky with no help around, up against an experienced killer, and God only knew how they had managed to bear up this long. He should never have brought them in here, he realized. He should have waited for the state police. For five years he had just been fooling himself that his department was as tough and disciplined as Louisville's, understanding now that over those years, little by little, his men had got used to their routine and had lost their edge. And so had he. Thinking about how he had argued with Orval instead of concentrating on the kid, about how he had got them all ambushed, and how their equipment was lost and how the posse was split up gone to hell and Orval dead, he was coming to realize—the idea cropping up and him pushing it away and it cropping up again stronger—how really soft and careless he had turned.

Like punching Mitch.

Like not warning Orval to stay low.

The first noise confused with the thunder, and he could not be certain that he had actually heard it. He stopped and looked at the others. "Did you hear?"

"I don't know exactly," Shingleton said. "Up ahead, I think. Off to the right."

Then three more came, and they were unmistakable shots from a rifle.

"It's Lester," Ward said. "But he's not shooting this way."

"I don't think he saved his rifle anymore than we did," Teasle said. "That's the kid shooting."

There was one more shot, still from a rifle, and he listened for yet another, but it never came.

"He ran around and caught them at the break in the cliff," Teasle said. "Four shots. Four men. The fifth was to finish somebody. Now he'll be after *us*." He hurried to lead Mitch in the opposite direction from the shots.

Ward balked. "Hold it. Aren't we going to try and help? We can't just leave them."

"Depend on it. They're dead."

"And now he'll be coming for us," Shingleton said.

"You bet on it," Teasle said.

Ward looked anxiously toward the direction of the shots. He closed his eyes, sickened. "Those poor dumb bastards." Reluctantly he bolstered Mitch, and they moved off to the left, gaining speed. The rain eased off, then got heavier.

"The kid will probably wait for us at the cliff in case we didn't hear," Teasle said. "That will give us a lead. As soon as he's sure we're not coming, he'll set off across the bluff to find our trail, but this rain will wipe it out and he won't find anything."

"We're in the clear then," Ward said.

"Clear then," Mitch repeated stupidly.

"No. When he doesn't find our trail, what he'll do is run toward the far end of the bluff and try to get ahead of us. He'll find a spot where he thinks we're most likely to climb down, and he'll lie waiting for us."

"Well then," Ward said, "we'll just have to get there first, won't we?"

"First, won't we," Mitch repeated, staggering; and Ward made it sound so easy, Mitch's echo sounded so funny, that Teasle laughed, nervously. "Hell yes, we'll just have to get there first," he said, looking at Shingleton and Ward, impressed by their control, and he suddenly thought that things might work out after all.

13

At six the rain changed to big cracking chunks of hail, and Shingleton was hit so hard in the face by some that they had to grope close under the shelter of a tree. The leaves had already fallen from the tree, but there were enough bare branches for most of the hail to glance off of, and the rest of it came down striking sharply against Teasle's bare back and chest and the arms he had raised protectively over his head. He was desperate to start moving again, but he knew it would be crazy to try: a few wallops from chunks of hail this size could lay a man flat. But the longer he stayed huddled by this tree, the more time the kid had to catch up, and his only hope was that the hail had forced the kid to stop and take cover also.

He waited, glancing around, braced for an attack, and then at last the hail stopped and no more rain came, and with the light clearing and the wind dying, they worked fast across the bluff. But without the distraction of the wind and rain, the noises they made hurrying through the underbrush were loud, a signal to the kid. They tried going slower, but the noises were almost as loud, so they hurried on again, crashing.

"Doesn't this top have an end?" Shingleton said. "We've been going for miles."

"For miles," Mitch echoed. "Four miles. Five. Six." He was dragging his feet again.

Next he sagged; Ward heaved him up; and then Ward himself heaved up, careening backward. The report from the rifle was rolling through the trees, and Ward was now on his back, arms and legs stuck out in a death frenzy, and from where Teasle lay on the ground, he saw that Ward had taken the bullet directly in the chest. He was surprised to be lying on the ground. He didn't remember diving there. He was surprised that he had his pistol out.

Christ, Ward dead now too. He wanted to crawl to him, but what was the use. What about Mitch? Not him too. He was fallen into the mud, lying still as if he had been shot as well. No. He was all right, eyes opening, blinking at a tree.

"Did you see the kid?" Teasle said fast to Shingleton. "Did you see where he shot from?"

No answer. Shingleton was flat on the ground, staring blankly ahead, his face drawn tight around his massive cheekbones.

Teasle shook him. "Did you see, I asked you. Snap out of it!"

Shaking him was like pressing a release valve. Shingleton broke into motion, fist up close to Teasle's face. "*Keep your fucking hands off me.*"

"Did you see him, I asked you."

"No, I said!"

"You didn't say *anything*!"

"Anything," Mitch echoed dumbly.

They looked at him. "Quick, give me a hand," Teasle said, and they dragged him forward into a slight hollow ringed with bushes, a rotting tree fallen across the forward rim. The hollow was full of rain water, and Teasle sank slowly into it, cold against his chest and stomach.

His hands were shaking as he checked his pistol to be sure no water plugged the barrel. He knew what had to be done now and it frightened him, but he did not see any other way, and if he thought about it too much, he might not be able to make himself go through with it. "Stay here with Mitch," he said mouth-dry to Shingleton. His tongue had not been moist in hours. "If somebody comes back through these bushes and doesn't first say it's me, shoot him."

"What do you mean stay here? Where—"

"Out ahead. If we try running back the way we came, he'll only follow us. We might as well save ourselves the trouble of running and try to end this right here."

"But he's trained to fight like this."

"And I was trained for night patrol in Korea. That was twenty years ago, but I haven't forgotten all of it. I might be slow and out of practice, but I don't hear any better ideas."

"Stay here and wait for him. Let him come to us. We know he'll come. We're ready for him."

"And what happens when it gets to be night and he sneaks right on to us before we hear him?"

"We'll move out when it's night."

"Sure, and make so much noise he won't even need to see us to shoot us. He'll just have to aim toward where he hears us. You just said it. He's trained to do this, and I'm betting that's our edge. With any luck he won't expect me to go out there and play it his way. He'll expect me to run, not attack."

"Then I'm going with you."

"*No*. Mitch needs you to stay with him. Two of us crawling around out there might make enough noise to warn the kid."

He had another reason for doing it alone, but he didn't wait to explain anymore. He had waited too long as it was. Immediately he crawled up out of the hollow, to the left around the fallen tree. The mud was so chill against his stomach that he had to force himself down along it. He squirmed forward several feet, and paused to listen, and squirmed forward again, and each time he dug his shoes into the mud to push ahead, the mud gave a sucking noise and he tensed. The suck increased until finally he stopped using his feet to push and switched to wriggling forward on his elbows and knees, always careful to keep his pistol free of the mud. Drops of water spilled icy onto his spine as he wormed under bushes. He stopped and listened and crawled on.

Shingleton wouldn't understand his other reason for doing this anyhow, he thought. It wasn't Shingleton who had been in charge and made the mistakes that killed Orval and Lester and the young deputy and Ward and Galt and the two men in the helicopter and all the rest. So how could Shingleton understand why he couldn't bring himself to let anybody else die for him? This time it would be just himself and the kid and nobody else, just the way this thing started, and if there were going to be anymore mistakes, this time it would be just himself who would pay.

His watch hands had been at six-thirty when he set out. He was so busy concentrating on the movements and sounds around him that it was seven when he next looked at his watch. A squirrel scrambling up a tree startled him into guessing it was the kid, and he came close to shooting at it. The light was dimming again, not from the clouds now, but from the start of evening, and the air was colder and he was shivering as he crawled. Even so, there were rivulets of sweat trickling down his face and back and under his arms.

It was fear. The hot pressure of his anus. The adrenalin squirting into his stomach. He wanted desperately to turn and go back, and because of that, he urged himself to go farther on. God in heaven, if he missed this chance at the kid, it wasn't going to be because he was afraid to die. Jesus no. He owed that to Orval. He owed it to the rest of them.

Seven-fifteen. He had crawled far out now, and he had worked back and forth across the forest, pausing, peering deeply into groves and thickets to see if the kid was hiding there. Small noises made him jumpy, noises he could not account for, the snap of a branch that could be the kid adjusting his position to aim, the brush of leaves that could be the kid circling behind him. He crawled slowly, fighting his panic to speed up and get this over, fighting to concentrate on everything around him. The slightest piece of cover was all the kid needed. All he himself had to do was get careless once and not check one bush or one stump or one dip in the ground, and that might be the end. It would be so abrupt that he would never hear the burst of the shot that killed him.

Then it was seven-thirty and the shadows had merged deep enough to trick him. What looked like the kid was only the dark trunk of a crooked tree set far back in the gloom. A fallen log in back of a bush deceived him the same way, and he knew he had done the best he could. It was time to head back. That was the worst part. His eyes were tired and the shadows were touching him, and he just wanted to hurry back to Shingleton and relax a minute and let Shingleton keep watch for the kid. But he could not dare give up searching to speed up back there. Even as he returned, he still had to take his time and check every bush and tree before he made a move. He had to look behind, afraid the kid was sneaking toward him. His back felt so naked, so white in the gloom that he kept expecting to glance around and see the kid aiming with a smile at the cleft between his shoulder blades. The bullet would blast apart his backbone and rupture his insides and instantly he would be dead. In spite of himself he hurried to return.

He almost forgot to let Shingleton know it was himself coming. Wouldn't that be a laugh. To risk searching for the kid and then be shot by his own man. "It's me," he whispered. "It's Teasle."

But nobody answered.

I whispered too low and he didn't hear me, Teasle thought. "It's me," he repeated, louder. "It's Teasle." But again nobody answered, and Teasle knew something had to be wrong.

He circled the hollow and crept up from behind, and something was more than wrong. Shingleton wasn't there, and Mitch was flat on his back in the water, his throat neatly slit from ear to ear, his blood steaming in the cold. Shingleton. Where was Shingleton? Worried and tired of waiting, he must have gone after the kid too, and left Mitch, and the kid came up and slit his throat to kill him quietly. The kid, Teasle realized, the kid must be very close. He crouched and spun, and the sight of Mitch, the frenzy of trying to protect himself from all angles made him want to cry out, Shingleton, get back here, Shingleton! Two men facing in opposite directions would maybe see the kid before he rushed them. Shingleton, he wanted to call.

Instead Shingleton called to him from some place on the right. "Look out, Will, he's got me!" His cry was punctuated by a rifle shot, and that was all Teasle could stand. He finally had his breakdown, running before he knew it, screaming, racing away, charging through the shadows, through the trees and bushes. Aaaeeiii, he was screaming. The niche in the cliff, was all he could think. *The cliff the cliff!*

14

He shot at Teasle, but the light was bad and the trees were too thick, and anyway, Shingleton grabbed the rifle so that the bullet jerked low. Shingleton ought to have been dead. He had been shot in the skull. He should not have been able to get back off the ground and grab the rifle to throw off its aim. Rambo really had to admire him as he shot him again, through one eye now, and this time Shingleton was dead for sure.

Without a pause he set off running after Teasle. It was obvious that Teasle's direction was back toward the niche in the cliff, and he planned on beating him there. He did not follow exactly on Teasle's path—Teasle might get control of himself and lie somewhere waiting—so he ran in a line parallel to Teasle, racing to beat him to the cliff.

He just missed him. He came hurrying through the woods, able to see the cliff edge now and the top of the niche, and he dropped to his knees, hiding for Teasle. But then he heard chips of stone rattling down the cliff and the sound of heavy breathing down there, and he rushed over just in time to see Teasle jump the last few feet down the niche, ducking around the side of the cliff wall. He saw too the bodies of the four deputies where he had shot them at the bottom of the cliff, and he didn't like the position he was in. Now Teasle had the advantage. To climb down the niche after him, he would be as easy a target for Teasle as the four deputies had been for himself.

He knew damn well that Teasle was not going to stand down there all night waiting for him. Shortly Teasle was going to take his chance and clear out, and he would be left up on top, suspecting that Teasle was gone but not willing to risk that he was still there. To be safe he had to find another way down off this bluff, and that way had to be in the direction Teasle would take for home.

He raced back toward where he had killed Shingleton, and passed his body, and continued racing toward where he hoped the bluff would slope down into the draw, and it did slope down, and in half an hour he was into the draw, running through the woods toward a stretch of grass he had dimly spotted from above. The light was fading worse, and he was hurrying to get to the grass before the dark could blot out Teasle's trail. He reached the grass and ran through the line of trees that bordered it, not wanting to show himself as a target while he searched for tracks that led out of the trees into the open space. He looked and ran to look farther along, but still no tracks in the wet earth, and he thought that maybe Teasle had been slow to leave the cliff, began to worry that Teasle was behind him, coming, watching. Just as it started to rain again and made everything even darker, he found the grass pushed down.

There.

But he had to take a handicap, give Teasle a headstart. Because in spite of his temptation to rush across the open grass after him, he had to wait until the night was fully black: Teasle might not be running ahead at all, he might be lying in the bushes on the other side, aiming. Then he supposed it dark enough so he could run across without showing himself as a target, but his caution was needless because when he got over there Teasle was not around. The rain was falling lightly through the trees, it muffled sounds very little, and there, up ahead, something was working to break through the thick underbrush.

He set out after it, stopped and listened, corrected his direction toward the noise, then set on again. He expected that fairly soon Teasle would give up running and try to ambush him, but as long as he could hear Teasle running, it was safe to keep after him and make all the noise he had to. Then one time he stopped and listened, and the running up ahead was stopped as well, so he sank to the ground and began crawling quietly forward. In a minute the running up ahead continued again, and he leapt to his feet, charging after it. That was the pattern for an hour: running, stopping, listening, crawling, running. The rain kept on in a cold faint drizzle, and the belt that was cinched around his ribs loosened, and he had to tighten it to ease the pain. He was certain now that his ribs were broken and that sharp bones were lancing his insides. He would have given up, but he knew he would have Teasle soon; he doubled over in agony, but Teasle was still running up there, so he straightened, pushing himself on.

The chase went up a slope of trees, over a spine of rock and down a patch of shale to a stream, then along the bank of the stream, across the stream into more woods, across a ravine. The pain in his chest cut sharply as he jumped across, and he almost slipped down into the ravine, but he pulled himself up, listened for Teasle, heard him and chased after him. Each time his right foot hit the ground, the jolt went all the way up his right side, grating his ribs. Twice he was sick.

15

Up and down, the pattern of the country repeated itself. Stumbling up a slope of rocks and brush, Teasle felt like he was back on the ledge, trying to get up the rise to the woods. In the dark he couldn't see the top; he wished he knew how far it was; he couldn't keep on climbing much longer. The rain was making the rocks slippery, and he was losing his balance, falling hard. He took to crawling up, and the rocks tore at his pants, cut into his knees, while behind him, down in the trees at the bottom, he heard the kid breaking through the undergrowth.

He scrambled faster. If he could just see the top and know how far he had to go. The kid must be out of the woods now and starting up the slope, and Teasle thought of shooting blindly down to hold him back. He couldn't: the flashes from his pistol would give the kid a target, but Christ, he had to do something.

In one desperate lunge he reached the top but didn't know it was the top until he tripped and barely grabbed a rock in time to stop from rolling down the other side. Now. Now he could shoot. He stretched out and listened to where the kid was rushing up the slope, and he fired six times in a line across the noises. Then he hugged the ground in case he had missed, and a shot came from below, zinging over him. He heard the kid climbing off to the left, and he fired once more at the noise before he started racing down the other side of the slope. Again he tripped, and now he struck his shoulder solidly against a rock and couldn't keep from rolling as he grabbed his shoulder and tumbled to the bottom.

He lay there dazed. The wind was knocked out of him, and he fought to breathe but he couldn't. He gasped and pushed his stomach muscles in, but they wanted to push out, and then he managed to suck in a little air and a little more, and he was almost breathing normally again when he heard the kid clambering on the rocks above. He groped to his knees, then to his feet—and discovered that in his fall he had lost hold of his pistol. It was somewhere up on the slope. No time to go back for it. No light to find it.

He staggered through woods, circling he guessed, going nowhere, winding around and around until he'd be brought to bay. Already his knees were buckling. His direction was wobbly. He was bumping against trees, a crazy vision in his head of him in his office, bare feet on the desk, head tilted sipping hot soup. Tomato soup. No, bean with bacon. The rich expensive kind where the label said don't add water.

16

It was only minutes now before he'd have him. The noises ahead were slowing, more erratic, clumsy. He could hear Teasle breathing hoarsely, he was that close to him. Teasle had given him a good race, that was sure. He had figured to tag him several miles ago, and here they were still at it. But not for long. A few minutes now. That was all.

The pain in his ribs, he had to slow, but it was still a fair pace, and since Teasle had slowed too, he wasn't bothered much. His hand was over his ribs, helping the belt to press. All his right side was swollen. In the rain the belt was even looser than before, and he had to keep his hand pressing.

Then he stumbled and fell. He hadn't done that before. No, he was wrong about that. He had stumbled at the ravine. Then he stumbled again, and rising to his feet, working on, he decided it might take slightly more than a few minutes before he caught up to Teasle. It would be soon, though. No question about it. Just a little more than a few minutes. That was all.

Had he said that out loud?

The brambles caught him full in the face as he came up to them in the dark. They were spikes lashing into him, and he recoiled, clutching his ripped cheeks. He knew it wasn't rain wetting his cheeks and hands. But it did not matter, because off in there in the brambles was the sound of Teasle crawling. This was it. He had him. He bore to the left along the edge of the brambles, waiting for it to curve down and lead him to the bottom of the patch where he could rest and wait for Teasle to crawl out. In the dark he would not be able to see the surprised look on Teasle's face when he shot him.

But the longer he hurried along the edge of the brambles, the farther it stretched on, and he began to wonder if the brambles covered all this section of the slope. He hurried farther, and still the brambles did not curve down, and then he was sure they stretched all along this rise. He wanted to stop and double back, but he had the thought that if he kept on just a little more, the brambles would at last curve down. Five minutes became what he judged was fifteen, and then twenty, and he was wasting his time, he should have gone right in after Teasle, but now he could not. In the dark he had no idea where Teasle had entered.

Double back. Maybe the brambles did not go far along the other end of this ridge, maybe they curved down over there. He rushed back, holding his side, moaning. He hurried a long while until he no longer believed they would ever curve down, and when next he stumbled and fell, he remained face down in the muddy grass.

He'd lost him. He had given up so much time and strength to come so close and lose him. His face stung from the gashes of the brambles. His ribs were on fire, his hands pulpy, his clothes ripped, his body slashed. And he had lost him, the rain coming down in a gently cooling drizzle as he lay there splayed out, breathing deeply, holding it, letting it out slowly, breathing deeply again, letting the dead weight of his arms and legs relax with every slow exhale—for the first time he could remember, crying, softly crying.

17

Any moment the kid would be breaking through the brambles after him. He crawled hysterically. Then the brambles got lower and thicker until he had to press himself flat and wriggle. Even so, the lowest branches scraped across his back and snagged in the seat of his pants, and when he twisted to unsnag them, other branches gouged his arms and shoulders. He's coming, he thought, and squirmed desperately forward, letting the barbs dig into him. His belt buckle scooped into the mud, funneling it into his pants.

But where was he going? How did he know he wasn't completing a circle, returning to the kid? He stopped, frightened. The land sloped down. He must be on the side of a hill. If he kept wriggling downward, he'd be headed straight away. Or would he? Hard to think, suffocated in the dense black tangle and the constant rain. You bastard kid, I'm going to get away and kill you for this.

Kill you for this.

He lifted his head off the mud. And couldn't recall having moved for a while. And gradually understood he had passed out.

He stiffened and glanced all around. The kid could have crept up to him in his stupor and slit his throat just like he did to Mitch. Christ, he said out loud, and his voice was a croak that startled him. Christ, he said again—to free his voice—but the word broke like a crust of ice.

No, I'm wrong, he thought, his brain slowly unclouding. The kid wouldn't have crept up in my sleep to kill me. He would have wakened me first. He'd want me to know what was happening.

So where is he? Watching close? Finding my trail, coming? He listened for noises in the brush and didn't hear anything and had to keep moving, had to keep distance between them.

But when he tried crawling fast, he only managed a sluggish strain to pull forward. He must have been unconscious a long time back there. The light wasn't black now, it was gray, and he could see the brambles everywhere, thick and ugly, spines an inch long. He fingered his back, and he was like a porcupine, dozens of barbs hooked in his skin. He stared at his hand all bloody and struggled worming on. Maybe the kid was very close, watching him, enjoying him suffer.

Then it all confused, and then the sun was up, and through the tops of the brambles, he saw the sky bright and stark blue. He laughed. What are you laughing at?

Laughing at? I don't even remember the rain stopping, and now the sky is clear and it's daylight for crissake. He laughed again and realized he was turning giddy. And that was funny and he laughed at that. He had crawled ten feet out of the brambles into an autumn-plowed field before he understood that he was out. It was quite a joke. He squinted and tried to see the end of the field and couldn't, and tried standing and couldn't, and the inside of his head was spinning so much that he had to laugh again. Then he suddenly quit. The kid would be around here somewhere aiming. He'd enjoy watching me come out sliced to pieces before he shot. The sonofabitch I'll

Bean with bacon soup.

His stomach heaved up.

And that was a joke too. Because what on earth did he have in his stomach to heave up? Nothing. That's right, nothing. So what was this stuff on the ground in front of him? Raspberry pie, he joked. And that made him sick again.

So he crawled through it over a couple of furrows and collapsed, and then he crawled over a few more. There was a pool of black water between two furrows. He had been twisting his face toward the sky all night to drink the rain, but his tongue was still choking him, his throat was still swollen dry, and he drank from the muddy water, poking his face down close and lapping and almost passing out with his face in the water. There was sweet gritty dirt in his mouth. A few more feet. Just try to do a few more feet. I get away, I'll kill that bastard kid...tear him

Because I'm a, but then the idea fell apart on him.

I'm a, but he couldn't remember, and then he had to stop and rest, chin on the top of a mulchy furrow, the sun warming his back. Can't stop. Pass out. Die. Move.

But he couldn't move.

He couldn't raise himself to crawl on his hands and knees. He tried clawing at the dirt ahead of him to pull himself forward, but he couldn't force himself to move that way either. Got to. Can't pass out. Die. He braced his shoes against a furrow and pushed and pushed harder and this time he budged a little. His heart swelling, he pushed his shoes against the furrow even harder and inched forward through the mud, and he didn't dare let himself stop: he knew he would never be able to raise the strength to go again. Shoes against furrow. Push. Worm. The kid. That's it. He remembered now. He was going to fix the kid.

I'm not as good a fighter.

Oh yes, the kid's a better fighter.

Oh yes, but I'm, and then the idea fell apart again as he lapsed into the mechanical rhythm of shoes against furrow—push—one more time—and push—*one more time*. He didn't know when his arms had started back to work, hands clawing the dirt, dragging him along. Organize. That was the word he'd been searching for. And then he clawed forward and he touched something.

It took a while to register.

A wire.

He looked up, and there were other wires. A fence. And sweet God, through the fence was something so beautiful that he didn't believe he was really seeing it. A ditch. A gravel road. His heart was pounding wildly and he was laughing, sticking his head through the wires, shimmying through, the fence barbed wire, ripping his back some more, but he didn't care, he was laughing, rolling into the ditch. It was full of water and he tumbled on his back, the water trickling into his ears, and then he was struggling up the rise toward the road, sliding down, groping up, sliding, flopping himself over the top, one arm touching the gravel of the road. He could not feel the gravel. He could see it sure. He was squinting directly at it. But he could not feel.

Organize. That was it. Now he remembered it all.

I know how to organize.

The kid's a better fighter. But I know how...to organize.

For Orval.

For Shingleton and Ward and Mitch and Lester and the young deputy and all of them.

For me.

I'll kill him.

He lay there at the side of the road, repeating that over and over to himself, closing his eyes to the glare of the sun, snickering at how his pants were in shreds, at how bloody he was, the blood seeping through the mud on him while he grinned, repeating his idea, telling it to the state trooper who said "My God" and gave up trying to lift him into the cruiser and ran for the car radio.

PART THREE

1

IT WAS NIGHT, and the back of the truck smelled of oil and grease. A sheet of stiff canvas had been pulled across the top to form a roof, and in under it Teasle sat on a bench, staring at the big map that hung on one wall. The only light was from an unshielded bulb dangling over the map. Next to the map was a bulky two-way radio on a table.

The radioman wore earphones. "National Guard truck twenty-eight in position," he was saying to a deputy. "Three miles down from the bend in the stream." The deputy nodded, shoving one more red pin into the map next to the others along the south side. To the east, yellow pins showed the deployment of state police. Black pins in the west were police from nearby towns and counties; white pins to the north were police from Louisville, Frankfort, Lexington, Bowling Green, and Covington.

"You're not going to stay here all night, are you?" someone said to Teasle from outside the back of the truck. Teasle looked, and it was Kern, the captain of the state police. He was out far enough that the glare from the bulb lit just part of his face, his eyes and forehead in shadow. "Go home and get some sleep, why don't you?" Kern said. "The doctor told you to rest, and nothing serious will happen here for a while."

"Can't."

"Oh?"

"Reporters are looking for me at my place and the office. The best way I know to rest is not go through everything again for them."

"They'll be coming around here looking for you soon anyhow."

"No. I told your men at the roadblocks not to let them pass."

Kern shrugged and stepped toward the truck into the full light. It was stark and accented the lines in his forehead, the pinched skin around his eyes, making him look older than he was. It did not reflect off his red hair, making even that seem lusterless and dull.

He's the same age I am, Teasle thought. If he looks like that, then after these last few days, how must I look?

"That doctor came close to making a career out of bandaging your face and hands," Kern said. "What's that dark stain soaking through your shirt? Don't tell me you're bleeding again."

"Some kind of ointment he spread on too thick. I have bandages under my clothes too. The ones around my legs and knees are so tight I can hardly walk." He made himself smile, as if the tight bandages were a practical joke from the doctor. He did not want Kern to realize how very bad he felt, sick, dizzy.

"Any pain?" Kern said.

"I hurt less before he put these bandages on so tight. He gave me some pills to take every hour."

"Any help?"

"Enough." That sounded right. He had to be careful how he talked about it to Kern, minimizing his pain, but not so much that

Kern would stop believing him and insist that he go back to the hospital. Before, at the hospital, Kern had shown up damn mad at him for rushing into the forest after the kid without waiting for the state police. "*It's my jurisdiction, and you took advantage, and now you can just stay the hell out of this,*" Kern had said. Teasle had taken it all, letting Kern get rid of his anger, and then slowly he had done his best to convince Kern that more than one person was needed to organize this wide a search. There was another argument that he did not use, but he was sure that Kern was thinking it: as many men could die this time as at the start, and somebody ought to be around to share the responsibility. Kern was that sort of weak leader. Teasle had seen him rely on others too often. So now Teasle was here helping, but not necessarily for long. Despite Kern's faults, he did worry about his men and how much work they could stand, and if he once thought that Teasle was in too great pain, he could easily decide to send him away.

Outside, trucks were rumbling by in the night, big trucks that Teasle knew would have soldiers in them. A siren started, coming up the road fast, shrieking by toward town, and he was glad to talk about something besides how he felt. "What's the ambulance for?"

"Another civilian who just got himself shot."

Teasle shook his head. "How they're dying to help."

"Dying is about the word for it."

"What happened?"

"Stupidity. A bunch of them were up camping in the woods, figuring to be right with us when we start in the morning. They heard a noise out in the dark and guessed it might be the kid trying to sneak down and across the road, so they grabbed their rifles and went out to see. First thing, they mixed up in the dark. One guy heard another guy and thought it was the kid, started shooting, the other guy shot back, everybody else started shooting. God's mercy nobody was killed, just hit bad. I never saw anything like it."

"I did." For a time earlier, when he had been staring at the map, his head had felt like it was stuffed with satin, and now without warning it was like that again. His ears felt stuffed too, and the words "I did" seemed to have come in an echo from outside him. Off balance, faintly nauseous, he wanted to stop and lie down on the bench, but he could not let Kern know what was happening to him. "When I worked in Louisville," he said, and almost could not continue. "About eight years ago. There was a little town near us where a six-year-old girl had been kidnapped. The local police thought she might have been assaulted and left somewhere, so they organized a search, and some of us off-duty that weekend drove over to help. Trouble was that the people who were organizing the search put out a call for help over the radio stations and in the newspapers, and any guy who wanted a free meal and some excitement decided to come."

He was determined not to lie down. But the light was going gray on him, the bench he sat on seemed to be tilting. He finally had to compromise and lean back against the wall of the truck, hoping he looked at ease. "Four thousand," he said, concentrating to keep the words straight. "No place for them all to sleep, to eat. No way to coordinate that many. The town just grew overnight and split at the seams. Most of them drank half the time and then showed up hung-over on the buses going out to the search area. One guy nearly drowned in a swamp. One group got lost, and the search had to be stopped so everybody else could go find them. Snake bites. Broken legs. Sunstroke. It finally got so confused that all civilians had to be ordered home, and just the police kept on the search."

He lit a cigarette and dragged deeply on it, trying to numb his dizziness. He looked and the radioman and the deputy were turned to him, listening. How long had he been talking? Ten minutes it seemed, although it could not have been. His mind was skimming up and down in a smooth undulating pattern.

"Well don't stop," Kern said. "What about the girl? Did you find her?"

Teasle nodded slowly. "Six months later. In a shallow grave off a side road about a mile from where the search originally ended. Some old guy drinking in a bar in Louisville made a few jokes about feeling little girls, and we heard about it. A long chance there was a connection, but we followed up anyhow. Since I had been on the search and knew the case, they had me question him, and forty minutes after I started on him, he came out with the whole story. How he'd been driving by this farm and saw this little girl splashing in a plastic pool in the front yard. It was her yellow swimsuit attracted him, he said. Grabbed her right out of the front yard and into the car without anybody seeing. He took us directly to the grave. It was the second grave. The first grave had been in the middle of the search area, and while the civilians had been wandering around screwing things up, he had come back one night and moved her." He took another deep drag on his cigarette, feeling the smoke fill his throat, his bandaged fingers thick and numb holding the cigarette. "Those civilians will screw things up here too. Word about this should never have been let out."

"It's my fault. There's a reporter who comes around my office who heard my men talking before I could keep them quiet. I've got some of them herding all outsiders back to town right now."

"Sure, and that bunch in the woods might get jumpy again and take a shot at your men. Anyway, you'll never round everyone up.

Tomorrow morning there'll be civilians all through those hills. You saw the way they've taken over town. There's just too many of them to control. The worst hasn't come yet. Wait until the professionals show up."

"I don't know what you mean by professionals. Who in hell are they?"

"Amateurs really, but they call themselves pros. Guys with nothing better to do than chase around the country to every place that has a search. I met a few of them when we were looking for that little girl. One guy had just come from the Everglades where they were tracking down some lost campers. Before that he'd been to California helping search for a family out hiking caught in a brush fire. That winter he'd been to Wyoming after skiers hit by an avalanche. Between times he went where the Mississippi was flooding or where miners were sealed off by a cave-in. The trouble is, types like him never work with the people in charge. They want the power of organizing their own groups and going off on their own, and before long they confuse the search pattern, interfere with official groups, run ahead to places that look exciting, like old farms, leaving whole fields unsearched—"

Teasle's heart suddenly fluttered, missed a beat, sped up, and he held his chest, gasping.

"What's the matter?" Kern said. "You're—"

"Fine. I'm fine. I just need another pill. The doctor warned me this would happen." It wasn't true. The doctor had not warned him at all, but this was the second time his heart had done that, and the first time a pill had brought it back to normal, so now he quickly swallowed another. He certainly could not let Kern know there was anything the matter with his heart.

Kern did not look satisfied with his answer. But then the radioman adjusted his earphones as if he were listening to a report, and told the deputy "National Guard truck thirty-two in position." He traced his finger down a list on a page, "That's at the start of Branch Road," and the deputy shoved one more red pin into the map.

The chalk taste of the pill remained in Teasle's mouth. He breathed, and the tightness around his heart began to relax. "I never could understand why that old guy moved the little girl's body to a different grave," he said to Kern, his heart relaxing even more. "I remember when we dug her up, and how she looked from six months in the ground and what he had done to her. I remember thinking, God, it must have been a lonely way to die."

"What just happened to you?"

"Nothing. Fatigue, the doctor said."

"Your face matched the gray of your shirt."

More trucks rolled by outside, and in their noise Teasle did not have to answer. Then a patrol car pulled up behind Kern, its headlights flooding him, and Teasle knew he would not have to answer at all.

"I guess I have to go," Kern said reluctantly. "These are the walkie-talkies to hand out." He stepped toward the cruiser, hesitated, then turned back. "Why don't you at least lie down on that bench and catch a little sleep while I'm gone. Staring at the map won't tell you where the kid is, and you'll want to be fresh when we start tomorrow."

"If I get tired. I want to make double sure that everybody is where he should be. I'm in no shape to go into those hills with you, so I might as well be good for something here."

"Listen. What I said at the hospital about the poor way you went after him..."

"It's done. Forget it."

"But listen. I know what you're trying. You're thinking about all your men shot and you're straining your body to punish your-self. Now maybe it's true what I said—that Orval might still be alive if you had worked with me from the beginning. But the kid is the one who pulled the trigger on him and the rest. Not you. Remember that."

Teasle did not need to be reminded. The radioman was saying "State police unit nineteen in position," and Teasle was dragging on his cigarette, watching intently as the deputy shoved another yellow pin into the eastern side of the map.

2

The map had almost no interior details. "Nobody ever wanted a breakdown of these hills before," the county surveyor had explained when he brought it. "Maybe if a road goes through there someday, we'll have to chart it. But surveying costs a lot of money, especially in that kind of rough country, and it just never seemed practical to use up our budget on something nobody would ever likely need." At least the surrounding roads were accurate. To the north they formed the top part of a square; but the road to the south curved like the bottom part of a circle, joining with the roads that went straight up on either side. Teasle's communication truck was parked on the lowest part of the south road's arc. That was where he had been found by the state trooper, and since the kid was last near there, it was the point from which the search was being directed.

The radioman looked at Teasle. "A helicopter's coming in. They're talking, but it's not clear enough to understand."

"Our two just left. None of them should be coming back this soon."

"Motor trouble maybe."

"Or it's not one of ours at all. It might be another news crew flying by taking pictures. If it is, I don't want them to land."

The radioman called it, asking for identification. No reply. Then Teasle heard the roar of the approaching rotor blades, and he rose stiffly from the bench, walking with difficulty to the open back of the truck. Next to the truck was the plowed field that he had crawled across that morning. It was dark, and then he saw the furrows, a harsh white as the searchlight on the bottom of the helicopter swooped down and across the field. It was the kind of searchlight the camera crew had used to take pictures earlier.

"They're hovering," he told the radioman. "Try them again. Make sure they don't land."

But already the chopper was setting down, motor quieting, blades whipping through the air in a recurrent whistle that came less and less often. There was a light in the cockpit, and Teasle saw a man climb out, and from the bearing of this man as he walked across the field toward the truck, steady and lithe and straight, Teasle knew even without being able to make out his clothes that this was no reporter, nor any state policeman coming back with motor trouble. This was the man he had sent for.

He climbed down slowly and in pain from the back of the truck and limped to the edge of the road. The man had just reached the barbed wire fence where the field ended.

"Excuse me, I've been up and down the line to find someone," the man said. "I wonder if he's here. They said he might be. Wilfred Teasle."

"I'm Teasle."

"Well, I'm Col. Sam Trautman," he said. "I've come about my boy."

Three more trucks drove by, National Guardsmen standing in back holding rifles, their faces pale under their helmets in the dark; and as the headlights flashed, Teasle could see Trautman's uniform, his colonel's insignia, his green beret tucked neatly under his belt.

"*Your* boy?"

"Not exactly, I suppose. I didn't train him myself. My men did. But I trained the men who trained him, so in a sense he's my boy. Has he done anything more? The last I heard he killed thirteen men." He said it clearly, directly, without emphasis, but all the same Teasle recognized the things subdued in his voice; he had listened to them too often before, too many fathers at night in the station, shocked, disappointed, embarrassed over what their children had done.

But this was not the same, not that simple. There was something else hidden in Trautman's voice, something so unfamiliar in this kind of situation that Teasle was having trouble identifying it, and when he did, he was bewildered.

"You sound almost proud of him," Teasle said.

"Do I? I'm sorry. I don't mean to. It's just that he's the best student we ever turned out, and things would certainly be wrong with the school if he hadn't put up a good fight."

He pointed to the barbed wire fence and began climbing over it, the same smooth economy of movement as when he had got out of the helicopter and walked across the field. Coming down into the ditch on Teasle's side of the fence, he was close enough for Teasle to see how his uniform molded perfectly to his body, not a fold or a wrinkle. In the dark his skin seemed the color of lead. He had short black hair combed straight back, a thin face, a sharp chin. The chin pointed forward a little, and Teasle was reminded of how Orval sometimes used to think of people in terms of animals. Not Trautman, Orval would have said now. Not trout. But feist. Or ferret. Or weasel. Some type of slick fleshhunter. He remembered career officers he had come up against in Korea, professional killers, men totally at home with death, and they always made him want to stand back. I don't know if I really want you here after all, he thought.

Maybe asking you to come was a mistake.

But Orval had taught him to judge a man by his grip as well, and when Trautman came in three steps out of the ditch, his handshake was not what Teasle expected. Instead of rough and overbearing, it was strangely gentle and firm at the same time. It made him very comfortable.

Maybe Trautman would be all right.

"You came sooner than I expected," Teasle told him. "Thank you. We need all the help we can get."

Because he had just been thinking of Orval, he was suddenly struck that he had gone through this another time, two nights ago when he had thanked Orval for coming, in almost the same words that he had just used to thank Trautman.

But now Orval was dead.

"You do need all the help," Trautman said. "To be honest I was planning to come even before you called. He's not in the service anymore, this is strictly a civilian matter, all the same I can't help feeling partly responsible. *One thing though*—I'm not about to involve myself in any butcher job. I'll only help if I see that this thing is done properly, to capture him, not to kill him without a chance. He might get killed yet, but I wouldn't like to think that was the point. Are we together on that?"

"Yes." And he was telling the truth. There was no way he wanted the kid shot to pieces out of his sight up in the hills. He wanted him brought back, wanted to see every damn thing that happened to him.

"All right then," Trautman said. "Although I'm not sure my

help will do you any good. It's my guess that none of your people will get close enough to even see him, let alone catch him. He's much smarter and tougher than you can imagine. How is it he didn't kill you too? I don't see how you ever managed to get away from him."

There it was again, that faintly mixed tone of pride and disappointment. "Now you sound like you're sorry I did."

"Well in one sense I am, but there's no need to take that personally. Strictly speaking, he shouldn't have slipped up. Not with his skill and training. If you had been an enemy he let get away, it could have been very serious, and I would like to find out why it happened in case there's a lesson I can pass on to my men. Tell me how you've planned this so far. How did you get the National Guard mobilized this fast?"

"They had war games scheduled for the weekend. Their equipment was ready, so all they had to do was activate their men a few days early."

"But this is a civilian command post. Where are headquarters for the military?"

"Down the road in another truck. But the officers are letting us give the orders. They want to learn how their men do alone, so they're only monitoring, just as they would have in the war games."

"Games," Trautman said. "Christ, everybody loves a game. What makes you sure he's still around?"

"Because every road around these hills has been watched since he went up there. He can't have gotten down without being seen. Even if he had, I would have felt it."

"What?"

"It's nothing I can explain. A kind of extra sense I've been having after what he put me through. It doesn't matter. He's up there all right. And tomorrow morning I'll be pouring men after him until there's one for every tree."

"Which isn't possible of course, so he still has the advantage. He's an expert in guerrilla fighting, he knows how to live off the land, so he doesn't have the problem that you do of bringing up food and supplies for your men. He's learned patience, so he can hide somewhere and wait out this fight all year if he has to. He's just one man, so he's hard to spot. He's on his own, doesn't have to follow orders, doesn't have to synchronize himself with other units, so he can move fast, shoot and get out and hide some place else, then do the same all over again. Just like my men taught him."

"That's fine," Teasle said. "Now you teach me."

3

Rambo woke in the dark on cold flat stone. He woke because of his chest. It was swollen so painfully that he had to ease the belt he had cinched around it, and each time he breathed, his ribs lanced him and he had to wince.

He didn't know where he was. He guessed it must be night, but he couldn't understand why the dark was so complete, why there were no grays mixed in with the black, no stars flickering, no faint radiance from cloud cover. He blinked, the dark remained the same, and fearing some damage had been done to his eyes, he quickly spread his hands over the stone he lay on, groped frantically around, touched walls of damp rock. A cave, he thought puzzled. I'm in a cave. But how? And still dazed he began to stagger out.

He had to stop and go back to where he had wakened because he didn't have his rifle in his hand, but then his stupor cleared a little and he realized that his rifle had been with him all along, wedged between his equipment belt and his pants, so he started out again. The floor of the cave sloped gradually down though, and he knew that the cave mouth would likely be somewhere up, not down, so once again he had to turn around and start out. The direction of the breeze coming down the tunnel from outside should have told him which way to go, but he didn't figure that until he had stumbled around a bend and reached the mouth.

Outside it was a crystal night, brilliant stars, a quarter moon, the outlines of trees and rocks distinct below. He didn't know how long he had been passed out, nor how he had come to be in the cave. The last things he recalled were struggling up at sunrise from where he lay near the ridge of brambles, wandering through the forest, and collapsing by a stream to drink. He had deliberately rolled into the stream he remembered, and had let the cool water flow over him reviving him, and now he was at the mouth of this cave and it was night, and there was an entire day plus a passage of territory that he could not account for. At least he guessed it was only one day. He suddenly thought, could it have been longer?

Far down and away, there were lights, what looked like hundreds of bright speckles, except that these were off and on, coming and going, yellow and red mostly, traffic on a road he thought, a highway maybe. But there was too much of it to be ordinary. And something else: it did not seem to be going anywhere. The lights were slowing. Then they stopped, a sweeping string of them from his left to his right about two miles off. He could have been wrong calculating the distance, but he was positive now that the lights had to do with coming after him. That much activity down there, he thought, Teasle must want me worse than anything he ever wanted before.

The night was very cold, and there were no insects sounding nor any animals moving around in the brush, just a slight wind that was rustling fallen leaves and scraping bare branches together. He hugged his outside wool shirt and shivered and then he heard the helicopter chugging up from his left, building to a roar, dimming as it flew off far behind him. There was another one behind it, and another to his right, and to his right as well, he heard the faint echoes of dogs barking. The wind shifted then, coming toward him from the direction of the lights down there, bringing with it the yelp of more dogs, and the accumulated far-off murmur of heavy truck engines. Since the lights had been left on, the engines would need to be kept idling, he thought. He tried counting the lights, but in the distance they confused him, and he multiplied their countless number by the amount of men each truck could carry, twenty-five, perhaps thirty. Teasle certainly wanted him. And this time he was not taking any chance of failure, he was going to come with every man, every piece of equipment he could muster.

But Rambo did not want to fight him anymore. He was sick and in pain, and sometime between losing Teasle in the brambles and waking in this cave, his anger had gone. It had started to go even as the chase for Teasle had drawn on, him exhausted, wanting desperately to catch the man, not anymore for the pleasure of teaching him, but just so he could do it and get it over and be free. And after killing all those men, after sacrificing so much time and strength that he needed for escape, he had not even won. The stupid useless waste, he thought. It made him feel empty and disgusted. What had it all been for? He should have taken his chance in the storm and run away.

Well, this time he was going. He'd had his fight with Teasle, and it had been fair, and Teasle had survived: that was the end of it.

What kind of crap-screen is that you're throwing up now? he told himself. Who are you fooling? You were hungry to be in action again, and you were damn sure you could beat him, but you lost and now it's dues time. He won't be looking for you just yet, not in the dark, but by sunrise he'll be coming after you with a small army that you don't have a chance against. You're not going because he won fairly and it's over. You just want to get out while you damn well still can. Even if he's leading them all, right at the head in plain sight, you had just better clear out and stay alive.

Then he knew it would not be that easy. Because as he stood there shivering, wiping the sweat from his forehead, his eyebrows, there was a flash of heat from the root of his spine to the base of his skull, then a sudden chill. The sequence repeated itself, and he understood now that he was not shivering from the breeze and the cold. It was fever. And extremely high to make him sweat this much. If he tried moving off, maybe to see if he could sneak through that line of lights down there, he would end up collapsed. He was having trouble standing as it was. Heat—that's what he needed. And shelter, someplace to sweat out the fever and rest his ribs. And food, he had not eaten since he had found the dried meat on the body of the old man who had been washed off the cliff, however long ago that was.

He shook and swayed and had to put out a hand to steady himself against the cave entrance. This was it then, the cave would have to do, he didn't have the strength to find anyplace better. He was going weak so fast that he wasn't even sure he would have the strength to get the cave ready. Well then, don't stand here telling yourself how weak you are. Do it.

He picked his way down a strip of shale to the trees he had seen in outline. The first trees he came to had sharp branches from where the leaves had fallen, and that was no good, so he shuffled through the leaves until at last they changed to soft springy fir needles underfoot, and then he searched among these trees, feeling for lush branches that might easily be broken off, always careful to take only one from each tree so that it would not be obvious he had gone through here gathering them.

When he had five, the motion of raising his arms to break off the boughs became too great a strain on his ribs. He would have liked more, but five would have to do. He lifted them painfully onto the shoulder away from his damaged ribs, and worked back toward the cave, the weight of the boughs making him stagger even worse than he already had been. The climb up the slope of shale was the really bad time. He kept teetering off to one side instead of straight up. Once he lost his footing and slipped face forward, wincing.

Even when he made it to the top, setting the boughs at the cave entrance, he still had to go back down the slope, this time gathering dead leaves and bits of wood that were scattered on the ground. He stuffed what he could inside his wool shirt and filled his arms with large dead branches and carried them back to the cave where he made two trips inside, first with the dead branches he already had in his arms, then with the fir boughs. He was thinking better, doing what he should have done when he had first moved around in the cave. As soon as he was deep in, past where he had wakened, he tested the floor ahead with his feet to be careful of sudden drops. The farther in he went, the lower the roof came, and when he had to crouch, bunching his ribs, he quit. The pain was too much.

This part of the cave was clammy, and he hurried to pile the dead leaves on the floor and spread chips of wood on them and lit the leaves with the matches the old man with the still had given him nights before. The matches had been soaked in the rain and the stream, but there had been time enough for them to dry, and while the first two wouldn't strike, the third did, going out, and the fourth stayed lit, setting flame to the leaves. The

flame spread, and he patiently added more leaves, more chips of
wood, nursing each lick of fire until they all came together in
a blaze that was big enough to add larger chunks of wood and
then the dead branches.

The wood was so old that it did not smoke much, and the little
smoke that did come off was tugged at by the breeze from the entrance and wafted down the tunnel. He stared at the fire, hands
out, warming them, shivering, and directly he looked around at
the shadows on the cave walls. He had been wrong. It wasn't a
cave, he saw now. Years ago somebody had worked this place as
a mine. That much was obvious from the symmetry of the walls
and the roof and the flatness of the floor. There were no tools
left around, no rusty wheelbarrows or broken picks or rotting
buckets—whoever gave up this place had respected it all right,
and left it neat. He should have closed the entrance, though. That
was strangely careless of him. By now the timber pilings and support beams were old and sagging, and if children ever came in
to explore, they might knock against a beam or make too much
noise and bring down a part of the roof on them. But what would
children be doing out here anyhow? This was miles from where
anybody lived. Still, he had found it; others could too. Sure and
they would find it tomorrow, so he had better watch his time and
leave before then. The quarter moon outside had been up to what
he imagined was eleven o'clock. A few hours of rest. That was all
he needed, he told himself. Sure. Then he could be gone.

The fire was warm and soothing. He brought the fir boughs
next to it and spread them on top of each other in imitation of
a mattress, stretching out on them, his bad side towards the fire.
Here and there the points of the needles stuck through his clothes
and pricked him, but there was nothing he could do about that:
he needed the boughs to keep him off the dampness of the floor.

In his exhaustion the boughs became soft and restful beneath him, and he closed his eyes and listened to the low crackle of the burning wood. Down the tunnel, water was dripping, echoing.

On first sight of the mine walls he had almost expected to see drawings, paintings, animals with horns, men clutching spears, stalking them. He had seen photographs of something like that, but he could not remember when. In high school maybe. Pictures of hunting had always fascinated him. When he was a young boy at home in Colorado, he had often gone hiking by himself into the mountains, and once when he had stepped cautiously into a cave, rounding a corner, flashing his light, there had been a drawing of a buffalo, just one, in yellow, perfectly centered on the wall. It had looked so real, as if it would bolt at the sight of him and run, and he had watched it all afternoon until his flashlight dimmed. He had gone back to that cave at least once a week after that, to sit there, and watch. His secret. His father had one night beaten him repeatedly in the face for not saying where he had been. Remembering, Rambo nodded his head at not having told. It was a long time now since he had been in that cave, and this place made him feel secret like in the other. One buffalo, high-humped, squat-horned, staring at him. So high up in the mountains, away from its native plains, and how long had it been there and who had drawn it? And who had worked this mine and how long ago was that? The cave had always reminded him of a church, and this place did too, but now the association embarrassed him. Well, he had not been embarrassed when he was a child. First Communion. Confession. He remembered what it had been like to push away the heavy black cloth and slip into the dark confessional, his knees on the padded board, the voice of the priest, muffled, giving absolution to the penitent in the other side of the box. Then the wood slide snicking back and him confessing. Confessing what? The men he had just killed. It was in self-defense, Father.

But did you enjoy it, my son? Was it an occasion of sin?

That embarrassed him more. He did not believe in sin, and he did not like to entertain ideas about it. But the question repeated itself: was it an occasion of sin? And his mind drowsing with comfort from the fire, he wondered what he would have said as a child. Probably yes. The sequence of killings was very complicated. He could justify to the priest that it was self-defense to kill the dogs and the old man in green. But after that, when he had his opportunity to escape, when instead he went after Teasle and shot his deputies while they were in rout, that was sin. And now Teasle would be coming for good, he thought as he had before, and now it was time for his penance. Down the tunnel the water was dripping hollowly.

Down the tunnel. He should have checked it at the first. A mine was a natural place for a bear. Or snakes. What was the matter that he had not checked it already? He took a flaming brand from the fire and used it for a torch down the tunnel. The roof came lower and lower, and he hated stooping, torturing his side, but this needed to be done. He came around a curve where the water he had heard was dripping from the roof, gathering in a pool and draining through a crack in the floor, and that was the end. His torch sputtering to go out, he came to a final wall, a two foot gap in it that angled down, and he decided he was safe. By the time his torch did go out, he was well on his way back to the fire, so near he could see the shimmering reflection of the flames.

But now he remembered there were other things to do. Check outside to be certain the light from the fire could not be seen. Get food. What else? Resting in this mine had seemed so simple an idea at the start, but it was getting more bothersome as he went along, and he was tempted to forget the whole thing and make a try at sneaking through that line of lights down there. He managed as far as the entrance before he swayed so dizzily that he had to sit down. This had to be it. He didn't have a choice. He was going to have to stay for a while.

Just for a while.

The first rifle shot echoed up from somewhere down on his right. Three more came immediately after. It was too dark and they were too far off for him to be the target. Another three shots echoed up and then the faint wail of a siren. What the hell? What was going on?

Food. That's all you need to worry about. Food. And he knew exactly what kind: a big owl he had seen take off from a tree down there when he had come out of the cave the first time. It had swung off, and in a couple of minutes had drifted back. He had seen that happen in silhouette twice now. The bird was already gone again, and he was waiting for it to complete its round.

There was more shooting far off to the right. But what for? He stood and shivered and waited, puzzling. At least his shot would only blend with all the other shots down there; it would not tell his position. Aiming at night was always difficult, but with the luminous paint the old man with the still had put on the sights of this rifle, he had a chance. He waited, and waited, and just as the sweat on his face, the chill in his spine became too much, he heard the single flap of wings and looked to see the quick silhouette swoop and settle in the tree. One, two, and he had the rifle up to his shoulder, aiming at the black spot of the owl. Three, four, and he was shivering, clenching his muscles to control them. Carack! the recoil jarred his ribs and he staggered in pain against the cave entrance. He was thinking that he might have missed, fearing that the owl might take off and not fly back, when he saw it move, just a little. And then it plummeted gracefully from the tree, hit a branch, toppled off, disappeared in the dark. He heard it strike rustling into fallen leaves, and he slipped hurriedly down the shale toward the tree, not daring to take his eyes off where he thought the bird had landed. He lost his bearings, couldn't find the bird; only after a long search did he happen upon it.

At last returned to his fire in the cave, he collapsed head spinning onto the boughs, shivering violently. He struggled to ignore his pain by concentrating on the closed talons of the owl, by smoothing its ruffled feathers. It was an old owl, he decided, and he rather liked the wizened face of it, but he could not keep his hands steady enough to smooth its feathers well.

He still could not understand what all the shooting outside was for, either.

4

The ambulance wailed past the communications truck, speeding back toward town, three pickup trucks rumbling up behind it, loaded with civilians, some complaining loudly, shouting indistinctly at the National Guardsmen along the road. Directly after the pickup trucks two state cruisers swept by, keeping watch on them all. Teasle stood at the side of the road, the headlights flashing by him in the dark, shook his head and walked slowly over to the communications truck.

"No word yet how many more were shot?" he asked the radioman in the back.

The radioman was haloed by the glare of the lightbulb dangling farther inside. "Just now, I'm afraid," he said, slowly, quietly. "One of them. One of us. The civilian was hit in the kneecap, but our man got it in the head."

"Oh." He closed his eyes a moment.

"The ambulance attendant says he might not live to reach the hospital."

Might nothing, he thought. The way things have been going the last three days, he won't make it. There's no doubt. He just won't make it.

"Do I know who he was? No. Wait. You'd better not tell me. I already have enough men dead that I knew. Are those drunks at least all gathered up now so they can't shoot anybody else? Was that the last of them in the pickup trucks?"

"Kern says he thinks so but he can't be positive."

"Which means there could still be as much as another hundred camped up there."

Christ, don't you wish there was another way to do this, that it was just you and the kid again. How many others are going to die before this is over?

He had been walking around too much. He was going dizzy once more, leaning against the back of the truck to hold himself up, legs becoming limp. His eyes felt like they would roll up into their sockets. Like doll's eyes, he thought.

"Maybe you ought to climb back inside and rest," the radioman said. "Even when you're almost out of the light, I can see you sweating, your face, through the bandages."

He nodded weakly. "Just don't say that when Kern's here. Hand me your coffee, will you?" His hands were shaking as he took the coffee and swallowed it with two more pills, his tongue and throat balking from the bitter taste, and just then Trautman returned from where he had been speaking with the shadowed forms of National Guardsmen down the road. He took one look at Teasle and told him, "You ought to be in bed."

"Not until this is over."

"Well, that's likely going to take a while longer than you expect. This isn't Korea and the Choisin Reservoir all over again. A mass-troop tactic would be fine, provided you had two groups against each other: if one flank got confused, your enemy would be so large that you could see it coming in time to reinforce that flank. But you can't do that here, not against one man, especially

him. The slightest bit of confusion along one line and he's so hard
to spot he can slip through your men without a signal."

"You've pointed out enough faults. Can't you offer something
positive?"

He said it stronger than he intended, so that when Trautman
answered "Yes," there was something new, resentment, hidden in
that even voice: "I have a few details to settle on yet. I don't know
how you run your police department, but I like to be sure before
I go ahead on something."

Teasle needed his cooperation and immediately tried to ease
off. "Sorry. I guess it's me who sounds wrong now. Don't pay attention. I'm just not happy unless I get miserable every once in a
while."

Again it came, that strange intense doubling of past and
present: two nights ago when Orval had said "It'll be dark in an
hour," and he himself had snapped "Don't you think I know it"
and then had apologized to Orval in almost the same words he
had just said to Trautman.

Maybe it was the pills. He didn't know what was in them, but
they certainly worked, his dizziness leaving now, his brain slowly
revolving to a stop. It bothered him that the periods of dizziness
were coming more and more often and lasting longer, though. At
least his heart was not speeding and missing anymore.

He gripped the back of the truck to climb up, but he did not
have the strength to raise himself.

"Here. Take my hand," the radioman said.

With help then, he managed to get up, but too fast, and he had
to wait a moment before he was steady enough to go and sit on
the bench, shoulders at last relaxing against the wall of the truck.
There. Done. Nothing to do but sit, rest. The pleasure of fatigue
and relief he sometimes had after vomiting.

Trautman climbed up with apparently unconscious ease and stood at the back, watching him, and there was something that Trautman had said a while ago that puzzled Teasle. He could not decide what it was. Something about—

Then he had it.

"How did you know I was at the Choisin Reservoir?"

Trautman looked in question.

"Just now," Teasle said. "You mentioned—"

"Yes. Before I left Fort Bragg I called Washington and had your file read to me."

Teasle did not like that. At all.

"I had to," Trautman said. "There's no need to take that personally either, as if I was interfering in your privacy. I had to understand what kind of man you were, in case this trouble with Rambo was your fault, in case you were after blood now, so I could anticipate any trouble you might give me. That was one of your mistakes with him. You went after a man you didn't know anything about, not even his name. There's a rule we teach—never engage with an enemy until you know him as well as yourself."

"All right. What does the Choisin Reservoir tell you about me?"

"For one thing, now that you've told me a little of what happened up there, it explains part of why you managed to get away from him."

"There's no mystery. I ran faster." The memory of how he had bolted in panic, leaving Shingleton, made him disgusted, bitter.

"That's the point," Trautman said. "You shouldn't have been able to run faster. He's younger than you, in better condition, better trained."

The radioman had been sitting by the table, listening to them.

Now he turned from one to the other and said, "I wish I knew what you guys were talking about. What's this reservoir?"

"You weren't in the service?" Trautman said.

"Sure I was. In the navy. Two years."

"That's why you never heard of it. If you had been a marine, you'd know the details by heart and you'd brag about them. The Choisin Reservoir is one of the most famous marine battles of the Korean war. It was actually a retreat, but it was as fierce as any attack, and it cost the enemy thirty-seven thousand men. Teasle was right in the center of it. Enough to earn a Distinguished Service Cross."

The way Trautman referred to him by name made Teasle feel strange, as if he were not in the same place with them, as if he were outside the truck listening, while Trautman, unaware he was being overheard, talked about him.

"What I want to know," Trautman asked Teasle, "was Rambo aware that you were in that retreat?"

He shrugged. "The citation and the medal are on my office wall. He saw it. If it meant anything to him."

"Oh, it meant something to him, all right. That's what saved your life."

"I don't see how. I just lost my head when Shingleton was shot, and ran like a goddamn scared rat." Saying it made him feel better, publicly confessing it, out in the open, nobody criticizing him for it when he wasn't near.

"Of *course* you lost your head and ran," Trautman said. "You've been out of that kind of action for years. In your place who wouldn't have run? But you see, he didn't expect you to. He's a professional and he naturally would think that somebody with that medal is a professional too—oh, a little out of practice and certainly not as good as him, but still he would think of you as a professional—and it's my guess he went after you on that basis. Did you ever watch a chess match between an amateur and a pro? The amateur wins more pieces. Because the pro is used to playing with people who have a reason and pattern for every move, and here the amateur is shifting pieces all over the board, not really knowing what he's up to, just trying to do the best he can with the little he understands. Well, the professional becomes so confused trying to see a nonexistent pattern and allow for it, that in no time he's behind. In your case, you were in blind flight, and Rambo was behind you trying to anticipate what somebody like himself would do for protection. He would have expected you to lie in wait for him, try to ambush him, and that would have slowed him down until he understood, but then it would have been too late."

The radioman had just slipped on his earphones to listen to a report that was coming through. Now Teasle saw him staring blankly at the floor.

"What's wrong? What's happened?" Teasle said.

"Our man who was shot in the head. He just died."

Sure, Teasle thought. Dammit, sure.

So what are you letting it bother you for, like it was something you didn't expect? You were already certain he was going to die.

That's the trouble. I was certain. Him and how many others before this is through.

"God help him," Teasle said. "I can't think of another way to go after that kid except with all these men, but if I could have anything in the world, I'd want it to be just me and him again."

The radioman took off his earphones and stood soberly from the table. "We were on different shifts, but I sometimes used to talk to the guy. If you don't mind, I'd like to go walk around for a while." He climbed distracted down the open end of the truck to the road, and paused a moment before he spoke again. "Maybe that supply van is still parked down the road. Maybe I'll get some doughnuts and more coffee. Or something." He paused a moment longer, then walked off, disappearing into the darkness.

"If it was just you and the kid again," Trautman said, "he'd know how to come after you this time. On a straight run. He'd kill you for sure."

"No. Because I wouldn't run now," Teasle said. "Up there I was afraid of him. I'm not anymore."

"You should be."

"No, because I'm learning from you. Don't go after a man until you understand him. That's what you said. Well, I know enough about him now that I could take him."

"That's just stupid. I hardly told you anything about him. Maybe some party-game psychiatrist could build up a theory about his mother dying of cancer when he was young, his father being an alcoholic, about when his father tried to kill him with a knife, and how he ran from the house that night with a bow and arrow that he shot at the old man, nearly killing him. Some theory about frustration and repression and all that. How there wasn't enough money to eat and he had to quit high school to work in a garage. It would sound logical, but it wouldn't mean anything. Because we don't accept crazies. We put them through tests, and he's as well-balanced as you or I."

"I don't kill for a living."

"Of course not. You tolerate a system that lets others do it for you. And when they come back from the war, you can't stand the smell of death on them."

"At the start I didn't know he was in the war."

"But you saw he wasn't acting normally, and you didn't try very hard to find out why. He was a vagrant, you said. What the hell else could he have been? He gave up three years to enlist in a war that was supposed to help his country, and the only trade he came out with is how to kill. Where was he supposed to get a job that needed experience like that?"

"He didn't need to enlist, and he could have gone back to work in the garage."

"He enlisted because he figured he was going to be drafted anyhow, and he knew the best trained cadres that gave a man the best chance to stay alive didn't take draftees, only enlisted men. You say he could have gone back to the garage. That's some cold comfort, isn't it? Three years, and he gets a Medal of Honor, a nervous breakdown, and a job greasing cars. Now you talk about fighting him one-to-one, yet you imply there's something diseased about a man who kills for a living. Christ, you haven't fooled me, you're as military as he is, and that's how this mess got started. I hope you do get a one-to-one fight with him. It'll be the last surprise of your life. Because he's something special these days. He's an expert at his business. We forced him into it over there, and now he's bringing it all back home. To second-guess him even once, you'd have to study him for years. You'd have to go through every course he took, every fight he was in."

"For a colonel, the way you're talking, you don't seem to like the military very much."

"Of course I don't. Who in his right mind would?"

"Then what are you staying in it for, especially doing that job of yours, teaching men to kill?"

"I don't. I teach them to stay alive. As long as we send men anywhere to fight, the most important thing I can do is make damn sure at least some of them come back. My business is saving lives, not taking them."

"You say I haven't fooled you, that I'm as military as he is. I think you're wrong. I do my job as fair as I know how. But let's leave that for a second. Because you haven't fooled me, either. You talk about coming here to help, but so far that's *all* you've done— talk about it. You claim you're out to save lives, but you haven't done one thing yet to help prevent him from killing more people."

"Suppose something," Trautman said. He slowly lit a cigarette from a package that was on the radio table. "You're right. I have been holding back. But suppose I did help. Now think about this. Would you really *want* me to help? He's the best student my school ever turned out. Fighting against him would be like fighting against myself, because I suspect he was pushed into this—"

"Nobody pushed him into killing a policeman with a razor. Let's get that straight."

"I'll put it differently: I have a conflict of interests here."

"You have what? Dammit he's—"

"Let me finish. Rambo is a lot like myself and I wouldn't be honest if I didn't admit that I sympathize with the position he's in, enough so that I'd like to see him get away. On the other hand, Christ, he's gone wild. He didn't have to chase after you once you were in retreat. Most of those men didn't have to die, not when he had a chance to escape. That was inexcusable. But no matter how I feel about that, I still sympathize. What if, without knowing it, I work out a plan against him that allows him to escape?"

"You won't. Even if he escapes here, we still have to keep hunting him, and someone else is bound to be shot. You've already agreed that's your responsibility as much as mine. So if he's your best, then dammit prove it. Put every obstacle against him that you can dream of. Then if he still breaks free, you'll have done everything you could and you'll have double reason to be proud of him. In a couple of ways you can't afford not to help."

Trautman looked at his cigarette, drew deeply on it, then flipped it out of the truck, sparks showering in the dark. "I don't see why I lit that in the first place. I gave up smoking three months ago."

"Don't avoid the question," Teasle said. "Are you going to help now or aren't you?"

Trautman looked at the map. "I suppose none of what I'm saying matters. In a few years a search like this won't even be necessary. We have instruments now that can be mounted on the underside of an airplane. To find a man all you have to do is fly over the spot where you think he is, and the machine will register his body heat. Right now there aren't enough of those machines to go around. Most of them are in the war. But when we come home from there, well, a man on the run won't have a hope. And a man like me, he won't be needed. This is the last of something. It's too bad. As much as I hate war, I fear the day when machines take the place of men. At least now a man can still get along on his talents."

"But you're avoiding the question."

"Yes, I'm going to help. He does have to be stopped, and I'd rather the person who manages it be someone like myself who understands him and goes through his pain with him."

5

Rambo held the owl's soft pliant back, clutched a fistful of feathers on the belly, and pulled. They made a dull tearing sound as they came away. He liked the feel of the feathers in his hand. He plucked the carcass bare, cut off the head and the wings and the claws, then pressed the point of his knife in at the bottom of the rib cage, drawing the sharp edge of the blade down to between its legs. He spread the flaps of the carcass, reached inside for the warm wet offal, and smoothly steadily drew it out, getting most of the entrails in a bunch on his first try, and scraping the inside with his knife to get the rest. He would have gone to rinse the carcass where the water was dripping from the roof of the mine, but he could not tell if the water had poisons in it, and anyway, rinsing the bird would just be another complication when all he wanted was to get this over, eat and get out. He had already wasted too much energy as it was. He took a long branch that was not in the fire, sharpened it and spitted the point into the owl, extending it over the fire. The bits of feathers and stubs that were still on it sparked in the flames. Salt and pepper, he thought. Since the owl was old, it would likely be solid and tough. The smell of its blood burning was acrid, and the meat would probably taste like that, and he wished he at least had salt and pepper.

So this is what he had been reduced to, he thought. From camping in his sleeping bag in the forest, and eating hamburgers washed with Coke in the dusty grass at the side of a road, to this, a bed of fir boughs in a mine and the carcass of an owl and not even goddamn salt and pepper. Not all that different from camping in the forest, but living then on a minimum had been a kind of luxury, because he wanted to do it. Now, though, he might be forced to live like this for a long while, and it really did seem like a minimum. Soon he might not even have this much, and he would look back on this good night when he slept for a few hours in a mine and cooked this tough old owl. Mexico was not even on his mind anymore. Only his next meal and what tree he would sleep in. A day at a time. A night at a time.

Chest throbbing, he raised his two shirts and looked at his ribs, fascinated by how swollen and inflamed they were. It was like he had a tumor in there or something growing in him, he thought. A few more hours sleep weren't going to cure that. At least he wasn't dizzy anymore. Time to move. He built up the fire to make the bird cook faster. The heat from the fire touched his forehead and the stretch of his nose. Or maybe it was the fever, he thought. He lay back flat on the fir boughs, face turned sweating toward the fire. The mucus in his mouth was dry and sticky, and he wanted to drink from his canteen, but he had already drunk too much from it, he needed to save some for later. But whenever he parted his lips, a thin web of sticky mucus clung between them. Finally he sipped and swirled the warm metallic water around in his mouth, collecting the mucus, debating whether he could afford the waste of spitting it out, deciding not and swallowing thickly.

The voice startled him. It echoed indistinctly down the tunnel, sounding as if a man were outside with a loudspeaker talking to him. How could they have known where he was? He hurriedly checked that his pistol and knife and canteen were attached to his equipment belt, grabbed his rifle and the stick in the owl, and rushed toward the mouth. The breeze coming down the shaft was fresh and cool. Just before the opening, he slowed, taking care that men were not out there in the night waiting for him. But he could not see anyone, and then he heard the voice again. It was definitely from a loudspeaker. From a helicopter. In the dark the motor was roaring over the rise, and throughout a man's voice was booming "Groups twelve to thirty-one. Assemble toward the eastern slope. Groups thirty-two complete to forty. Spread out north." Far down and away, the line of lights was still there, waiting.

Teasle wanted him all right. He must have a small army down there. But what was the loudspeaker for? Weren't there enough field radios to coordinate the groups? Or is this just noise to get on my nerves? he thought. Or to scare me, to let me know how many are coming for me. Maybe it's a trick and he doesn't have any men at all north and east. Maybe he just has enough for south and west. Rambo had heard a loudspeaker used like this by Special Forces in the war. It generally confused the enemy and tempted them to second-guess what Special Forces was about to do. There was a counter-rule: when somebody wants you to second-guess them, that's when you don't try. The best reaction is to go on as if you never heard it.

Now the voice was repeating itself, dimming with the helicopter over the rise. But Rambo didn't care about anything it said. For all he cared, Teasle could bring men into these hills from every side. It wouldn't matter. Where he was going, they would pass right by him.

He glanced east. The sky was gray now over there. Sunup in a while. He eased down on the cold rocks at the entrance to the mine and tested the bird with his finger in case it was too hot to eat. Then he carved off a strip and chewed, and it was just awful. Worse than he had expected. Stiff and dry and sour. He had to force himself to bite into another piece, and he had to chew and chew before he could swallow.

6

Teasle did not sleep at all. An hour before dawn, Trautman lay down on the floor and closed his eyes, but Teasle kept sitting on the bench, his back against the wall, told the radioman to switch the sound from the earphones to the speakers, then listened to the position reports coming in, his eyes seldom leaving the map. The reports soon came in less frequently, and the radioman leaned forward onto the table, head on his arms, and Teasle was alone again.

Every unit was where it should be. In his mind he saw policemen and National Guardsmen strung along the edges of fields and woodlots, stamping out cigarettes, loading their rifles. They were in sections of fifty, and each section had a man with a field radio and at six o'clock the order would go down the line over the radios to move out. Still spread in a wide line, they would sweep across the fields and through woods, moving in from the main points of the compass. It would take days to cover this much territory and converge in the middle, but eventually they would have him. If one group came into tangled country that slowed them, its man with the field radio would broadcast to the other groups to ease their pace and wait. That would prevent one group from slowing so much that it fell behind the main line, imperceptively shifting its direction until it was far to one side, searching an area that had already been covered by the others. There could be no gaps in the line except those which had been planned as traps, a band of men ready to catch the kid in case he tried to take advantage of that open space. The kid. Even now that Teasle knew his name, he couldn't get used to calling him by it.

The air seemed to dampen toward sunup, and he pulled an army blanket over Trautman on the floor, then wrapped one around himself. There was always something left to do, some flaw in any plan: he remembered that from his training in Korea, and Trautman had said it too, and he was going over the search from every angle for something he might have forgotten. Trautman had wanted helicopters to drop patrols on the highest peaks, from where they could spot the kid if he ran ahead of the search line. It had been dangerous lowering the patrols on ropes in the dark, but they had been lucky and there had been no accidents. Trautman had wanted the helicopters to fly back and forth out there broadcasting fake directions to confuse the kid, and that was being taken care of. Trautman had suspected the kid would make a break south: that was the direction he had used escaping in the war, and there was a good chance he would try that way again, so the southern line was reinforced except for the intentional weak spots that were traps. Teasle's eyes were burning from lack of sleep, but he couldn't sleep, and then when he could not find any part of the plan that he had forgotten to check, he began to think about other things that he *did* want to forget. He had been putting them out of his mind, but now, his head starting to ache, the ghosts came of their own accord.

Orval and Shingleton. The Friday dinners week after week at Orval's place. "A good way to start the weekend," Mrs.

Kellerman said, always phoning him at the police station on Thursday to find out what he wanted to eat the next day. In the old days she would have been phoning today, and tomorrow they would have been eating—eating what?—no, the idea of food filling his mouth was intolerable. Never Beatrice. Always Mrs. Kellerman. That was what they had decided when his father had been killed and he had gone to live with them. He couldn't bring himself to call her "Mother," and "Aunt Beatrice" never sounded right, so it was always Mrs. Kellerman, and Orval liked that, having been raised to call his own parents "Sir" and "Ma'am." With Orval's name it was different. Orval had been around his father's house so often that Teasle had got used to calling him Orval, and the habit was hard to break. Friday dinners. She'd be cooking, and he and Orval would be outside with the dogs and then they'd come in for a drink before dinner, but Orval had given up drinking by then, so it would be just Mrs. Kellerman and himself, and Orval would have tomato juice with salt and Tabasco sauce. Thinking about it now, Teasle's mouth salivated bitterly, and he tried not to think of food, thought instead of how the arguments had started and how the Friday dinners had then stopped. Why hadn't he given in to Orval? Was it really so important which way to holster a gun or train a dog that they had to argue about it? Was it that Orval was afraid of getting old and had to show that he was still as able as ever? Maybe they were just so close that every disagreement was a betrayal and they *had* to argue. Or maybe I was so proud that I had to show him I wasn't a kid anymore, Teasle thought, and Orval couldn't bear a stepson talking to him the way he himself had never dared talk to his own father. Mrs. Kellerman was sixty-eight. She had been married to Orval for forty years. What was she supposed to do now without him?

All her life was linked with his. Who would she cook for now? Who would she have to clean for and wash clothes for now?

Me, I guess, Teasle thought.

And what about Shingleton and the shooting tournaments they had been in together, representing the department? Shingleton had a wife too, and three young children, and what was she supposed to do? Get a job, sell the house, pay for babysitters while she worked? And how am I supposed to explain to both of them about the way their husbands died? he thought. He should have phoned them hours ago, but he couldn't bring himself to do it.

His paper cup had soggy cigarette butts in the coffee. He lit his last one, crumpling the package, throat dry, thinking about his panic on the bluff, Shingleton crying, "Look out, Will! He's got me!" And then the shot and then his bolting. Maybe if he had stayed, he might have been able to get a shot at the kid, maybe if he had somehow reached Shingleton, he might have found him still alive and been able to save him. Reliving his hysterical race from the bluff, he shook with disgust. You're some tough guy, he told himself. Oh yes, a lot of mouth. And if you had it to do over, you'd do the same.

No, he thought. No, I'd die before I ran again.

The bodies up on the bluff. The state police had tried going after them with a helicopter, but from the air all the bluffs looked alike and the police had not found the right one, and finally they had been called back to help with the search. Had the rain half-covered the bodies with dirt and leaves? Were there animals nosing around them, insects crawling across their cheeks? What would Orval be like after his drop from the cliff? Galt's funeral had been yesterday morning, while he himself had been struggling across the field. He was glad that he had not been to it. He wished that he would not have to go to the funeral for all the others when at last they were found and brought back, what was left of them after several days in the forest. A mass funeral. All the coffins in a row before the altar, lids closed, the whole town there looking at him and then at the coffins and then at him once more. How was he supposed to explain to those people why it had to happen, why he had thought it best to keep the kid moving away from town, and why the kid in his bitterness had needed to defy him, both of them unable to stop pushing at each other once the thing had started?

He looked at Trautman asleep under the army blanket on the floor, and realized that he was coming to see the kid from Trautman's view. Not totally, but enough to understand why the kid had done it all, and even to sympathize a little.

Sure, but you didn't kill anyone when you came back from Korea, and you had been through almost as much as him.

But thinking that the kid should have been able to control himself was not going to revive Orval and Shingleton and the rest, and his anger at the kid for shooting Orval was too great to sustain. For the last hours his fatigue had been overpowering it. He no longer had the strength of emotion to rouse great brutal images of what he would enjoy doing to the kid.

He thought about it, and in his daze from lack of sleep, it seemed to him in a crazy way that everything had been out of control even before he and the kid had met, himself and Anna, the kid and the war. Anna. He was surprised that he had not remembered her in two days, not since the killing had started. Now she seemed farther off in his mind than California, and the pain of losing her was dwarfed by all that had happened since Monday. Still, though small, it was pain, and he did not want any more.

His stomach cramped. He had to swallow two more pills, the bitter chalk taste worse now because he was anticipating it.

Through the open back of the truck he saw the sun barely above the horizon, pale and cold, troops ready along the road, frost coming from their mouths. The radioman was calling each group to be certain they were prepared.

Teasle leaned over and nudged Trautman on the floor to wake him. "It's starting."

But Trautman was already awake. "I know."

Kern drove up and climbed hurriedly into the back of the truck. "I've been checking up and down the lines. Everything looks good. What about National Guard headquarters?"

"They're all set to monitor. Whenever we're ready," the radioman said.

"That's it then."

"Why are you looking at me?" Teasle said.

"Since you started things, I thought you might want to give the order to go."

7

Sprawled on the spine of a high ridge, Rambo looked down and saw them coming, first small bands roaming through the woods far off, then a well-organized methodical sweep of the land by more men than he could count. They were about a mile and a half from him, tiny points that were growing fast. There were helicopters flying over, broadcasting orders which he dismissed, unable to decide if they were real or fake.

He guessed that Teasle expected him to retreat from the line of men and pull back farther inland. Instead he scurried down the ridge toward the men, staying low, using every clump of cover. At the bottom he raced toward the left, one hand holding his side. He would be able to stop running soon. He couldn't let his pain slow him. The men were only fifty minutes off, maybe less, but if he could get to where he was going before they did, then he would have all the chance he needed to relax. He labored up a wooded rise, slowing in spite of himself, gasping, reached the top, and there it was, the stream. He had been searching for it since he left the mine. The stream where he had lain after Teasle escaped into the brambles. He had judged that it would be close to the

mine, and as soon as he had set out, he had climbed to the highest
place near to try and see it. No luck. The stream had been too low
and too sheltered by trees for him to make out a glint of water or
a zigzag depression in the land. He had almost given up when he
realized that the sign he was looking for had been there all along.
Mist. Early morning fog off water. So he had hurried for it, and
now in pain he was stumbling down through trees toward it.

He reached it where the water was a trickle over stones, a gentle bank of grass on either side. He hunted along it, coming to a
deep pool, and here at last the banks were steep, but they were
stitched with grass like the ones before. He moved farther on until
there was another pool and steep banks, these of mud. A tree on
his side of the pool had bare roots, their soil eroded by the water's flow. He could not step in the mud without leaving tracks.
He had to grope long-legged from the grass and leaves on the top
of the bank to the roots of the trees, and then he lowered himself cautiously into the stream, not daring to dislodge silt from
the bottom that might linger in the pool and give him away. He
slipped between the tree roots and the bank, in where there was a
hollow of sodden earth above him, and then slowly, meticulously,
he commenced burying himself, spreading mud over his feet and
legs, scooping mud over his chest, drawing the tree roots closer to
him, squirming, burrowing deep into the muck like a crab, wiping his face in it, pulling it onto him until he felt the cold wet
heavy weight of it all over, breathing with difficulty, just a twig
space to take air from. It was the best that he could do. Nothing
more to try. An old expression came to him as a joke—you made
your bed, now lie in it. So he did, and waited.

They were a long while coming. As much as he could tell, they
had been two rises away when he reached the stream, and he
estimated they would be fifteen minutes, perhaps a little longer,

before they came to him. But fifteen minutes seemed to go, and still there was no sound of them. He decided that his sense of time was off, that lying buried in the mud, nothing to do but wait, he was fooled into thinking a few minutes were a great deal more than that. Oppressed by the mud, he had much trouble breathing now. His air space wasn't enough, but he couldn't afford to make it wider: someone outside might see the hole and be curious. Moisture was beginning to condense in his nose, stuffing it like phlegm. His eyes were closed, the mud settling firmly onto his lids.

Still no sound of the searchers. He needed something to do, something to help him keep quiet and still, the pressure of the mud unnerving him, so he started counting off the seconds, at the end of each minute expecting to hear the men, sliding into another round of sixty when no sound came, expecting at the end of this minute to hear them, but still no sound. When he had gone through to sixty for the fifteenth time, he was positive that things had gone wrong. The mud. Maybe that was it, maybe the mud cut off the sound of the people going by and the hunt had gone past him long ago.

Sure and maybe not. If he had not heard them, they might still be coming. He couldn't take that chance of digging out to look; they might be just now approaching the stream, held up before this by thick underbrush on one of the rises. He waited, moisture filling his nose as if to drown him, frantic to breathe. The mud was pressing harder on his face and chest, and he wanted desperately to push out of it. He remembered playing by a sand cliff when he was a boy, digging into the sand to build a cave, crawling inside, then having the sudden urge to crawl out just as the whole cliff plunged down on him burying his head, him crazy with fear, clawing frenzied at the sand, worming out from under just as more sand spilled down on him. He had barely come out soon enough, and that night as he tried to sleep, he had been certain that in the sand cave a premonition of death occurred to him, that the premonition had been what spurred him to crawl out in time. Now, buried in the ooze and mud, he was thinking that if someone walked over and stood on the ground above him, a part of the bank might be dislodged, plopping down and cutting off his air space. He had the same instant premonition as in the sand cave: he was going to be buried alive, die in here. Already the moisture in his nose was completely clogging his breath. He had to get out, dear God, couldn't bear the suffocation, pushed at the mud.

And froze when he heard them. The faint dull plod of footsteps. A lot of them. All together on top. And muffled voices, splashing in the water, people walking along the stream. The footsteps came closer, one set of them stopping, then thundering close, directly on top, weighing on the mud, on his chest, his broken ribs, the pain. He couldn't move, hadn't been breathing. How long could he go without air? Three minutes? Not as tired as he was. Two minutes then. Try holding two minutes. But time for him was so distorted, and one minute seemed like two, and he might need to breathe so much that he would squirm and shove and push out before he had to. Four five six seven, he was counting. To twenty, to forty, and as the sequence drew on, the numbers in his head linked up with his heartbeats that were coming louder and faster, and his chest was contracting, crushing. There. The mud above him budged, the pressure eased, the man on top of him moved. But hurry, not fast enough. The voices, the churning in the stream mercifully diminished. But too slow, he couldn't dig out yet. There might be stragglers. There might be someone who by chance glanced back this way. Oh Christ, hurry. Midway through the second minute, thirty-five, thirty-six, thirty-seven, throat contorting, forty-eight, forty-nine. He never got to sixty, couldn't endure it anymore, suddenly thought he was so weak-headed from the lack of air that he didn't have the strength to dig out. Push. Push, dammit. But the mud would not part, and he struggled to raise himself, to heave away the mud, and then in a gathering rush, sweet Jesus, cool air was upon him and light and he was gasping, half in the stream. Gray turned to white in his head; his chest ballooned in an ecstasy of breath, then bit sharply in his ribs, drawing in huge gasps of breath, expelling them, sucking them in violently. Too much noise. They'll hear. He quickly looked to see them.

None around. Voices and rustling in the underbrush. But they were out of sight now, gone now, at last he was in the clear, only one more hard part to go, crossing the nearby roads. He slumped against the bank. On his own. Free.

Not yet you're not. There's a hell of a lot more to do before you go near those roads.

Dammit, you think I don't know that? he told himself. There's *always* something more to do. Always. It never ends.

Then get busy.

In a second.

No. Now. You'll have all the time to rest if they catch you.

He breathed and nodded and grudgingly propped himself up from the side of the stream, wading through the water to the exposed tree roots. He slipped mud into the hole where he had been behind the roots, arranging it so if another group came through here they could not tell that the first group had missed his hiding place. They had to think that he was deep in the hills, not close to the road.

Next, his rifle on top of the bank, he eased into the deepest section of the pool and rinsed the mud off him. It did not matter now that he was stirring up silt and dirt from the bottom that might linger; the men who had just gone through here had completely clouded the water, and if they came back or if another group came, they would have no reason to think of him. He dunked his head to clean away the dirt in his hair and wash his face, taking a scummy mouthful and spitting it out with the grit that was in his mouth, blowing his nose underwater to get rid of the mud he had sucked up it. Just because he was living like an animal, he thought, didn't mean he had to feel like one. That was from training school. Be clean whenever you can. It makes you go longer and fight better.

He climbed dripping out of the stream, chose a thin branch off the ground and used it to clean the mud from inside the barrel of his rifle, to pick dirt from the firing mechanism. Then he worked the lever on the rifle several times to ensure that it was smooth, reloaded the shells he had ejected, and he was finally off, moving cautiously through the bushes and trees toward the direction of the road. He was glad that he had washed the mud off in the stream; he felt better, more energetic, able to escape.

The feeling disappeared when he heard the dogs, two packs of them, one baying straight ahead, coming his way, the other to his left, moving fast. Those forward had to be trailing the scent from where he had lost Teasle on the slope of brambles, wandered to this stream and headed semiconscious into the highlands, eventually ending at the mine. Those to the left then were following the route he had taken when he chased Teasle into the brambles. That chase was over a day old, and unless one of the men with the dogs was an expert tracker, they would have no idea which scent was him running toward the brambles and which scent was him wandering away. So they weren't taking any chances; they were setting dogs on both trails.

BREWED & BOTTLED BY THREE FLOYDS Brewing LLC. MUNSTER, IN 3FLOYDS.com

CA CASH REFUND CT/MA/MI 10¢ NY/IA/OR/VC 5¢ REFUND

THIS INTENSELY HOPPED AND GUSHING UNDEAD PALE ALE WILL BE ONES ONLY RESPITE AFTER THE ZOMBIE APOCALYPSE. CREATED WITH OUR MARVELOUS FRIENDS IN THE COMIC INDUSTRY. ART BY TIM SEELEY

Figuring that out didn't help him much. He still had to get away from this pack of dogs rushing toward the stream, and he certainly couldn't outrun them, not with his side bursting with pain. He could ambush them and shoot them all as he had done with Teasle's group, but the sound of gunfire would reveal his position, and with this many searchers in the woods they would have no trouble cutting him off.

So. He needed a trick to fool the dogs off his trail. At least he had some time to do it. They would not be coming directly to this part of the stream. First they would follow his scent away from the water, up the hills to the mine, only then down here. He could try going for the road, but the dogs would eventually lead in that direction, and the men would radio ahead to set a trap for him.

He had one idea. It wasn't very good, but it was the best that he could come up with. In a rush he backtracked through the trees to where he had buried himself at the side of the stream; he quickly slid into the water, wading waist high downstream toward the road, imagining what the dogs would do. They would trail him down from the mine, find the path he had taken away from his hiding place into the woods, follow it and sniff in confusion when his scent stopped abruptly in the undergrowth. It would take everybody a long while to guess that he had doubled-back along his trail, returned to the stream and waded into it; and when at last they did guess what he had done, he would be far off. Maybe driving a car or truck that he would manage to steal.

But the police would radio their cruisers to look out for a stolen car.

Then he would dump it after he had gone a few miles.

What then? Steal another car and dump that one? Leave it and run into the country only to have dogs start trailing him again?

As he waded down the stream, thinking desperately how to escape, he gradually came to understand how difficult it was going to be, almost impossible. Teasle would keep after him. Teasle would never allow him to get free, never allow him even to rest.

Worried about the dogs baying nearby, head down looking to avoid stones and logs submerged in the water that he might stumble over, clutching his ribs, he did not see the man until he was directly upon him. He came around a bend in the stream, and there the man was, shoes and socks off, sitting on the bank, feet in the water. The man had blue eyes. He held his rifle, looking suspicious. He must have heard Rambo coming and readied himself just in case, but he evidently had not believed this would actually be Rambo because when it registered on the man who Rambo was, his mouth opened and he sat there paralyzed as Rambo lunged for him. No noise. There can't be any noise. No shooting. Rambo had his knife out, wrenching the man's rifle away, the man scrambling to get up the bank, Rambo stabbing him hard in the stomach, tugging the blade up to the rib cage.

"Jesus," the man said in surprise, the last syllable gliding into a high whine, and he was dead.

"What?" somebody asked.

Rambo jerked involuntarily. He had no chance to hide.

"Didn't I tell you quit complaining about your feet?" the voice was saying. No. No. "Come on, get your shoes on before we—" It was a man coming up from a hollow, buckling his pants, and when he saw, he was quicker than his friend. He leapt for a rifle that was leaning against a tree, and Rambo tried to race there first, but the guy managed to reach the gun and no *no*, his hand was on the trigger, pulling it, cracking off a wild shot that ended Rambo's hopes. The guy was fingering the trigger for another shot as Rambo blew his head in. You had to shoot and warn them, didn't you, you bastard? You had to fix me.

Dear God, what am I going to do?

Men were calling to each other off in the forest now. The underbrush was alive with the sound of branches snapping, men rushing. The pack of dogs that was near began barking toward him. There was nowhere to go, nothing to do. The men would be everywhere. I'm through.

He was almost grateful that he had lost. No more running, no more pain in his chest, they would take him to a doctor, feed him, give him a bed. Clean clothes. Sleep.

If they didn't shoot him here, thinking he still wanted to fight.

Then he would throw down his rifle and hold up his hands and yell that he was surrendering.

The idea revolted him. He couldn't let himself merely stand and wait for them. He'd never done it before. It was disgusting. There had to be something more to do, and then he thought again of the mine and the final rule: if he was going to lose, if they were going to capture him, at least he could pick the place where it would happen, and the place that gave him the best advantage was the mine. Who knew what might change? Maybe as he went to the mine, he would see another way to escape.

The men were calling closer through the underbrush. Not in sight yet. Very soon. All right, the mine then. No time to think about it anymore, and suddenly the thrill of going into action flashed through his body and he was no longer tired and he took off away from the stream deep into the woods. Ahead, he heard them charging through the thick bushes. He darted to the left, staying low. Far to his right, he saw them now, running loudly toward the stream. National Guardsmen he saw. Uniformed. Helmeted. In the night, watching the chain of lights miles off, he had joked badly about Teasle having a small army after him, but Jesus Christ, this really was the army.

8

The Guardsmen had been reporting descriptions of the country as they moved inland, cliffs and swamps and hollows that the deputy sketched onto the barren map, and now Teasle sank tired and empty onto the bench, watching him mark an X where the bodies of the two civilians had been found by the stream. He felt as if he were watching from far away, at last numbed by all the pills he had been swallowing. He had not let on to Trautman or Kern, but shortly after the report came in about the bodies stabbed and shot, he had experienced a sharp constriction near his heart so severe that it had scared him. Two more killed. How many did that make now? Fifteen? Eighteen? He jumbled the numbers in his mind, wanting to avoid a new total.

"He must have been heading for the road when he was discovered by those two civilians," Trautman said. "He knows that we expect him near the road, so he'll have to turn around and go back into the hills. When he thinks it's safe, he'll try a different route to another part of the road. Maybe east this time."

"Then that's it," Kern said. "We have him trapped. The line is between him and the high ground, so he can't go that way. The only direction open to him is toward the road, and we have another line there waiting for him."

Teasle had continued looking at the map. Now he turned. "No. Didn't you listen?" he said to Kern. "The kid is probably in the high ground already. The whole story is right there on the map."

"But that doesn't make sense to me. How is he going to make it up through the line?"

"Easily," Trautman said. "When those Guardsmen heard the shots behind them, a group broke from the main line to go back and investigate. When they did, they left a hole more than big enough for him to slip through and up into the hills. Like you, they all expect him to keep moving away from the line anyhow, so they wouldn't have been alert to sight him when he came near and slipped through. You had better tell them to continue into the hills before he gains more distance."

Teasle had been a long while expecting this from Kern. Now it came. "I don't know," Kern said. "It's getting too complicated. I don't know *what* I had better do. Suppose he didn't think like that. Suppose he didn't realize there was a break in the line and just stayed where he was, between the line and the road. Then if I order those men farther inland, I'll ruin the trap."

Trautman lifted his hands. "Suppose whatever the hell you want. It's no matter to me. I don't like helping in the first place. All the same I am. But that doesn't mean I have to explain over and over what I think should be done and then goddamn beg you to do it."

"Wait, don't misunderstand. I'm not questioning your judgment. It's only that in his position he might not do what's logical. He might feel closed in and run in a circle the way a flushed rabbit does."

For the first time the pride in Trautman's voice was completely open. "He won't."

"But if he does, if he just possibly does, you're not the one who answers for sending the men in the wrong direction. I do. I have to look at this thing from every angle. After all we're just talking theory here. We have no evidence to go on."

"Then let *me* give the order," Teasle said, and the truck seemed to drop three feet, jolting, as a new more serious constriction seized his chest. He struggled to go on talking, braced his body. "If the order's wrong, I'll gladly answer for it." He stiffened, holding his breath.

"Christ, are you all right?" Trautman said. "You'd better lie down quick."

He gestured to keep Trautman away. Abruptly the radioman said, "A report is coming through," and Teasle fought to ignore the racking misbeats of his heart and listen.

"Lie down," Trautman told him. "Or I'll have to make you."

"Leave me alone! Listen!"

"*This is National Guard leader thirty-five. I don't figure this. There must be so many of us that the dogs have lost their sense of smell. They want us to go up into the hills instead of toward the road.*"

"No, they haven't lost their sense of smell," Teasle said, clutching himself, voice strung out with pain, to Kern. "But we've lost a hell of a lot of distance on him while you tried to make up your mind. Do you think now you can bring yourself to give that order?"

9

As Rambo started up the slope of shale toward the mine, a bullet whacked into the rocks a few yards to his left, the rifle report echoing through the forest back there. Staring at the mine entrance, he hurried stumbling up the slope into the tunnel, shielding his face from chips of stone that two more bullets blasted off the right side of the opening. Far down the tunnel, out of reach of more bullets, he stopped exhausted, slumping against a wall, gasping. He had not been able to maintain his distance from them. His ribs. Now the Guardsmen were barely a half mile behind him, coming fast, so taken up in the hunt that they were shooting before they had a clear target. Weekend soldiers. Trained for this but not experienced, so they did not have the discipline and in the excitement might do anything. Rush in stupidly. Spray bullets down the shaft. He was right to have come here. If he had tried giving up at the stream, they would have been too quick, would have shot him. He needed a buffer between himself and them so they would not shoot before he explained.

He returned up the dark tunnel toward the light at the mouth, studying the roof. When he found where it was dangerously cracked, he pushed away the support beams, lurching back before the ceiling could cave in on him. He was not worried by the risk. If the collapse was so great that it buried the entrance and blocked off his air, he knew that they would dig him out before he died. But when he pushed away the beams, nothing happened, and he had to try the next beams ten feet farther down, and this time when he pushed, the roof did collapse, barely missing him with a crash and rumble of falling rock that made his ears ring. The passage was filled with dust and he was choking, standing back, coughing, waiting for the dust to settle so he could see how much rock had fallen. A faint beam of light was radiating through the dust, and then the dust was clouding to the floor, and there was a foot of space between the barrier of rocks and the nearly demolished roof. More rocks dislodged, and the space dwindled to six inches. The reduced breeze that was coming through wafted some of the dust down the tunnel. It became colder. He slid down the wall to the damp floor, listening to the roof crack and settle, and very soon he heard the dim voices out there.

"Do you think it killed him?"

"How would you like to crawl in and find out?"

"Me?"

Some of them laughed then, and Rambo smiled.

"A cave or a mine," another man said. His voice was loud and deliberate, and Rambo guessed that he was talking into a field radio. "We saw him run inside, and then the place dumped in on him. You should have seen the dust. We have him for sure. Wait a minute, hold it a second." And then as if to someone outside, "Get your dumb ass away from the entrance. If he's still alive, he might be able to see to shoot at you."

Rambo inched up the rockfall, his knees pressing hard on the blunt tips of stone, to peer through the space at the top. There were the sides of the entrance which framed the shale slope and the bare trees and the sky outside, and then a soldier ran into view from the left to the right, his canteen thumping on and off his hip as he ran.

"Hey, didn't you just hear me say to keep clear of the entrance?" the one man said, out-of-view on the right.

"Over there I can't hear what you're saying on the radio."

"Well Christ."

He might as well get this finished. "I want Teasle," he called through the small opening. "I want to give myself up."

"What?"

"Did you guys hear that?"

"Bring Teasle. I want to give myself up." His words rumbled in the tunnel. He listened carefully to the ceiling in case it might crack and drop onto him.

"In there. It's him."

"Hold on, he's alive in there," the man said into the radio. "He's talking to us." There was a pause and then the man spoke much closer to the entrance, though still out of sight. "What do you want in there?"

"I'm tired of saying it. I want Teasle out here and I want to give myself up."

They were whispering now, then the man was talking into the radio, repeating the message, and Rambo wished they would hurry and get this over. He had not believed that surrendering would make him feel this empty. Now that the fight was over, he was positive that he had exaggerated his fatigue and the pain in his ribs. Surely he could have gone on longer. He had in the war. Then he shifted position and his ribs bit and he had not exaggerated.

"Hey, in there," the man called, out-of-sight. "Can you hear me? Teasle says he can't come up."

"Dammit, this is what he's been waiting for, isn't it? You tell him to get the hell up here."

"I don't know anything about it. All they said was he can't come."

"You just told me it was Teasle. Now it's they. Have you been talking with Teasle or haven't you? I want him up here. I want his guarantee that nobody shoots me by mistake."

"Don't you worry. If one of us shoots you, it won't be by mistake. You come out of there careful and we won't have any mistakes."

He thought about it. "All right, but I need help pushing away these rocks. I can't do that all by myself."

He heard them whispering again, and then the man said, "Your rifle and knife. Throw them out."

"I'll even throw out my handgun. I have a revolver that you don't know about. Now I'm being honest with you. I'm not stupid enough to try fighting my way past all of you, so tell your men to keep their hands free of their triggers."

"When I hear you throw that stuff out."

"Coming."

He hated to shove them through. He hated the feeling of helplessness he would have without them. Peering through the space at the top of the rockfall, looking at the bare forest and sky out there, he liked the cool breeze on his face as it came in and down the tunnel.

"I don't hear that stuff yet," the man said out of view. "We have tear gas."

So. And that sonofabitch wouldn't bother himself to come up.

He was pushing the rifle through. He was just ready to let go of it when he understood. The breeze. The breeze down the tunnel. This strong it had to be going somewhere. It was blowing down to the fissure at the end, and from there it was being sucked away, sucked out another passage in the hill. Another way out, that was the only explanation. Otherwise the breeze couldn't move and circulate. Adrenaline scalded into his stomach. He had not lost yet.

"Where's the guns, I said," the man outside told him.

Up yours, Rambo thought. He slipped the rifle back in and heart pounding excitedly, he hurried down the darkness of the tunnel. The coals of his fire were dead, and shortly he had to grope to find where he had camped. He grabbed the fir boughs and the unburned sticks of wood and carried them down the remainder of the tunnel until, head stooped against the low ceiling, he heard the water dripping and bumped into the final wall. A new fire to guide him as far as it could. Smoke from the fir boughs to help him spot the direction of the breeze after that. Christ, maybe.

10

The pain came again, and Teasle bent forward on the bench, squinting at a dark oil stain in the wood floor. He knew he could not keep going much longer. He needed sleep. Oh how he needed it. Something from a doctor. There was no telling how much he had strained and damaged himself. Thank God this was almost over.

A little while, he told himself. That's all. Just hold on a little while more and he'll be caught.

He waited until Trautman and Kern were looking somewhere else and then fumbled to swallow two more pills.

"That box of them was full last night," Trautman said and surprised him. "You shouldn't be taking so many."

"No. I upset it and lost some."

"When was that? I didn't see."

"When you were asleep. Before dawn."

"You couldn't have lost that many. You shouldn't be taking them so much. Not with all the coffee."

"I'm fine. It's a cramp."

"Will you go to a doctor?"

"No. Not yet."

"Then I'm calling a doctor out here."

"Not until he's caught."

Now Kern was walking over. Why wouldn't they leave him be? "But he *is* caught," Kern said.

"No. He's just cornered. It's not the same."

"He might as well be caught. It's a question of time is all. What's so damn important about sitting there in needless pain until they actually put their hands on him?"

"I can't say it right. You wouldn't understand."

"Then call a doctor," Trautman told the radioman. "Get a car to take him back to town."

"I won't go, I said. I promised."

"Who? What do you mean?"

"I promised I'd see this to the last."

"Who?"

"Them."

"You mean your posse? This man Orval and the rest who died?"

He didn't want to talk about it. "Yes."

Trautman looked at Kern and shook his head.

"I told you that you wouldn't understand," Teasle said.

He turned to the open back of the truck, and the sun coming in was sharp on his eyes. Then he was afraid and it was dark and he was flat on his back on the floor. He remembered the boards rumbling when he hit.

"I'm warning you, don't call a doctor," he said slowly, unable to move. "I'm just down here resting."

11

The blaze lit the fissure, smoke wafting down it from the breeze. For a moment Rambo hesitated, then slid his rifle between his belt and his pants, handled a torch and squeezed between the two walls, the strip of rock under his shoes wet and slippery, tilting down. He pressed his back against one wall so that his ribs would not scrape much against the other wall, and the farther in and down he went, the lower the top of the fissure came, and then the orange reflection of his torch glistening on the wet rock showed him where the roof and the walls tapered into a hole directly down. He held his torch over the hole, but the flames radiated only part of the way, and all he could see was a widening funnel down in the rock. He took out a rifle cartridge and dropped it, counting to three before it struck bottom, the echo of a faint metallic ring. Three seconds wasn't deep, so he eased one leg into the hole and then the other leg and slowly squirmed himself down. When he was in as far as his chest, his ribs wedged and he could not go down more without great pain. He stared at the fire up at the entrance to the fissure, smoke enshrouding it, irritating his nostrils, and there were noises off in the mine. Another rockfall, he thought. No. Voices, shouts that merged and rumbled down to him. Already they were coming. He drew in his chest, sweating, forcing his ribs into the hole, closed his eyes, pushed, and then he was through.

The spasm in his chest nearly made him drop. He could not let himself. He had no idea what was below him. His head still above the hole, he persisted in supporting himself by his arms and elbows on the rim while he shifted his feet down there to find a ledge or a crack. The funnel was slippery and smooth, and he let himself down a little more, but still there was no place to rest his feet. The weight of his body stretched his chest, ribs cutting. He heard the men shouting indistinctly in the mine, and eyes watering from the smoke of his fire, he was about to release his grip and drop the rest of the way anyhow, hoping there were no rocks down there to break him, when his feet touched something slender and round that felt like wood.

The upper rung of a ladder. From the mine, he thought. It must be. The guy who worked the mine must have explored here. He lowered himself gingerly onto the rung. It bent but held; he stepped gently onto the second rung, it split and he snapped through two more rungs before he stopped. The sound of his fall drummed through the chamber, startling him. When it faded, he listened for the shouts of the men but he could not hear them now, his head below the rim of the hole. Then as he relaxed, the rung that held him bent, and fearing that he would crash through to the bottom, he quickly waved his torch to see what was below. Four other rungs and then a rounded floor. When it rains, he thought, water from outside must drain down here. That's why the smooth worn rock.

He touched bottom, trembling. Looked. Followed the one exit, a wider fissure that sloped down as well. An old pick was leaning against one wall, its iron rusty, its wood dirty and warped from the damp. In the flickering torchlight, the handle of the pick cast a shadow onto the wall. He could not understand why the miner had left tools here but not in the upper tunnel. He came around a curve, water plunking somewhere, and found him. What was left of him. In the shimmer of the orange light, the skeleton was as repulsive as the first mutilated soldier he had ever seen. His mouth tasted of copper coins as he stood away from the skeleton for a moment and then took a few steps toward it. The bones were tinted orange by his light, but he was certain that their real color was gray like the silt that had gathered around them, and they were perfectly arranged. Not a bone was out of place or broken. No sign at all of why he had died. It was as if he had lain down to sleep and never wakened. Perhaps a heart attack.

Or poison gas. Rambo sniffed apprehensively, but he smelled nothing except dank water. His head was not off balance or his stomach queasy or any of the other symptoms of gas poisoning.

So what in hell could have killed this man?

He shivered again and hated the sight of this perfect set of bones and hurriedly stepped over them, eager to get away. He went farther down, and the fissure became two. Which direction? The smoke had been a bad idea. By now it had dispersed so he could not see which way it was drifting, and it had dulled his sense of smell so he could not even detect its path with that. His torch was burning low in the damp air, flickering sporadically in no particular direction. What was left to him was a kid's game, moistening his finger in his mouth, holding it at one opening, then the other. He felt the breeze slightly cool on the wet of his finger going to the right, and uncertainly he followed down, sometimes forced to squeeze through, occasionally stooping. His torch was burning lower in the damp air all the time. He came to another set of openings and wished that he had rope or string to lay out behind him so that if he became lost he would be able to find his direction back.

Sure, and wouldn't you like a flashlight too? And a compass? Why don't you go on over to the hardware store and buy them?

Why don't you forget the jokes?

The breeze seemed to the right again, and as he moved along, the passage grew more complicated. More twists and turns. More offshoots. Soon he could not remember how he had come to where he was. The skeleton seemed a long confusing distance behind him. It was strangely funny to him that the moment he considered turning around and retracing his steps, he realized he was lost and could not do that. He did not actually want to return yet, he was just considering it, but all the same he would have preferred the option of being able to go back if the breeze suddenly ended. It was extremely faint even so, and he wondered if he had missed some crack in the rock where it seeped out of the hill. God, he could wander here until he died, end up like those bones.

The murmur saved him from panic, and he thought it was them coming, but how could they find him in this maze, and then he recognized the distant sound of water rushing. Before he knew, he had increased speed toward it, at last a perceptible goal in mind, shouldering against walls, staring into the darkness beyond his light.

Then the sound was gone and he was alone again. He slowed and stopped, leaning against a wall, hopeless. There had been no sound of rushing water. He had imagined it.

But it had seemed so real. He could not believe that his imagination could trick him so completely.

Then what happened to the sound? If it was so real, where was it?

A hidden turn, he realized. In his haste to reach the sound, he had failed to check for other entrances in the rock. Go back.

Look. And as he did, he heard it once more, and found the opening, on the blind side of a curve, and slipped into it, the sound
louder as he went.

It was deafening now. The flames of his torch diminishing to
go out, he arrived where the fissure came onto a ledge—and below him, far down, a stream was swirling through a hole in the
rock, roaring down into a channel and away under a shelf. Here.
This had to be where the breeze was going.

But it wasn't. The water foamed up over the shelf and there was
no space for air to be sucked through. But still he felt the breeze
strong here; there had to be another exit close by. His torch hissed,
and he glanced around frantic to memorize the shape of the ledge,
and then he was in darkness, a darkness that was more complete and
solid than any he had ever stood in, made overpowering by the cascade of water below into which he might easily fall if he did not grope
his way with care. He tensed, waiting to get used to the dark. He
never did get used to it. He began to lose his balance, swaying, and
at last he went down on his hands and knees, crawling toward a low
passage at the end of the ledge that he had seen just before his light
sputtered out. To go through the hole he had to slip flat on his belly.
The rock there was jagged. It tore his clothes and scraped his skin and
twisted his ribs until he repeatedly groaned.

Then he screamed as well. From something more than his ribs.
Because as he came blind through the hole into a chamber where he
had room to lift his head, he reached out his hand to claw himself
forward, and fingered mush. A drop of wet muck plopped onto his
neck, and something bit his thumb, and something tiny darted up
his arm. He was lying in thick scum that was soaking through his
two ripped shirts, streaking his belly. He heard squeaking above
him, and the cardboard ruffle of wings, and Jesus Christ, it was bats,
he was lying in their shit, and what were by now a half-dozen tickly

things scurrying over his hands, nibbling, they were beetles, the scavengers that feasted off bat dung and sick bats fallen to the floor. They could strip a carcass clean, and they were piercing the flesh of his arms, as he wriggled insanely backward through the hole, Jesus Christ, swatting them off his hands and arms, bumping his head, wrenching his side. Jesus, rabies, a third of any bat colony was rabid. If they woke and sensed him they might attack and cover him biting while he screamed. Stop it, he told himself. You'll bring them to you. Stop screaming. Already wings were flapping. Christ, he couldn't help it, screaming, wriggling back, and then he was out on the ledge, sweeping his hands and arms, rubbing, making sure and double-sure they all were off, still feeling their many-legged tickles on his skin. *They might follow*, he suddenly thought, scurrying back from the low entrance to the hole, disoriented in the dark, one leg toppling off the ledge, dangling. The fright of his near fall jolted him. He lurched in the opposite direction and bumped against a wall of rock and shook, hysterically wiping the mushy dung off his hands onto the rock, pawing at the slime on his shirt to get the stuff off. His shirt. Something was in there scratching on his skin. He shoved in a hand, grabbing it, snapping its brittle back so he felt its soft wet insides on his fingers as he threw it violently toward the sound of the cascade.

Bats. A pest hole. Disease. The putrid smell of the dung stinging his nose and throat. That's how the guy who worked the mine had died. Rabies. He had been bitten unknowingly, and days later the disease came driving him out of his mind; he wandered crazily through the forest, into the tunnel, out of the tunnel, in once more and down into the fissure, in and around until he crumpled and died. The poor bastard, he must have thought it was the loneliness that was getting to him. At the start anyhow. And when he became delirious, he was too far gone to help himself. Or maybe toward the end he knew he couldn't be helped and went down into the fissure where he could die without being a danger to anyone.

Maybe nothing. What in hell do you know about it? If he had rabies, then he would have hated water, even the smell of it, the idea of it, so he would never have gone down into the dampness of the fissure. You're just imagining that it'll be you who dies that way. If they don't eat you first.

What are you talking about? The bats can't eat you. Not the kind around here.

No, but the beetles.

He was still shaking, struggling to calm himself. The breeze had been strong in the chamber. But he could not go that way. And he did not know how to return to the upper tunnel. He had to face it. This was it. He was stuck.

Except that he could not let himself believe that he was stuck. He had to fight panic and pretend there was a way out; he had to sit against the wall of rock and try to relax and maybe if he thought long enough he might actually discover an escape. But there was only one escape and he knew it: toward the breeze into the bat's den. He licked his lips and took a sip of warm iron-pipe-tasting water from his canteen. You know you have to go in there with the bats, don't you, he told himself. It's either that or sit here and starve and get sick from the damp and die.

Or kill yourself. You were trained to do that too. If things became too much.

But you know you won't. Even if you're passing out and you're positive you're going to die, there's always the chance they'll search these fissures until they stumble into here and find you unconscious.

But they won't. You know you have to follow the breeze into there with the bats. Don't you. You know that.

12

Then go on, get started, get it over with, he told himself.

But instead he sat in the dark on the ledge, listening to the roar of the water below him. He knew what the sound was doing to him, its monotonous rush dulling his ears, little by little pressing him to sleep. He shook his head to keep awake and decided to go in with the bats while he still had the energy, but he could not move; the water rushed on, dinning; and when he woke, he was by the side of the ledge again, one arm dangling. But he was groggy from the sleep, and this time the danger of falling off did not disturb him as much. He was too tired to care. It was so luxurious resting stretched out, arm over the edge emptily. Lulled by the sleep, his body had no sensation, his ribs did not even bother him anymore, numb.

You'll die here, he thought. If you don't soon move, the darkness and the noise will leave you too weak and stupid for anything.

I *can't* move. I've come too far. I need to rest.

You went farther longer in the war.

Yes. And that's what finished me for this.

All right, then die.

I don't want to die. I just don't have the strength.

"God damn it, go on," he said out loud, and in the water's roar, his words were flat and echoless. "Do it quick. Just get in there quick and charge right through where they are and the worst will be done."

"Goddamn right," he said, waited, then repeated himself. But if there's anything worse beyond this, I won't be able to stand it, he thought.

No. This is the worst. There can't be anything beyond this.

I believe it.

Slowly, reluctantly, he crawled in the black toward the entrance to the chamber. He paused, gathered strength, and squirmed his body in. Pretend it's tapioca pudding that you'll touch, he told himself, mustering a smile at the joke. But when his hand reached out and grasped the muck, grasped something scabby in the muck, the hand shot back reflexively. He breathed in the sulfurous stench of dung and decay. The gas would be poisonous; once he was fully in, he would have to hurry. Well, here's batshit in your eye, he told himself, pretending another joke, hung back a moment, then charged into the slime, scrambling to his feet. Already he was dizzy and nauseous from the gas. The muck rose up to his knees, and things rattled against his pantlegs as he wallowed through. The breeze went straight ahead.

No. He was wrong again. The breeze *came* from straight ahead. This was a different air current. The one he had been following must have blown out a different way.

He was wrong about something else too. No matter how much he wanted to hurry, he remembered that he should not. There might be drops in the floor. He had to test each part of the floor ahead of him with his feet, and with each shuffle forward, he expected not to touch more muck and crud, but open space.

The sound in the chamber was changed: before there had been squeaks and the ruffle of wings, but now he heard nothing except the liquid slush of his legs through the deep mire and the dim cascade of water droning on the other side of the entrance. The bats must have gone. He must have slept longer than he knew, until it was night and the bats had gone to hunt and feed. He slogged forward toward the breeze, sick from the stench, but at least they were gone and he relaxed a little. A drop of rotten goo pelted his nose.

He whipped it off and the hair on his neck prickled as the cavern exploded in a thousand bursts of wind and wings. From being on the ledge so long, the roar of water must have partially deafened him. The bats were here all the time, squeaking and settling as before, but his ears had been too dulled to hear them, and now the bats were everywhere, swishing past him, his hands covering his head while he shrieked.

They bumped against him, leathery wings flapping on his face, their high-pitched screeches at his ears. He hit them away, flailed his arms in the air, then covered his head, then flailed again. He wallowed forward, desperate to get out, stumbled, slid to his knees, cold slime up to his hips now, soaking onto his genitals. The bats came and came, an endless swarm of them, tumbling, churning. He reeled to his feet, hands up, swatting sightless. The air was infested with them. He could not breathe. He hit out, crouched, shielding himself. They were swirling at him from the right, tapping him, flipping through his hair. He turned his back, crouched lower, his skin creeping. "Jesus! Jesus!" He shifted to the left, slipped again and fell cheekbone cracking against a wall. His mind was white inside from the pain of striking, and he barely had the will to straighten, swayed, clutched his swollen cheek as the bats continued swarming at him, past him, forcing him along the wall. Desperate, beaten, and half-senseless, he felt something inside expand and strain and at last rupture, nothing to do with his body, just the center of whatever it was that had kept him going this far, but it was everything. He ceased his fight with them, gave himself up to them, let them push him along, staggered with them, arms slowly sinking to his side, and in that wonderful release from fear and desperation, utterly hopeless and passive, never before so free from caring what happened to him, he came to understand what they were about. They were not attacking him. They were flying to get out. He could not control his laughter, trembling with relief. It had to be night outside. They had sensed it, the leader had given his signal, and as one, they had flushed off the cave roof toward the exit while he was in here with them, terrified that they were coming after him. You wanted a string so you could find your way? he told himself. You blind stupid asshole, you've got it. You've been fighting them, and here every second they've been showing you the way.

He climbed sharp ridges with them, felt for drops, pawed before him. Soon their squeaks and brush of wings became expected and familiar as if he and they had been meant to live in company, until they outdistanced him, a few stragglers fluttering past, and then he was alone, the only sounds the echoing scrabble of his hands and shoes on rock. The sweet cool breeze was blowing strongly on his face, and leaning his face toward it, thinking of how the bats had helped him to this direction out, he began to feel a strange affection for them, missing them now that they were gone, as if a bond had been broken between himself and them. He enjoyed breathing, clearing his nostrils and throat and lungs, erasing the taste of dung in his mouth. The touch of his hands on the

rough rock was a clear unfiltered sensation, for the first time con-
sciously real, and his heart beat fast when he climbed and touched
dirt, fingering it, wonderfully pebbled and gritty. He was not outside yet. This was silt that rain had washed into a crack in the hill,
but he was close he sensed, and he climbed steadily upward, in
no hurry, loving the grainy feel of the silt, crawling up a beautiful
hillside of it. When he sprawled at the top, he smelled the outside,
savoring it: crisp leaves, wind through long grass, woodsmoke in
the air. Just a few more feet. He reached carefully forward, his
hand stopped by a barrier of rock. He fingered around, and the
barrier was on all three sides before him. A basin. How high?
It might rise up forever, him so close to being free outside yet
trapped. As much as he was easy and content within himself, he
did not think he had the corresponding strength to climb high.

Then forget about the climb, he told himself. Don't worry
about it. Either you'll make it or you won't. Nothing you can do
if the basin is high. Forget about it.

All right, he thought, stayed seated in the comfortable soft dirt
and rested, accustoming himself to the change in him. He had
never been so aware of things before, so with them. It was true
that in the past in moments of action he had felt a little like this.
He would be performing each gesture smoothly and properly—
running, pivoting to aim, a gentle squeeze on the trigger, the recoil filling his body solidly, his life depending on his grace—and
he would be absorbed in himself, his mind gone, just his body
there in that instant, totally in tune with its operation. The native
allies in the war had called it the way of Zen, the journey to arrive
at the pure and frozen moment, achieved only after long ardu-
ous training and concentration and determination to be perfect. A
part of movement when movement itself ceased. Their words had
no exact English translation, and they said that even if there were,

the moment could not be explained. The emotion was timeless, could not be described in time, could be compared to orgasm but not so defined because it had no physical center, was bodily everywhere.

But this, what he felt now, was different. There was no movement involved, and the emotion was not isolated in one eternal second. It was every second; sitting there in the soft dirt, back conforming restfully with the rock, he sorted through words in his mind and finally decided on "good." He had never felt so good.

He wondered if he had gone crazy. The fumes must have affected him more than he knew and this was just quiet giddiness. Or maybe, having given himself up for dead, he was just overwhelmingly glad to be alive. Having gone through that hell, maybe he had to find everything else full of pleasure.

But you won't feel it much more if you let them come across you here, he told himself, and he stood in the dark, testing the emptiness above him so as not to bump his head against a shelf. Even then, he spiked his head, jerked down, and realized that what he had struck was the end of a branch. It was a bush up there, and when he put out his hands, he touched the rim of the basin, waist high. Out. He had been out all this while, the night sky clouded, fooling him that he was yet underground.

Careful of his ribs, he drew himself up under the bush and gulped air, tasting its freshness, smelling the woody bark of the bush. Down from him, quite a distance, there was a small fire in the trees. After the total darkness of the caves, the fire was bright and rich and alive.

He tensed. Someone had spoken muffled down near the fire. Someone else moved in the rocks nearby, and there was a vivid scratching sound that he saw now was a match being struck on its folder's abrasive paper. Then the flare of the match went out and he saw the gentle glow of a cigarette.

So they were out here waiting for him. Teasle had guessed why he went down into the fissures and caves. Teasle had deployed men around the hill in case he found an exit. Well, they could not see much in the dark, and after being underground, he was at home in the dark, and as soon as he had rested more, he would slip down past them. It would be easy now. They would be thinking he was still in the caves, and he would be miles off on his road. No one had better get in his way. Christ, no. He would do anything. What he had come to feel, he would do anything to anyone to keep.

13

It was dark again, and Teasle did not understand how he had come to be in the murk of the forest. Trautman, Kern, the truck. Where were they all? What had happened to the day? Why was he stumbling so urgently through the solid shadows of the trees?

He leaned breathless against the black trunk of a tree, the pain in his chest rousing from its numbness. He was so disoriented that he was afraid. Not directionless. He knew he had to keep moving straight ahead, he had to go, somewhere ahead, but he did not understand why, how.

Trautman. He remembered this. Trautman had wanted to take him to a doctor. He remembered lying on his back on the wood floor of the truck. He grasped for an explanation of how he had come from there to here. Had he struggled with Trautman not to go to the doctor? Maybe he had broken loose, had grappled from the truck across the field into the woods. Anything not to give up his vigil before it was time. To get closer to the kid. Help catch him.

But that was not right. He knew it was not right. In his condition he could not have fought off Trautman. He could not think.

He had to hurry forward in spite of his chest and the terrible sense that someone was after him, or would soon be after him. The kid. Was it the kid who was after him?

The cloud cover melted, the quarter moon shone through, lighting the trees, and all around him were the hulks of wrecked cars, piled atop each other, stacked against the trees, hundreds of them, twisted, gutted and decayed. It was like a graveyard, grotesque, moonlight on the oval outlines, reflecting.

And soundless. Even when he moved, through leaves and crumpled fenders and broken glass, he made no noise. He was gliding. And somehow he knew it was not the kid who was after him, but someone else. But why was he afraid at the sight of the road through the ghostly carcasses? Why was he afraid of the row of Guardsmen trucks parked along the road? Christ, what was happening to him? Had he lost his mind?

No people there. Nobody near the trucks. Fear draining. A police car empty, the last in the line, nearest town. Ecstatic now, creeping from the junked vehicles, doorless, seats ripped, hoods raised, into the field, silent, close to the earth, toward the car.

A sudden noise disturbed him, fracturing glass that split finely in his eardrums, and he blinked. He was on his back once more. Had somebody shot him in the field? He felt his body for the wound, felt a blanket, no earth beneath him. Soft cushions. A coffin. He started, in a panic, understood. A couch. But Christ where? What was going on? He fumbled for a light, knocked a lamp, and switching it, blinked, discovering his office. But what about the forest, the wrecks of cars, the road? Christ, they had been real, he knew. He looked at his watch, but it was gone, glanced at the clock on his desk, quarter to twelve. Dark outside through the venetian blinds. The twelve must be midnight, but the last he remembered was noon. What about the kid? What's happened?

He faltered to sit up, clutching his head to keep it from throbbing apart, but something had raised the floor of his office, tilting it high away from him. He cursed, but no words came from his mouth. He wavered uphill to the door, grabbed the knob with both hands and swung it, but the door was stuck, and he had to tug with all his might, the door jolting open, almost reeling him downhill to the couch. He threw out his arms, steadying himself like a tightrope walker, his bare feet off the soft rug of his office onto the cold tile of the corridor. It was in gloom, but the front office was lit; halfway there he had to put a hand against a wall.

"Awake, Chief?" a voice said down the corridor. "You O.K.?"

It was too complicated to answer. He was still catching up to himself. On his back on the bright floor of the truck, blearing up at the greasy tarpaulin that was the roof. The voice from the radio: "My God, he isn't answering. He's run deep into the mine." The fight with Trautman to keep from being carried to the cruiser. But what about the forest, the dark—

"I said are you O.K., Chief?" the voice said louder, footsteps coming down the hall. There was an echo enveloping.

"The kid," he managed to say. "The kid's in the forest."

"What?" The voice was directly next to him, and he looked. "You shouldn't be walking around. Relax. You and the kid aren't in the forest anymore. He's not after you."

It was a deputy, and Teasle was sure he ought to know him, but he could not recall. He tried. A word came to him. "Harris?" Yes, that was it. Harris. "Harris," he said proudly.

"You'd better come up front, sit and have some coffee. I just was making fresh. Broke a jug carrying water from the washroom. Hope that didn't wake you."

The washroom. Yes. Harris was echoing, and the imagined taste of coffee squirted sourly into Teasle's mouth, gagging him. The washroom. He staggered through the swinging door, sick in the urinal, Harris holding him, telling him, "Sit down here on the floor," but it was all right, the echoing had stopped now.

"No. My face. Water." And as he splashed his cheeks and eyes coldly, the image flashed in him again, no longer a dream, real. "The kid," he said. "The kid's in the forest by the road. In that junkyard of cars."

"You'd better take it easy. Try and remember. The kid was trapped in a mine and he ran deep into a maze of tunnels. Here. Let me have your arm."

He waved him off, arms down supporting himself on the sink, face dripping. "I'm telling you the kid isn't in there now."

"But you can't know that."

"How did I get here? Where's Trautman?"

"Back at the truck. He sent men with you to the hospital."

"That sonofabitch. I warned him not to. How did I get here instead of the hospital?"

"You don't remember that either? Christ, you gave them all kinds of trouble. You yelled and fought in the cruiser and kept grabbing the wheel to stop them from turning toward the hospital. You were shouting that if they were going to take you anyplace, they were going to take you here. Nobody was going to strap you into any bed if you could help it. So finally they got afraid they would hurt you if they fought with you anymore, and did what you said. Tell you the truth, I think they were just as glad to be rid of you, the racket you were making and all. Once when you grabbed the wheel, you almost hit a transport truck. They had you on a couch here, and as soon as they left, you went out and got in a patrol car to drive yourself back, and I tried to stop you but it was no problem, you passed out behind the wheel before you could find the ignition switch. You really don't remember any of it? There was a doctor came right away, and he checked you over, said you were in half-decent shape, except you were exhausted and you'd been taking too many pills. They're some kind of stimulant and sedative all in one, and you'd swallowed so many you were flying. Doctor said he was surprised you didn't crash even harder and sooner than you did."

Teasle had the sink full of cold water, dunking his face in it, swabbing himself with a paper towel. "Where's my shoes and socks? Where did you put them?"

"What for?"

"Never mind what for. Just where did you put them?"

"You're not planning to try and go back there again, are you? Why don't you sit down and relax? There's all sorts of men swarming through those caves. Nothing more you can do. They said not to worry, they'd call here the minute they found a sign of him."

"I just told you he's not—. Where the hell are my shoes and socks, I asked you."

Far off in the front room the phone started ringing faintly. Harris looked relieved to get away and answer it. He swung out through the door of the washroom, and the phone rang again, then again, then abruptly stopped. Teasle rinsed his mouth with cold water and spat it out milky. He did not dare swallow it in case it would make him sick again. He peered at the dirty checkered tiles on the washroom floor, thought incongruously that the janitors weren't doing their job, and swung through the door out into the corridor. Harris was standing up at the end of the hall, his body blocking off part of the light, uncomfortable about speaking.

"Well?" Teasle said.

"I don't know if I should tell you this. It's for you."

"About the kid?" Teasle said and brightened. "About that junkyard of cars?"

"No."

"Well what is it then? What's the matter?"

"It's long distance—your wife."

He did not know if it was fatigue or shock, but he had to lean against the wall. Like hearing from somebody buried. With everything that had happened because of the kid, he had gradually so managed to keep her out of his mind that now he could not remember her face. He tried but he could not. Dear God, why did he want to remember? Did he still want the pain?

"If she's going to upset you more," Harris said, "maybe you shouldn't talk to her. I can say you're not around."

Anna.

"No. Plug it through to my office phone."

"You're sure now? I can as easily tell her that you're out."

"Go on, plug it through."

14

He sat in the swivel chair behind his desk and lit a cigarette. Either the cigarette would clear his head or else it would cloud his head and spin him, but it was worth a try because he could not talk to her as unsteady as he was. He waited and felt better and picked up the phone.

"Hello," he said quietly. "Anna."

"Will?"

"Yes."

Her voice was thicker than he recalled, throaty, a little broken in some of the words. "Will, are you hurt? I've been worried."

"No."

"It's true. Believe it or not, I *have* been worried."

He drew slowly on his cigarette. There they went again, misunderstanding. "What I meant is no, I'm not hurt."

"Thank God." She paused, then exhaled steadily as if she had a cigarette too. "I haven't been watching TV or reading newspapers or anything, and then suddenly tonight I learned what was happening to you and I got scared. Are you sure you're all right?"

"Yes." He thought about describing it all, but it would only sound like he wanted sympathy.

"Honestly, I would have called earlier if I'd only found out. I didn't want you to think I don't care what happens to you."

"I know." He looked at the rumpled blanket on the couch. There were so many important things to say, but he could not bring himself to do it. They did not matter to him anymore. The pause was too long. He had to say something. "Do you have a cold? You sound like you have a cold."

"I'm getting over one."

"Orval's dead."

He heard her stop breathing. "Oh. I liked him."

"I know. It turns out I liked him even more than I knew. And Shingleton's dead and so is that new man Galt and—"

"Please. Don't tell me any more. I can't let myself know any more."

He thought about it longer, and there really was not much to say after all. The quality of her voice did not make him long for her the way he feared it might have, and at last he felt free, at the end of it. "Are you still in California?"

She did not answer.

"I guess that's none of my business," he said.

"It's O.K. I don't mind. Yes, I'm still in California."

"Any troubles? Do you need any money?"

"Will?"

"What?"

"Don't. I didn't call for that."

"Yes, but do you need any money?"

"I can't take your money."

"You don't understand. I—I think it's going to be all right now. I mean, I feel a lot better about everything now."

"I'm glad. I've been worrying about that too. It's not as if I want to hurt you."

"But what I mean is I feel a lot better, and you can take some money if you need it without the idea that I'm trying to make you beholden and have you come back."

"No."

"Well at least let me pay for this call. Let me accept the charges."

"I can't."

"Then let me put it on the office bill. It won't be me paying, it'll be the town. For Christ sake, let me do something for you."

"I can't. Please stop it. Don't make me regret calling. I was afraid this would happen and I almost didn't."

He felt the telephone sweaty in his palm. "You're not coming back, are you?"

"This is all wrong. I didn't want to go into this. It's not why I called."

"But you won't be coming back."

"Yes. I'm not coming back. I'm sorry."

All he wanted was to hold her, not do anything but hold her. Slowly he crushed out his cigarette, lit another one. "What time is it there?"

"Nine. I'm still confused about the time zone shift. I slept fourteen hours when I got here, getting used to the different time. For them it was eleven o'clock, and for me it was already two hours after midnight. What is it, midnight now, where you are?"

"Yes."

"I have to go, Will."

"So soon? Why?" Then he caught himself. "No. Never mind. That's none of my business either."

"Are you positive you're not hurt?"

"They've bandaged me up, but it's mostly scratches. Are you still living with your sister? Can you at least tell me that much?"

"I moved out into an apartment."

"Why?"

"I really have to go. I'm sorry."

"Keep me in touch with what you're doing?"

"If it'll help you. I didn't know it would be this hard. I don't know how to say this." She sounded like she was sobbing. "Good-bye."

"Good-bye."

He waited, trying to be with her as long as possible. Then she broke the connection and the dial tone was buzzing and he sat there. They had slept together four years. How could she make herself a stranger? Not easily. Her sobbing. She was right, this was hard for her too, and he was sorry.

15

It's over. Do something. Move. Get your mind on the kid where it belongs. The kid. Behind the wheel of a car. Driving fast.

He saw his shoes and socks by the file cabinet and hurriedly put them on. He took a Browning pistol from his gun case, slipped a full magazine into the handle and strapped on a holster, slanting it backward he noticed, the way Orval always had told him to. As he came down the hall, through the front room toward the door, Harris looked at him.

"Don't say it," he told Harris. "Don't say I shouldn't go back out there."

"Fine, then I won't."

Outside the streetlights were on, and he breathed the fresh night air. A cruiser was parked at the side. He was just getting in when he glanced to the left and saw the side of town light up, flames reflecting in waves across the night clouds.

Harris was shouting on the front steps. "The kid! He got out of the caves! They just called that he stole a police car!"

"I know that."

"But how?"

The force of the explosions rattled the windows in the police station. WHUMP, WHUMP, WHUMP! A string of them from the direction of the main road into town. WHUMP, WHUMP!

"Christ almighty, what's that?" Harris said.

But Teasle already knew and he was ramming the car into gear, racing it out of the parking lot to get there in time.

16

Roaring deeper into town, swerving to pass a motorcyclist who was stopped looking back astonished, Rambo saw in his rearview mirror the street behind him flooded with fire leaping high into the trees that bordered it. The fierce red flames radiated into the cruiser. He pressed the accelerator to the floor, whipping down the main street, explosions flaring in the night behind him, bursting the pattern of the fire. Now they would have to waste time going around. Just in case, he needed to do it again. The more diversions, the more they would be confused. They would have to put off chasing him and stop to control the fire.

One of the streetlights ahead was burned out. Under it the brakelights of a car flashed on, its driver opening his door to stare back at the flames. Rambo sheered into the left lane, bearing down fast on the low headlights of a sports car. It swung into the right lane to avoid him just as he swung into his own lane too, and he continued sweeping toward it until it leapt up onto the sidewalk, snapped off a parking meter and crashed through the front display window of a furniture store. Sofas and chairs, Rambo thought. Here's to a soft landing.

Foot solidly on the throttle, he was surprised there were not more cars on the street. What kind of town was this anyhow? A few minutes after midnight and everybody was asleep. Store lights off. Nobody coming out of bars singing. Well, there was a little life in town now. There sure as hell was. The rush of the cruiser, the hefty surge of the engine, he was reminded of Saturday nights years ago racing stock cars, and he loved it all again. Himself and the car and the road. Everything was going to be fine. He was going to make it. Working unnoticed down through the hills to the highway had been easy. Creeping through the forest of junked cars, into the field and up to the cruiser had been easy. The policemen from the car must have been in the hills with the rest, or else down the road to see the drivers of the troop trucks. There had been no key in the switch, but tripping the ignition wires had been no problem, and now streaking through the red light of an intersection, the power of the motor seeming to rise up through the accelerator, flooding his body, he knew it would be only a matter of hours before he was free. He felt too good not to make it. The police would radio ahead to try and stop him, of course, but most of their units were probably behind him with the searchers, so there could not be much resistance ahead. He would make it through town and take to the side roads and hide the car. Then run overland. Maybe hitch on to a freight train. Maybe sneak into a transport. Maybe even hijack a plane. Christ, there were any number of possibilities.

"Rambo."

The voice startled him, coming from the car radio.

"Rambo. Listen to me. I know you can hear me."

The voice was familiar, years off. He could not place it.

"Listen to me." Each word smooth, sonorous. "My name is Col. Sam Trautman. I was director of the school that trained you."

Yes. Of course. Never in sight. The persistent voice over the camp's loudspeaker. Any hour. Day after day. More running, fewer meals, less sleep. The voice that never failed to signal hardship. So that was it. Teasle had brought in Trautman to help. That explained some of the tactics the searchers had been using. The bastard. Turning on his own kind.

"Rambo, I want you to stop and surrender before they kill you."

Sure, you bastard.

"Listen to me. I know this is hard to understand, but I'm helping them because I don't want you killed. They've already begun to mobilize another force ahead of you, and there'll be another force after that, and they'll wear you down until there's nothing left of you. If I thought there was the slightest chance of your beating them, I'd gladly tell you to keep on the move. But I know you can't get away. Believe me. I know it. Please. While you still can, give up and get out of this alive. There's nothing you can do."

Watch me.

Another chain of explosions rumbling behind him, he veered the cruiser, tires squealing, into the empty lot of a gas station, lights off for the night. He ran from the car, kicked through the glass of the station's door, stepped inside and switched on the electricity for the pumps. Then he grabbed a crowbar and hurried outside to wrench the locks off the pumps. There were four, two hoses on each, and he squeezed them on, spewing gasoline into the street, setting their latches in place so they would not shut off when he let go. By the time he drove the car up the street and stopped, the pavement back there was flowing with gasoline. A struck match and whoosh, the night flared into day, a huge lake of fire from sidewalk to sidewalk, twenty feet high, storefronts crackling, windows shattering, heat streaking over him, singeing.

He raced the cruiser away, the blaze of gasoline spreading behind him, streaming to parked cars. WHUMP, WHUMP, they exploded, rocketing. WHUMP. Their own fault. The sign on the light pole had said no parking after midnight. He thought about what would happen when the pressure in the underground gasoline storage tanks went low. The fire would back up into the hoses and down into the tanks and half the block would explode. That would hold them from following. It certainly would.

"Rambo," Trautman said from the radio. "Please. I'm asking you to stop. It's no use. There's no sense to it."

Watch me, he thought again and shut off the radio. He was almost through the heart of town. A few minutes and he would be out the other side.

17

Teasle waited. He had the patrol car blocked across the main road through the town square, and he was leaning over the front fender onto the hood, pistol in hand. There were specks of headlights coming from the flames and the explosions. The kid might have been quicker than himself, might already have sped past and out of town, but he did not believe it. He saw as if from two angles at once—through the kid's eyes as the front of the stolen car hurtled toward the town square—from his own point of view as the headlights loomed into bright discs, the dome on the roof of the car distinct now. A siren dome, a police car, and he pulled back the injection slide on top of his gun, releasing it, aiming steadily. He had to do this just right. There would be no other chance. He had to make absolutely certain this was the kid and not a stray patrolman. The engine was revving louder. The headlights were glaring onto him. He squinted at the outline of the driver. It had been three days since he had seen the kid, but there was no misjudging the shape of his head, hair cut short in clumps. It was him. Now at last, one against one, not in the forest, but in town where he knew best, and on his terms.

The headlights blinding him, he shot one out, then the other, his ejected cartridges clinking across the pavement. How do you like it now? He aimed, and as the kid dove below the dashboard, he fired and shattered the windshield and immediately shot out the front tires, the triple jolt from his pistol drumming his hand on the hood. The cruiser came rushing out of control, spinning, Teasle jumping out of the way as the car hit his in a crash of metal and glass that flung his in a circle and rebounded the kid's toward the far sidewalk. A hubcap rattled down the street, a spray of gasoline spattered the pavement, and Teasle was crouched running toward the kid's car, firing repeatedly at the door, up to it, leaning inside shooting below the window. But the kid was not there, just the front seat dark with blood, and Teasle dove to the road, elbows scraping, glancing furtively around, seeing underneath the car the kid's shoes running across the sidewalk into an alley.

He started after him, reached the brick wall next to the alley, and braced himself to go in firing. He did not understand the spots of blood across the concrete. He did not think any of his bullets had connected. Maybe the kid had been hurt in the crash. It was a lot of blood. Good. Slow him down. From in the alley he heard something heavy smashing against wood as if the kid were breaking in a door. How many shots left? Two at the headlights, one at the windshield, two at the tires, five at the door. That left three. Not enough.

Hurriedly he slipped out the magazine from the handle, slapped in a full one, held his breath, trembling, and then in a rush went down the alley, firing one two three, empty shells winging through the air as he sprawled behind a row of garbage cans and saw the door to Ogden's Hardware open. The garbage cans were too thin to protect him from a bullet, but at least they hid him while he decided if the kid was actually in the store, or if the open door was a trick and the kid was in ambush farther down the alley. He scanned the alley and did not see the kid. He was heading for the door when the thing came flipping out in sparkles. What the—? Dynamite, the fuse too short for him to snub it out in time, too short for him to grab the stick and throw it far enough in time. Like recoiling from a snake, he was back out of the alley, hugged against the brick wall, hands over ears, the explosion stunning him, strips of wood and metal and fiery cardboard bursting out of the alley onto the street. He stopped himself from running again to the broken door. Think it through. Think it through. The kid has to run before other people get here. He can't stay and fight. The dynamite is just to hold you back. Forget the alley. Check the front door.

He darted around the corner of the street, and the kid was long out of the store, well up the block, charging across the road into the shadows of the courthouse. The range was difficult to aim with a pistol. He tried it anyhow, dropping to one knee as if in genuflection, leaving the other knee raised, supporting an elbow on it, steadying the gun with both hands while he sighted and fired. And missed. His bullet smacked loudly into the stone wall of the courthouse. There was a pinpoint flash, the crack of a rifle by the courthouse, a bullet rang through a mailbox next to Teasle. He thought he saw the dark form of the kid ducking around to the back of the courthouse, and he was running after him when three explosions in a row lit the courthouse into flames, debris slashing out the windows brilliantly. Christ, he's gone out of his mind, Teasle thought, running faster. This isn't just to try holding me back. He wants to blow up the whole town.

The wood inside the courthouse was old and dry. The blaze ate into the upper rooms. Running, Teasle grabbed at a muscle cramp in his side, determined not to let it slow him, pressing to go as far as he could before the little energy he had mustered gave out and col-lapsed his body. The fire in the courthouse was breaking, snapping, its smoke filling the street up there so that he could not see where the kid was. To the right, across the street from the courthouse, there was somebody moving on the front steps of the police station, and he guessed it was the kid, but it was Harris, out looking at the fire.

"Harris!" he shouted, urgent to get it all out at once. "The kid! Get back! Get away!"

But his words were swallowed in the thunder of the biggest ex-plosion yet that heaved the station and disintegrated it outward, obliterating Harris in a sweep of flame and rubble. The shock wave of the blast struck Teasle motionless. Harris. The station. It was all he had left, and now it was gone, the office, his guns, the trophies, the Distinguished Service Cross; and then he thought of Harris again and cursed the kid and screamed, his new anger suddenly charging him farther up the sidewalk toward the flames. You sonofabitch, he was thinking. You didn't have to, you didn't have to.

Ahead, to the right of the sidewalk, there were two more storefronts and then the lawn of the police station, littered with burning wood. As he ran up cursing, a shot cracked into the concrete by his feet and ricocheted off. He sprawled into the gut-ter. The street was bright, but the rear of the station was still in shadow, and he returned the kid's shot, aiming at where he had seen the flash of the rifle back there. He shot twice more and now, when he rose, his knee gave out and he toppled across the side-walk. His strength was finally gone. The beating he had taken in the last few days had finally caught up to him.

He lay on the sidewalk and thought of the kid. The kid was bleeding and he'd be weak too. That wasn't stopping the kid any, though. If the kid could keep on, then so could he.

But so tired, so hard to move.

Then all that about fighting the kid one-to-one, nobody else in the way to get hurt, that was all a lie, was it? And Orval and Shingleton and the rest, the promise you made, that was all a lie too, was it?

You can't promise dead men. A promise like that doesn't count.

No, but you promised yourself, and that does count. If you don't start moving, you won't be worth a poor goddamn to yourself or anyone else. You're not tired. You're afraid.

He sobbed, crawled, staggered up. The kid was to the right behind the station. But he could not escape that way because the backyard of the station ended with a high barbed-wire fence, and on the other side of the fence was a long sheer drop to the foundation of the new supermarket. The kid would not have the time or strength to climb safely over and down. He would run farther up the street, and that way there were two houses, then a playground, then a field the town owned that was thick with tall grass and wild raspberry bushes and a listing shed some children had built.

He stalked forward, using the slope of lawn in front of the police station for cover, peering through the smoke to catch sight of the kid, not wanting a second glance at what was left of Harris spread apart on the street. Now he was between the courthouse and the station, their flames lighting him, smoke burning his eyes, heat stinging his face and skin. He stooped closer to the slope of lawn to hide himself in the light. The smoke cleared a moment, and he saw that people who lived in the two houses up from the station were out on their porches, talking, pointing. Lord, the kid might blow up their houses too. Kill them just like Harris.

He struggled to hurry toward them, watching for the kid. "Get the hell away!" he shouted. "Get back!"

"What?" someone up there called.

"He's near you! Run! Get away!"

"What? I can't hear you!"

18

He huddled next to the porch on the far side of the last house and aimed at Teasle. The man and the two women on the porch were so distracted calling to Teasle that they did not see he was hiding below them. But when he pulled back the hammer on his rifle, they must have heard the click because there was an abrupt sound of movement on the wood up there, and a woman leaned over the rail at him, saying "My God! My God!"

That was enough warning; Teasle scurried off the sidewalk, up the lawn to the first house and the shelter of its porch. Rambo fired anyhow, not counting on a hit, but sure at least of frightening him. The woman up there screamed. He levered out his empty cartridge and aimed at the corner of the porch down there. Teasle's shoe was sticking out, lit by the flames. He pulled the trigger, but nothing happened. His rifle empty, no time to reload, he dropped it and drew the police revolver, but Teasle's shoe was gone now. The woman was still screaming.

"Oh, for chrissake shut up, lady," he told her, and ran to the rear corner of the house, studying the shadows of the backyard. Teasle would not risk coming around the front where the flames made him a bright easy target. He would slip into the dark at the back of the first house, and then work his way to the back of this house. Rambo drew close to the corner, staring past a bicycle and a tool shed, waiting. His forehead was cracked open from when his car had struck Teasle's, slamming his face against the police radio, and his sleeve was sticky from wiping away the blood that streamed down into his eyes. The collision had also wakened the pain in his ribs so that he did not know which hurt him worse.

He waited longer, went drowsy briefly, then alerted himself. There was no sound, but a black figure seemed to be gliding along the rear fence in among evergreen shrubs. He wiped blood from his eyes, aimed, but could not let himself fire. Not until he was certain it was Teasle. If the gliding figure was just a trick of the eyes, then shooting at it would reveal his place. It would also be wasting a bullet: he only had five in his handgun, the chamber beneath the firing pin was bare. Teasle's Browning held thirteen. Let *him* waste shots. He could afford to.

There was another reason he did not fire immediately at the figure: when last he had wiped blood from his eyes, they had not focused properly, seeing double, as if the blood remained. He could not distinguish now between the dark shape and the shape of the evergreens, all blurred together, and he was enduring a headache so sharp that it seemed ready to split his skull.

Why wasn't the shadow moving? Or was it moving and he could not see it? Teasle ought to have made some sound, though. Come on, make a sound, why didn't he? It was getting too late. Already sirens were wailing close. Fire sirens maybe. But maybe police. Come on, Teasle. He heard the people from the porch in the house now, talking frightened. He sensed something, and looked behind to see if anyone was still on the porch with a gun or something that might hurt him, and Christ, there was Teasle coming up the front lawn. In his surprise Rambo fired before he knew it, Teasle crying out, careening backward down the lawn in an arc that landed him on the sidewalk, but Rambo could not puzzle out what was happening to himself, the way he was jerking back weightless, whipping to one side, striking facedown in the grass. His hands were warm and wet on his chest, then directly sticky. Oh Jesus he was hit. Teasle had managed a shot and hit him. His chest was stunned, nerves paralyzed. Got to move. Have to get away. Sirens.

He could not stand. He squirmed. A wire fence to the side of the house. Beyond it vague hulking objects in the night. The flames from the station and the courthouse surged high, illuminating them orange, but still he could not see them distinctly. He strained his eyes. His vision cleared and he saw. Seesaws, the word a hollow jingle in his head. Swings. Slides. A playground. He inched toward them on his belly, the sound of the flames down behind him like the roar of a windstorm snapping through trees.

"I'll get my gun! Where's my gun?" the man shouted inside the house.

"No. Please," a woman said. "Don't go out there. Stay out of it."

"Where's my gun? Where did you put my gun? I told you to quit moving it."

He dug his elbows into the lawn, squirming faster, reached the fence, a gate, opened it, kneed himself through. Behind him there were hollow footsteps on the wood of the backstairs.

"Where is he?" the man was saying, his voice clear outside. "Where'd he go?"

"There!" the second woman said hysterically, the voice of the one who had seen him from the front porch. "Over there! The gate!"

Well you bastards, Rambo thought and looked. The blazes were flaring high, and the man was standing by the tool shed, aiming a rifle. The man was too awkward aiming, but he went instantly graceful when Rambo shot him, smoothly clutching his right shoulder, spinning easily, toppling perfectly over the bicycle next to the tool shed, and then he was awkward again as the bicycle gave way under him and the two jumbled to the ground in a tinny jangle of chain and spokes.

"Christ, I'm hit," the man was groaning. "He hit me. I'm hit."

But the man did not know how lucky he was. Rambo had aimed at his chest, not his shoulder. No longer able to see to shoot straight, no longer able to hold his gun steady, his chest rapidly draining blood, he had no hope of getting away, no means of efficiently protecting himself, nothing. Except perhaps the stick of dynamite still in his pocket. The dynamite, he thought. Screw the dynamite. With the little strength remaining in him, he would not be able to lob the stick five feet.

"He hit me," the man was groaning. "He hit me. I'm hit."

Well, so am I, buddy, but you don't hear me whining about it, he thought, and since he could not accept merely waiting for the men in the siren cars to come for him, he began crawling again. Into a dry wading pool at the center of the playground. Into the center of the wading pool. And there his nerves tingled, stretched to life, and gradually registered his pain. Teasle's bullet had torn through his cracked ribs, and it was like lancing a giant fester, poison spewing forth. The pain grew to overwhelm him. He was scratching at his chest, clawing, ripping. He shook his head, clenched his body, so convulsed with pain that he raged to his feet up out of the wading pool, head stooped, shoulders hunched, tottering toward the fence at the edge of the playground. It was low, and he leaned over it gasping, kicked his feet in the air; in a grotesque somersault came down on the other side, expecting his back to hit ground; instead snagged thorns and leafless branches. A field of brambles. Wild raspberries. He had been here before. He did not remember when, but he had been here before. No. No, he was wrong. It was Teasle who had been here before, up in the mountains, when he had escaped into that whole slope of brambles. Yes, that was it. Teasle had gone in. Now it was the other way around. Now it was his own turn. The barbs dug him. They felt so good, helping him to rip at his pain. Teasle had escaped this way, through brambles like these. Why couldn't *he*?

19

Teasle lay on his back on the concrete of the sidewalk, ignoring the flames, staring up fascinated at a yellow streetlight. If this were summer, he thought, there would be moths and mosquitoes flying around the bulb. Then he wondered why he had thought that. He was losing his stare, blinking now, holding both hands over the hole in his stomach. It amazed him that except for a compulsive itch in his intestines, he had no sensation. There was also a big hole in his back, he knew, but that too was just an itch. So much damage and so little pain, he thought. Almost as if his body no longer belonged to him.

He was listening to the sirens, first a few, then a cluster of them, wailing somewhere beyond the fire. Sometimes they sounded far off, sometimes just down the street. "Just down the street," he said to hear himself, and his voice was so distant that his mind had to be separate from his body. He moved one leg, then the other, raised his head, arched his back. Well then, at least when the bullet had gone through it had not shattered his spine to break his back. The thing is, though, he told himself, you're dying. That big a hole and this little pain, you're dying all right, and that too amazed him—that he could think about it so calmly.

He glanced away from the streetlight toward the burning courthouse, even its roof on fire, toward the police station, flames seething out every window. And I just had those inside walls painted, he thought.

Someone was behind him. Kneeling. A woman. An old woman. "Is there anything I can do?" she gently asked.

You're some old woman, he thought. All this blood and still you made yourself come to me. "No. No, thank you," he said, his voice very distant. "I don't believe there's anything you can do. Unless. Did I hit him, do you know? Is he dead?"

"He fell I think," she said. "I'm from the next house down. By the station. I'm not sure exactly about it all."

"Well," he said.

"My house is catching fire. The people in this house, someone was shot I think. Can I get you a blanket? Some water? Your lips are dry."

"Are they? No. No, thank you."

It was certainly fascinating, his voice far off, but hers close, unfiltered against his eardrum, and the sirens, oh the sirens, wailing louder deep inside his head. It was all reversed, him outside of himself, but everything out there within him. Fascinating. He had to tell her about it. She deserved to know. But when he looked she was gone, and it was like a ghost had been with him. What kind of sign was it that he didn't know when she had gone? The sirens. Too loud. Shrieking like knives through his brain. He raised his head and looked between the fires down toward the bottom of the town square, police cars veering around the corner down there, speeding this way up the street, flashers spinning. Six, he counted. He had never seen anything with such distinct clarity, each detail in pure focus, especially each color of the light, flashers quick intermittent red, front-beams constant glaring yellow, men behind the windshields orange in the shimmering radiance of the flames. The vision was too powerful. It set the street spinning, and he had to close his eyes or be sick. That would be all he needed. To retch and tear his stomach more, and maybe die right there before he could discover how this would end. It was a grace that he had not already been sick. He was long overdue. Hold together. That was all he could do. If he was going to die, and he was sure that he was, he could not let it come over him just yet. Not until the end.

He heard their tires squealing, and when he looked again, they were braking with a lurch below the station, policemen jumping out before the cars were at full stop, sirens ebbing. One policeman pointed up the street toward him, and they all came running between the fires, shielding their faces from the heat, shoes scuffling on the pavement, and in among them he saw Trautman. They had their guns drawn. Trautman had a pump shotgun that he must have taken from one of the cruisers.

Now he saw Kern among them too. Kern was telling a man, running as he spoke, "Go back to the car! Radio for an ambulance!" Kern was pointing up and down the street, telling others, "Get these people out of here! Push them back!"

What people? He did not understand. He looked, and dozens of people had materialized. Their abrupt appearance startled him. They were watching the fires. Something about their faces. They were crowding toward him, eyes aglow, bodies stiff, and he raised his hands to keep them away, irrationally afraid, about to cry, "Not yet!" as the policemen reached him, blocking them off, encircling him.

"The kid," he said.

"Don't talk," Kern told him.

"I think I hit him." He said it calmly. He concentrated, trying to imagine he was the kid. "Yes. I hit him."

"You need your strength. Don't talk. A doctor's coming. We would have been here sooner, but we had to go around the fires on the—"

"Listen."

"Relax. You've done everything you could. Let us handle it now."

"But I've got to tell you where he is."

"Here!" a woman screamed from the front lawn of the house. "Back here! Get a doctor!"

"You eight come with me," Kern said. "Spread out. Half on that side of the house, half on this side. Be careful. The rest of you help scatter this crowd."

"But he's not back there." Too late. Kern and his men were gone.

"Not back there," he repeated to himself. "Kern. What's the matter with him that he can't listen?" It was just as well he had not waited for Kern to help that evening at the start of the chase, he decided. With Kern along, the posse would have been twice as confused, and the men Kern brought would have died with the others.

Trautman had not yet spoken. The few policemen who remained were trying to avoid the sight of all the blood. Not him, though.

"No, not you, Trautman. You don't mind the blood at all. You're used to it."

Trautman did not answer, just kept staring.

One policeman said, "Maybe Kern is right. Maybe you should try not to talk."

"Sure, and that's what I told Orval when *he* was shot. But he didn't want to die quiet anymore than I do. Hey, Trautman, I did it. I said I would, didn't I? And I did."

"What's he talking about?" one policeman said. "I don't get it."

"Look at him. His eyes," another said. "He's gone crazy."

Still staring, Trautman gestured for them to be quiet.

"I told you I'd outguess him, didn't I?" His voice was a victorious child's. He did not like the sound of it, but he could not stop himself. Something inside him was rushing it on, getting it all out, the secret. "He was up there by the side of that porch, and I was the next house down beside that porch, and I could feel he was waiting for me to come. Your school trained him well, Trautman. He did exactly what he was trained to do, and that's how I outguessed him." His wound was itchy, he scratched it, his blood pooling out, and it was more fascinating to him with every moment how he could go on talking this way. He should be gasping, squeezing out each word, he knew, and here they were coming on and on in a fluent rush like an unspooling ribbon. "I pretended I was him. Do you see? I've been thinking about him so much it's like I know what he's doing. And just then, the two of us beside the porches, I was imagining what he would do and suddenly I could tell what he was figuring—that I wouldn't come for him on the street side where there was light from the fires, that I'd come around the back through the yard and the trees. Through the trees, Trautman. Do you see it? Your school trained him for guerrilla fighting in the hills, so he instinctively turned to the trees, and the lawn, and the bushes back there. And me, after what he did to me in the hills, I was God damned if I'd ever fight him again on his terms. On *my* terms. Remember that's what I told you? *My* town. And if I was going to get it, I was going to be on *my* street near *my* houses with the light from *my* office burning. And I did it. I outguessed him, Trautman. He took my bullet in the chest."

Still Trautman did not speak. He looked so long at it before he pointed to the gore of the stomach wound.

"This? You mean this, you're pointing at? I told you. Your school trained him well. My Christ, what reflexes."

Off in the night, beyond the roar of the fires, there was a full roaring ca-whump that illuminated all that part of the sky. The echo from it rumbled in return over the town.

"Too soon. It went too soon," one deputy said in disgust.

"Too soon for what?"

Kern was coming from behind the house, scrambling down the slope of lawn to the sidewalk. "He isn't back there."

"I know. I tried to tell you."

"He shot some guy in the shoulder. That's what the woman was yelling about. My men are looking for a trace of him. There's blood they're following." He was distracted, glancing at the waves of light in the sky at the side of town.

"What is it? What was that explosion?" Teasle said.

"God, I doubt they had enough time."

"Time for what?"

"The gas stations. He set two of them burning. We heard on the radio about the fire department over there. The pumps and main buildings are so deep in the flames that they couldn't get in to shut off the gasoline. They were going to disconnect the electricity to that whole part of town when they realized—if they stopped the pumps, the pressure would reverse the fire down into the main tanks and the entire block would go up. I called a squad of my men over to help evacuate. One of the fires was in a section of houses. God, I hope they were in time before it went, and there's another one yet to go, and how many will be dead when this is over."

A shout from the side of the house: "He went across a playground over here!"

"Well, don't yell so loud that he knows we're on to him!"

"Don't worry," Teasle said. "He's not in the playground."

"You can't be sure of that. You've been lying here too long. He might have gone anywhere."

"No, you have to be in his place. You have to pretend that you're him. He crawled through the playground and pushed himself over the fence there and he's in the wild raspberries, the brambles. I got away from him through brush like that, and now he's trying it, but he's wounded too bad. You can't believe the pain in his chest. There's a shed there some children built and he's crawling toward it."

Kern frowned in question at Trautman and the two policemen. "What's been going on with him while I was back there? What's happened?"

The one policeman shook his head queerly. "He thinks he's the kid."

"What?"

"He's gone crazy," the other said.

"You two watch him. I want him quiet," Kern said. He knelt beside him. "Hang on for the doctor. He won't be long. I promise you."

"It doesn't matter."

"Try. Please."

There were bells clanging and more sirens as two big fire engines lumbered up the square, slowing heavily to a stop beside the police cars. Firemen were jumping off, rubber-coated, running for tools to open the water hydrants, reeling out hoses.

Another shout from the side of the house: "He went clean through the playground! There's blood all through it! There's some kind of field and bushes!"

"Don't shout, I told you!" Then, down to him on the sidewalk, "O.K., let's find out for you. Let's see if you're right about where he is."

"Wait."

"He'll get away. I have to go."

"No. Wait. You have to promise me."

"I did. The doctor is coming. I promise it."

"No. Something else. You have to promise me. When you find him, you have to let me be there for the end. I have a right. I've been through too much not to see the end."

"You hate him that much?"

"I don't hate him. You don't understand. He wants it. He wants me to be there."

"Jesus." Kern looked astounded at Trautman and the others. "Jesus."

"I shot him and all at once I didn't hate him anymore. I just was sorry."

"Well of course."

"No, not because he shot *me*, too. It wouldn't have made a difference if he shot me or not. I still would have been sorry. You have to promise to let me be there at the end. I owe it to him. I have to be with him at the end."

"Jesus."

"Promise me."

"All right."

"Don't lie. I know you're thinking I'm so badly hurt that I can't be moved up to that field."

"I'm not lying," Kern said. "I have to go." He stood, motioned to his men at the side of the house, and they joined him, spread out, staring nervously up the street toward the playground and the field beyond.

Except for Trautman.

"No, not you, Trautman," Teasle said. "You want to stay out of it yet, don't you? But don't you think you ought to see? Don't you think you ought to be there and see how he finally maneuvers himself?"

When Trautman now spoke at last, his voice was as dry as the wood in the courthouse must have been when it caught, tinder for the fire. "How bad are you?"

"I don't feel a thing. No. I'm wrong again. The concrete is very soft."

"Oh." Another full billowing ca-whump lit up the sky over there. Trautman watched it blankly. The second gas station.

"Score another point for your boy," Teasle said. "My yes, your school really trained him well. There's no question."

Trautman looked at the firemen hosing the flames of the courthouse and the police station, at the jagged hole in Teasle's stomach, and his eyes flickered. He pumped his shotgun, injecting a shell into the firing chamber before he started up the lawn toward the back of the house.

"What did you do that for?" Teasle said. But he already knew. "Wait."

No answer. Trautman's back was receding through the reflection of the flames toward the few shadows that were left at the side of the house.

"Wait," Teasle said, panic in his voice. "You can't do that!" he shouted. "That's not yours to do!"

Like Kern before him, Trautman was gone.

"Dammit wait!" Teasle shouted. He rolled on his stomach, pawing the sidewalk. "I have to be there! It has to be me!"

He groped to his hands and knees, coughing, blood dripping from his stomach onto the sidewalk. The two policemen grabbed him, pushing him down.

"You've got to rest," the one said. "Take it easy."

"Leave me alone! I mean it!"

They were struggling to control him. He was thrashing.

"I have a right! I started this!"

"Better let him go. If he tries fighting us anymore he'll rip himself wide open."

"Look at his blood on me. How much more can he have inside him?"

Enough, Teasle was thinking. Enough. He groped again to his hands and knees, drew up one leg, then the other, concentrating to stand. He had the salt taste of blood in his mouth. I started this, Trautman, he was thinking. He's mine. Not yours. He wants it to be me.

He braced himself, rose, walked a step, then listed, contending for his balance. If he fell, he was certain he would never be able to raise himself again. He had to hold himself steady, balancing as he wove up the lawn toward the house. I know it, Trautman, he was thinking. He wants it to be me. Not you. Me.

20

In agony, Rambo crawled through the brambles toward the shed. The firelight extended weakly onto it, and he saw how one wall leaned inward, the roof on an angle, but he could not see it through the half-open door, stark black in there. He crawled, but he seemed to be taking a very long while to go a short space, and then he found he was just doing the motions of a crawl, not getting anywhere. He worked harder, slowly managing some distance toward the shed.

But when he came to the black entrance, he refused. In there it was too much like the hole where he had been held prisoner in the war, dark, compressed, constricting. It reminded him strangely of the shower stall Teasle had made him go into, and of the cell Teasle had wanted to lock him in. They had been brightly lit, that was true, but the repulsion had been the same. Everything he was running from, he thought, and how could he have been so tired as to consider making a fight from in there.

A fight was out of the question now anyway. He had seen too many men die from bullet wounds not to know that he was bleeding to death. The pain continued in his chest, in his head, sharply accented by each pump of his heart, but his legs were cold and numb from the loss of blood, that was why he had trouble crawling, and his fingers were senseless, his hands, nerve extremities gradually shutting off. He did not have much life to go. At least he still had the choice of where it would leave him. Not in there, as in the caves. He was determined never to experience that again. No, in the open. Where he could see the sky unhampered, and smell the night air's unrestricted flow.

He groped to the right of the shed, burrowing awkwardly farther into the brush. The correct spot. That was the necessary thing. Someplace comfortable and friendly. Proper to him. Soothing. He needed to find it before it was too late. A shallow, body-long trough seemed promising, but when he lay face up in it, the trough was too much like a grave. Plenty of time to lie in his grave. Someplace else he needed, just the opposite, high, boundless, his last moments for a taste of it.

Crawling, he peered forward through the brush, and there was a gentle rise ahead, and when he reached the top it was a mound, slopes of brush down every side, the dome a clearing of drooped autumn grass. Not as high as he had wanted. Still it was above the field, and stretching back on top of the grass was pleasant, as if on a straw-stuffed blanket. He peered up at the glorious orange patterns that the flames projected onto the night clouds. At ease. This was the place.

At any rate his mind was at ease. But his pain quickened, racking him, and in contrast, the numbness crept to his knees, his elbows. Soon it would creep to his chest, cancelling the pain, and where after that? His head? Or would he be gone before then?

Well. He had better think if there was anything more to do, anything important he had forgotten. He stiffened in pain. No, there didn't seem anything more to do.

What about God?

The idea embarrassed him. It was only in moments of absolute fear that he had ever thought about God and prayed to him, always embarrassed because he did not believe and felt so hypocritical when he prayed out of fear, as if in spite of his disbelief there might be God after all, God who could be fooled by a hypocrite. When he was a child, then he believed. He certainly did believe when he was a child. How did it go, the nightly Act of Contrition? The words came hesitantly, unfamiliarly to him. Oh my God, I am heartily sorry for—For what?

For everything that happened the last few days. Sorry that it all had to happen. But it all did have to happen. He regretted it, but he knew if this were Monday again, he would go through the next days the same as he had up to now, just as he knew Teasle would. There was no avoiding any of it. If their fight had been for pride, it had also been for something more important.

Like what?

Like what a lot of horseshit, he told himself: freedom and rights. He had not set out to prove a principle. He had set out to show a fight to anyone who pushed him anymore, and that was quite different—not ethical, but personal, emotional. He had killed a great many people, and he could pretend their deaths were necessary because they were all a part of what was pushing him, making it impossible for someone like him to get along. But he did not totally believe it. He had enjoyed the fight too much, enjoyed too much the risk and the excitement. Perhaps the war had conditioned him, he thought. Perhaps he had become so used to action that he could not ease off.

No, that was not quite true either. If he had really wanted to control himself, he could have. He simply had not wanted to control himself. To live his way, he had been determined to fight anyone who interfered. So all right then, in a way he had fought for a principle. But it was not that simple, because he had also been proud and delighted to show how good he was at fighting. He was the wrong man to be shoved, oh yes he was, and now he was dying and nobody wanted to die, and all that he was thinking about principles was a lot of crap to justify it. To think that he would do everything again the same was just a trick to convince himself that what was happening right now could not have been avoided. Christ, it *was* right now, and he could not do one damn thing about it, and neither principles nor pride had any matter in the face of what was to come. What he should have done was cherish more smiling girls and drink more icy water and taste more summer melons. And that was a lot of horseshit too, what he should have done, and all that about God was merely complicating what he had shortly decided: if the numbness creeping up his thighs and forearms was an easy way to die, it was also poor. And helpless. Passively defeating. The one choice left to him was how to die, and it was not going to be like a holed-up wounded animal, a quiet, pathetic, gradually senseless deterioration. At once. In a great burst of feeling.

Since his first sight of tribesmen mutilating a body in the jungle, he had been afraid of what would happen to his own body when he died. As if his body still would have some nerve responses, he had imagined with chilling repulsion what it would be like having the blood drained from his veins, embalming fluid pumped in, his central organs removed, his chest cavity treated with preservatives. He had imagined what it would be like having the undertaker sew his lips together and his eyelids down, and he had been sickened. Death—strange that death should not bother him so much as what would happen to him after. Well, they could not do all that to him if there was nothing of him to have it done to. At least this way, doing it to himself, there was the chance of pleasure.

He took the final stick of dynamite from his pocket, opened the softly packed box of fuses and exploders, slipped one set of them into the stick, then arranged the stick between his pants and his stomach. He hesitated to light the fuse. This damn business about God, complicating things. It was suicide he was about, and that could send him to hell forever. If he believed. But he did not, and he had lived with the idea of suicide for a long while, in the war carrying the poison capsule his commander had given him to prevent being captured, tortured. Then when he had been captured, he had not had time to swallow it. Now, though, he would light the fuse.

But what if there *was* God? Well, if God was, He could not fault him for being true to his disbelief. One intense sensation yet reserved for him. No pain. Too instantaneous for pain. Just one bright dissolving flash. At least that would be something. The numbness up to his groin now, he prepared to light the fuse. Then, with one last bleary glance across the field to the playground, he saw in the firelight the double-focused image of a man in a Beret uniform stalking low and carefully through the cover of the swings and slides. He carried a rifle. Or a shotgun. Rambo's eyes could no longer tell him which. But he could make out it was a Beret uniform and he knew that was Trautman. It could be no one else. And behind Trautman, stumbling across the playground, clutching his stomach, came Teasle, it had to be him, lurching against a rectangular maze of climbing bars, and Rambo understood then there was a better way.

21

Teasle clung to the bars, resting, then pushed himself away, staggering toward the fence. He had been frantic that Trautman would get into the field before him, but now everything was going to be fine—Trautman was just a few steps ahead of him, crouched beside a bench, studying the thick brush of the field. Just a few steps ahead of him. He reached out and grabbed the bench to stop from falling, stood against it, breathing hoarsely.

Without a glance away from the field, Trautman told him, "Get down. He'll see you for sure."

"I would, but I'd never stand again."

"So what would be the need? You can't do any good the way you are. Stay out of it. You're killing yourself."

"Lie down and let you finish it for me? Screw. I'm dying anyhow."

Trautman looked at him then.

Kern was nearby, out of sight, yelling. "Christ, get yourselves down! He has perfect cover and I'm not risking any men to go in! I sent for gasoline! He likes to play with fire, we'll burn him out!"

Yes, that's your style, Kern, he thought. He grabbed at the itch in his stomach, holding himself wetly in, and shuffled clumsily forward, propping himself against the fence.

"Get down!" Kern yelled again.

Screw. Burn him out, will you, Kern? That's the kind of idea I expected from you, he thought. And you can bet that before the fire gets to him, he'll come through here shooting to take a few of your men with him. There's only one way to do this, and that's for somebody like me who doesn't have a hope anyhow to go in and take him. You haven't lost enough men yet, or you'd know that.

"What the hell was that?" Kern shouted, and Teasle realized that what he had been thinking he had said out loud. That startled him, and he had to get over the fence while he still was able. There was blood here on the fence. The kid's. Good. He would be going over where the kid had. His blood dripping on the kid's, he gathered himself and toppled over the fence. He guessed that he struck the ground hard, but his brain did not register the impact.

In a quick rush, Trautman came from the bench, vaulted the fence and landed in a near crouch in a clump of brush beside him.

"Stay out of here," Teasle told him.

"No, and if you don't shut up, he'll be on to everything we do."

"He's not anywhere around to hear. He's way over in the center of the field. Look, you know he wants it to be me. I have a right to be there at the end. You know that."

"Yes."

"Then stay out of what doesn't concern you."

"I started this long before you, and I'm going to help. There's no disgrace in taking help. Now shut up, and let's go while you still can."

"All right, you want to help? Then help me stand. I can't do it on my own."

"You mean it? What a mess this is going to be."

"That's what Shingleton said."

"What?"

"Nothing."

Trautman had him on his feet now, and then Trautman was crawling into the brush, disappearing, and Teasle stood, his head above the brush, surveying it, thinking, Go. Go on and crawl as fast as you can. It won't make a difference what you do. I'll get to him before.

He coughed and spat something salty and shifted forward through the brush in a straight line toward the shed. It was clear that the kid had gone this way, the branches broken down in a crude trail. He kept his pace slow, not chancing the helplessness of a fall. Even so, he was surprised at how soon he reached the shed. But as he prepared to go inside, he realized instinctively that the kid was not in there. He glanced around, and as if drawn toward a magnet, he shambled swaying down another broken path toward a large mound. There. The kid was there. He knew it, could feel it. There was no doubt.

When he had been spread out on the sidewalk, someone had said he was delirious. But that had been wrong. He had not been delirious. Not then. Now. Now he was delirious, and his body seemed to be melting from him, just his mind floating over the brush toward the mound, and the night was becoming glorious day, the orange reflection of the flames growing brighter, dancing wildly. At the bottom of the mound he ceased floating and hovered transfixed, the splendrous sheen illuminating him. It was coming. He had no more time. As if his will belonged to another, he saw his arm rise up before him, his pistol aiming toward the mound.

22

The numbness was at Rambo's shoulders now, at his navel, and steadying the gun was like aiming with two stumps of wood. He saw Teasle dispersing into triple focus down there, eyes bright, aiming, and he knew there should be no other way. No passive lapse into nothing. No lit fuse, self-disruption. But this way, the only proper way, in the last of the fight, trying his best to kill Teasle. Eyes and hands betraying him, he did not think he could hit Teasle. But he had to try. Then if he missed, Teasle would see the flash of his gun, and fire at it. And at least then I'll have died trying, he thought. He strove to squeeze his finger on the trigger, directing his aim at Teasle's center image. The barrel was wobbling, and he would never hit him. But he could not fake it. He had to try as hard as he could. He told his hand to squeeze on the trigger, but his hand would not work, and as he concentrated on it, clenching, the gun went off unintended. So careless and sloppy. He cursed himself. Not the real fight he had hoped for, and now Teasle's bullet would come when he did not deserve it. He waited. It should have come already. He squinted to clear his vision, looking down the mound where Teasle lay flat in the brush. Christ, he had hit him. God, he had not wanted that, and the numbness was so overwhelming by now that he could never light the fuse before it nulled him. So poor. So ugly and poor. Then death took him over, but it was not at all the stupefying sleep, bottomless and murky, that he had expected. It was more like what he had expected from the dynamite, but coming from his head instead of his stomach, and he could not understand why it should be like that, and it frightened him. Then since it was the total of what remained, he let it happen, went with it, erupted free through the back of his head and his skull, catapulted through the sky, through myriad spectra, onward, outward, forever dazzling, brilliant, and he thought if he kept on like this for long enough he might be wrong and see God after all.

23

Well, Teasle thought. Well. He lay back on the brush, marvelling at the stars, repeating to himself that he did not know what had hit him. He really did not. He had seen the flash of the gun and he had fallen, but he had been slow and gentle to fall, and he really did not know what had hit him, did not sense it, respond to it. He thought about Anna and then stopped that, not because the memory was painful, but because after everything she just didn't seem important anymore.

He heard someone stepping, cracking, through the brush. The kid coming, he thought. But slow, very slow to come. Well sure, he's hurt bad.

But then it was only Trautman standing there, head outlined against the sky, face and uniform lustrous from the flames, but eyes dull. "What's it like?" Trautman said. "Is it bad?"

"No," he said. "Actually it's kind of pleasant. If I don't think about what it's bringing. What was that explosion I heard? It sounded like another gas station."

"Me. I guess it was me. I took the top of his head off with this shotgun."

"What's it like for you?"

"Better than when I knew he was in pain."

"Yes."

Trautman pumped the empty shell from the shotgun, and Teasle watched its wide arc glistening through the air. He thought about Anna again, and she still did not interest him. He thought about his house he had fixed up in the hills, the cats there, and none of that interested him either. He thought about the kid, and flooded with love for him, and just a second before the empty shell would have completed its arc to the ground, he relaxed, accepted peacefully. And was dead.

A CONVERSATION WITH DAVID MORRELL

Let's start with some basics. *First Blood* **was your first novel, right?**

Yes, it came out in 1972. Debut novels almost always sink, but I was fortunate. Just about every major newspaper and magazine gave it glowing reviews. A film studio bought the movie rights before it was published. It was translated into 26 languages. It was taught in high schools and colleges. When Stephen King taught creative writing at the University of Maine, it was one of the two texts he used. (The other was James M. Cain's *Double Indemnity*.) This edition marks its 45th anniversary. It's never been out of print.

The book introduced Rambo, who turned out to be one of the five most iconic thriller characters of the twentieth century, along with Sherlock Holmes, Tarzan, James Bond, and Harry Potter. How does it feel to have created a character recognized around the world?

Rambo is mentioned almost daily in conversation or in the media. The word is in the Oxford English Dictionary.

Astrophysicists use the word Rambo to refer to a powerful group of stars. He continues to be referred to in countless movies and television series. He was a question on the television game show *Jeopardy*. He's so much a part of world culture that when I sign copies of *First Blood*, I often call myself "Rambo's father." It's like he's a son who grew up and went in unexpected directions. There's no way to predict the future of a character or a book. I tried to write the best novel I could. After that, it was out of my control. When I hear Rambo mentioned, I'm often caught by surprise and take a second to remember that I created him.

How did you get the idea for the story?

I was raised in southern Ontario. In the mid-1960s, I came to the United States to study American literature at Penn State. At that time, the Vietnam War was hardly mentioned in Canada, so I had no idea what the war was about when I met students recently returned from military duty there. I learned about their problems adjusting to civilian life: nightmares, insomnia, depression, difficulty in relationships, what's now called post-trauma stress disorder. In 1968, the two main stories on the television news were the many protests against the Vietnam War and the hundreds of riots that broke out in American cities after the assassinations of Martin Luther King, Jr. and Robert Kennedy. I got to thinking that the images of the war and the images of the riots weren't much different. Eventually I decided to write a novel about a returning Vietnam veteran who brings the war to the United States. The key to the novel is the way chapters alternate between Rambo's and Teasle's viewpoints. The reader doesn't know which character to cheer for. They represent the two sides of American culture as I saw it in the late 1960s. Teasle is old enough to be Rambo's father and exemplifies the generation gap of that era. He's a kind of Eisenhower Republican whereas Rambo has been radicalized by the war and under other circumstances might have demonstrated against it.

That alternating-viewpoints device wasn't used in the movie.

No. In the film, the police chief gets less screen time than Rambo while in the novel he and Rambo are equal. The only indication of Teasle's heroism in the Korean War is a display of medals behind his desk. In the novel that background is important because of the contrast between the traditional military tactics used in Korea and the guerrilla tactics used in Vietnam.

So, does that mean you don't like the film?

The opposite. I think the movie is excellent. Movies and books are different. Changes are inevitable. The film switches the locale from Kentucky to the Pacific Northwest. It removes the importance of Teasle's war experience in Korea. It makes Rambo a victim rather than somebody who's pissed off about what happened to him in Vietnam. Finally it changes the ending. But for all that, I love the movie. Ted Kotcheff's direction, Jerry Goldsmith's music, Andrew Laszlo's photography, Sylvester Stallone's acting, Richard Crenna, on and on. It's extremely well made and seems more realistic with each year because its action scenes don't use computer effects. The realism of the stunts is amazing.

You mentioned Stallone's acting.

It's all in the eyes and the body language. Richard Crenna had a long career. He appeared with countless film actors. He told me that, in all his years, he worked with only two actors who truly knew how to play to a camera, reacting rather than acting, using their eyes, skillfully handling props. Those actors were Steve McQueen and Stallone.

You talk about this sort of thing in detail in your audio commentary for the DVD of *First Blood*.

My full-length audio commentary is on most Blu-ray DVDs of *First Blood*. It's a detailed explanation about the differences between the novel and the film, along with a lot of fun details such as that the rat cave in the film was actually a much more horrifying bat cave in the novel. In the movie, the rats that Sly struggles with in the cave were actually white lab rats that were dyed brown. Some DVD versions also have an excellent documentary, "Drawing First Blood," that analyzes how the book became a movie.

How do you feel about the other Rambo films?

I didn't contribute to the scripts for any of them, so my reactions are partly those of an audience member. I enjoyed *Rambo (First Blood Part II)*. It's a cross between a Western and a Tarzan movie. The fight in the helicopter is like a fight on a stagecoach. The arrows with the grenades on them. The wall of mud that Rambo steps out of, magically appearing. It all makes me smile. I met an instructor from Fort Bragg who said that he and his unit went to see the second movie and couldn't stop laughing when Rambo shoots a rocket launcher through the shattered windscreen of his downed helicopter. The POWs Rambo rescued are in the back, and in real life, the back blast from the rocket would have killed them all. But the movie wasn't meant to be realistic, and despite the errors, the Fort Bragg instructor said that he and his team loved it. Thanks to director George Cosmatos, it has wonderful energy.

What about *Rambo III*?

I wrote novelizations for the second and third films, which means that I saw all the drafts of the scripts. *Rambo III*'s early versions featured a middle-aged Dutch female doctor, taking care of Afghan children injured or orphaned in the war with the Soviets. After Rambo rescues his mentor, Colonel Trautman, from the Soviets, the two join forces with the doctor and the children, helping them to get to safety. It was an emotional story that put soul into the action. In the final draft, all of that was gone. The story was reduced to: Trautman is captured; Rambo tries to rescue him and fails; Rambo tries to rescue him and succeeds. The repetition of rescue attempts hurts the film's structure. The day *Rambo III* opened in theaters, the Soviets pulled out of Afghanistan. I guess they heard he was coming.

And the fourth Rambo film?

Some people think that the first film is called *Rambo*. But it's not. It has the same title as my novel, *First Blood*. The fourth film is called *Rambo*, though, which must confuse a lot of people. It should have been called *Rambo IV*. Sly phoned me before making the movie and said that in retrospect he didn't care for the second and third films because they glorified the violence. He said he wanted to go back to the tone of my novel. This time around, the character is the way I imagined—angry and burned-out. There's a scene in which Rambo forges a knife and talks to himself, basically admitting that he hates himself because all he knows is how to kill. He spends a lot of time in the rain as if trying to cleanse his soul. At the start, he gathers cobras in the jungle, and he's comfortable with them because he knows he has nothing to fear from another creature of death. The most telling line of dialogue is, "I didn't kill for my country. I killed for myself. And for that, I don't believe God can forgive me."

Powerful stuff.

Yes, very daring. I just wish that the rest of the fourth film was like that. Many elements could have been better. The villains are superficial, and a lot could have been done with the connection between drug lords and the military in what the film calls Burma (the country's actual name is Myanmar), dramatizing how money earned from the heroin trade motivates the regime's ruthlessness. Instead, they're merely depicted as psychopaths. In a baffling moment, heroin somehow gets equated with meth, which is something entirely different and has nothing to do with the poppies grown in that area of the world. Otherwise, there are a lot of nice moments, especially after the final gun battle when Rambo is back in the United States, walking along a road, wearing the same clothes that he wore at the start of *First Blood*. If you think about it, the character in the first film, a victim, is different from the angry character in my novel. The character in the first film is also different from the jingoistic character in the second and third film and is different again in the fourth film, where he is close to the way I portray him in my novel. A lot of Rambos.

In a way, there's a fifth film.

Yes, a small British film called *Son of Rambow*. The misspelling is deliberate. It's set in England in the 1980s. Two kids from unhappy homes decide to distract themselves by making their version of a Rambo film. They dress up as Rambo and Colonel Trautman. It's a tender, charming story that features scenes from some of the other movies. There was also a half-hour TV cartoon series about Rambo.

You mentioned writing novelizations for *Rambo (First Blood Part II)* and *Rambo III*. Some people might not be familiar with the word.

In the 1980s, film producers began to hire writers who expanded scripts into books that helped generate publicity for the movies. It was mostly work for hire, and the authors couldn't change the dialogue or the scenes. Basically all the novelizers were allowed to do was add description and explore what the characters were feeling or thinking. When the second Rambo film was in production, the producers asked if I'd do a novelization. My instinct was to say no because of the limitations imposed on the writer. But for publicity purposes, the producers really, really wanted a novelization, and my contract stipulated that I was the only person who could write books about Rambo, so they couldn't go to anyone else. They finally agreed to give me the freedom that a novelizer almost never has.

What happened?

Well, the final draft script they sent me was about 85 pages long and was filled with lines like "Rambo jumps up and shoots this guy. Rambo jumps up and shoots the other guy." Not much to work with. So I asked if there were other scripts, and I was told, "Yes, the one that James Cameron wrote, but we only used bits of it."

You mean James Cameron of *Terminator 2*, *Titanic*, and *Avatar*?

Yes, but he wasn't that James Cameron yet. I asked to see the script and struck gold. In the end, my novelization was one-third original material from me, one-third adaptation of James Cameron, and one-third the final script. Those many differences between the film and the novelization had never been allowed before—or since. Most of the Cameron material involves the book's opening, where Colonel Trautman visits Rambo in a locked cell in the basement of an insane asylum. I can imagine what the producers thought when they opened Cameron's script to *that*. The scene probably wouldn't have worked in the movie, but I was happy to include it. I was also happy to include elements about the character that I thought were important but that weren't in the film. The book spent six weeks on the *New York Times* bestseller list, another first for a novelization.

What about the novelization for *Rambo III*?

Well, that was a difficult time for me. My son, Matthew, had been diagnosed with a rare bone cancer, Ewing's sarcoma. He had huge tumors growing out of his ribs and was in the hospital a lot, getting chemotherapy. Meanwhile I agreed to novelize the third Rambo film, partly to take my mind off what was happening to my son. The first script I received featured the middle-aged Dutch female doctor and the wounded children that I mentioned earlier. Rambo's journey to Afghanistan was epical, including a huge dust storm. At one point, horsemen had ropes around each of Rambo's arms and were pulling him apart.

Sounds wonderful.

I was very excited. But then a second script arrived, and the doctor and the kids weren't as important. Then a third script arrived, and the dust storm was gone. In the fourth script, the doctor and the kids were gone. With each successive draft, the story got simpler and simpler until it was merely a failed rescue attempt and a successful rescue attempt. Between visits to my son in the hospital, I finally phoned the producers (Andrew Vajna and Mario Kassar— I really liked them) and said, "I can't write a book this way. Pick a script for me to expand." But they told me there'd be more revisions, so we agreed that I'd use the script that featured the doctor and the kids. Once again, in violation of the rules of novelizations, at least half the book has material that isn't in the movie.

Your novel *First Blood* ends differently than the film. How did you justify being able to continue writing about the character?

I should warn people that what I'm going to say contains a major spoiler. Skip ahead two questions if you haven't read *First Blood* and don't want to be surprised. Now's your chance. Okay, at the end of my novel, Colonel Trautman kills Rambo with a shotgun. It's an allegory. Trautman's first name is Sam. He's Uncle Sam. He's the system that created Rambo, and that system destroys him. A version of that ending was filmed (Rambo commits suicide), but test audiences nearly rioted after cheering for Rambo and then seeing him die. So the producers went back to Hope, British Columbia, the location for the film, and shot a new ending in which Rambo lives. They had no intention of making sequels. They just wanted to have a movie that audiences liked. Then the film turned out to be so successful that they realized how lucky they were to be able to make sequels.

But you had a problem.

Again, just to alert people, this paragraph contains a spoiler also. Yes, my problem was that I killed Rambo, and now in the novelizations he would be alive. The logic really bothered me. One day, I crossed paths with my writer friend, Max Allan Collins (among other things, he wrote the wonderful graphic novel *The Road to Perdition*), who said that the problem was easily solved. "Just add an author's note," he told me, "in which you say something like, 'In my novel *First Blood*, Rambo died. In the films, he lives.'"

There's an amusing story about the way you describe the knives in the films.

The knives for the first two movies were designed by Jimmy Lile, the famed Arkansas knifemaker. Sly collects knives and knew Jimmy and asked him to design the first two knives. When I was researching the knives to write about them in the novelizations, I talked to Jimmy several times on the phone. He was fascinating. Then unfortunately he died, and another master knifemaker, Hall of Famer Gil Hibben, took over, I eventually got to know Gil very well. Anyway, in a foreword to the second novelization, I praised the Rambo knives as works of art. Pauline Kael, the film critic, somehow got her hands on the novelization and included it in her review, saying that she could hardly wait for her set to arrive.

Is it true that you thought of Rambo in terms of Audie Murphy, America's most decorated soldier of WWII?

Yes. The citations for the medals that Murphy received are astonishing for the heroism they describe. His war experiences traumatized him to the point that he often woke from nightmares and grabbed a pistol under his pillow to shoot at imaginary enemies in his bedroom. He had difficulty controlling his temper and was once accused of attempted murder for pistol-whipping a dog trainer who, Murphy said, had overcharged a friend of his. After his war experiences, Murphy became an actor in Western films. You can see a lot of anger in his eyes, especially in his action scenes. In *No Name on the Bullet*, a whole town goes crazy just from looking at him. I got to thinking about what would have happened if Murphy was in the Vietnam War and returned very confused, only to be hassled by a policeman who didn't like the beard and long hair that Murphy might have grown. How would Murphy have reacted? Not well. It's important to remember that the novel was written at a time when police officers reacted negatively to young people who had a beard and long hair, because of the way anti-war protestors looked. I grew my mustache at that time, and I can tell you from personal experience that I was not treated well. When the movie came out in 1982, things had changed so much that almost every man in the audience had long hair, so when Brian Dennehy tells Sly, "We don't like people who look like you coming to our town," the men in the audience whispered to each other, "What's wrong with the way he looks?" The film almost failed at that point, but then the fight in the jail happened, and audiences were hooked.

And what about the character's name? Is it true that it comes from an apple?

Yes. When I was a graduate student at Penn State, my wife came home from grocery shopping and said that she'd found a fabulous-tasting apple that she'd never heard about. I hadn't yet decided on the name for the character. All I knew was that it needed to have the sound of force. So I was sitting at my desk, working on the novel, trying to come up with a name, and my wife kept saying "You should taste this apple," and I kept saying, "Later. Right now, I'm trying to find a name." Finally she insisted so much that I bit into the apple (I love the symbolism) just so I could go back to work. Indeed the apple was very tasty. So I asked the natural question, "What's it called?" She said, "Rambo." I was stunned. "How do you spell that?" I asked, and that's how Rambo was named. It turns out that when Johnny Appleseed (his real name was John Chapman) went through Pennsylvania, Ohio, and Indiana, planting apple trees in the 1800s, that was one of the types of apples that he planted. It's a Scandinavian name, and it means "mountain dweller." In the film adaptation, the screenwriters gave him the first name of John as in the American Civil War song, "When Johnny Comes Marching Home." In the novel, he doesn't have a first name. Nor does he have a middle initial.

What happened to your son?

He had surgery that removed his right ribcage, but the surgeons couldn't get to all of the cancer, so Matt then had a bone marrow transplant. He eventually died from septic shock because his immune system was compromised. One of my granddaughters, Natalie, died from the same rare bone cancer. Only a few hundred people get the disease each year in the United States. When Matt was sick, Sly phoned him late one afternoon. As it happened, Matt had two friends with him, and (you wouldn't believe this in a novel) they happened to be watching the videotape of *First Blood*. So Matt's two friends watched him talk to Sly. I couldn't help smiling when Matt (a show-business fanatic like me) asked about the box office receipts on Sly's latest film. They talked for about twenty minutes. It was a nice thing for Sly to do. In my career, I've had tremendous luck. My private life, my son and my granddaughter dying so young, that's another matter.

Gaslit London is brought to
its knees in David Morrell's
brilliant historical thriller series.

  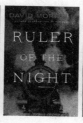 

"Evokes Victorian London with such finesse that you'll hear
the hooves clattering on cobblestones, the racket of dustmen,
and the shrill calls of vendors."

—*Entertainment Weekly*

"Edgar Allan Poe may have invented the modern detective
story, but now David Morrell has reinvented it."

—*Providence Journal*

"An absolutely terrific series."

—Dean Koontz

The following is an excerpt from *Murder as a Fine Art*, the first
book in the Thomas and Emily De Quincey series.

1

The Artist of Death

Something more goes to the composition of a fine murder than two blockheads to kill and be killed, a knife, a purse, and a dark lane. Design, grouping, light and shade, poetry, and sentiment are indispensable to the ideal murder. Like Aeschylus or Milton in poetry, like Michelangelo in painting, a great murderer carries his art to a colossal sublimity.

Thomas De Quincey
"On Murder Considered as One of the Fine Arts"

London, 1854

TITIAN, RUBENS, AND VAN DYKE, it is said, always practiced their art in full dress. Prior to immortalizing their visions on canvas, they bathed, symbolically cleansing their minds of any distractions. They put on their finest clothes, their best wigs, and in one case even a diamond-hilted sword.

The artist of death had similarly prepared himself. Dressed in evening clothes, he sat for two hours staring at a wall, focusing his sensations. When darkness cast shadows through a curtained window, he lit an oil lamp and put the equivalent of brushes, paint, and canvas into a black leather bag. Mindful of Rubens, he included a wig, which was yellow in contrast with the light brown of his own hair. A matching actor's beard was added to the bag. Ten years earlier, a beard would have drawn attention, but a recent trend made beards almost to be expected, as opposed to his increasingly unusual clean-shaven features. He set a heavy ship carpenter's mallet among the other items in the bag. The mallet was aged and had the initials J. P. stamped into its head. In place of the diamond-hilted sword that one artist had worn as he painted, the artist placed a folded, ivory-handled razor in his pocket.

He stepped from his refuge and walked awhile until he reached a busy intersection, where he waited at a cab stand. After two minutes, an empty hansom finally came along, its driver seated prominently behind the sleek vehicle. The artist of death didn't mind standing in plain view, despite the cold December night. In fact, at this point he wanted to be seen, although anyone observing him would soon find it difficult as fog drifted in from the Thames, casting a halo around gas lamps.

The artist paid eightpence for the driver to take him to the Adelphi theater in the Strand. Amid the bustle of carriages and the clop of hooves, he made his way toward a well-dressed crowd waiting to go inside. The Adelphi's gas-lit marquee indicated that the sensational melodrama *The Corsican Brothers* was being performed. The artist of death was familiar with the play and could answer any questions about it, especially its unusual device of two first acts, which occurred in sequence but were meant to be imagined as taking place simultaneously. In the first part, a brother saw the ghost of his twin. The next part dramatized how the twin was killed at the same time the brother saw his ghost. The revenge in the final part was so violent, with such copious amounts of stage blood, that many members of the audience claimed to be shocked, their outrage promoting ticket sales.

The artist of death joined the excited crowd as they entered the theater. His pocket watch showed him that the time was seven twenty. The curtain was scheduled to rise in ten minutes. In the confusion of the lobby, he passed a vendor selling sheet music of the "Ghost Melody" featured in the play. He exited through a side door, walked along a fog-shrouded alley, concealed himself behind shadowy boxes, and waited to determine if anyone followed him.

Feeling safe after ten minutes, he left the far end of the alley, walked across two streets, and hired another cab, no longer needing to wait inasmuch as numerous empty cabs were now departing from the theater. This time, he went to a less fashionable part of the city. He closed his eyes and listened to the cab's wheels shift from the large, smooth, granite pavers on the main streets to the small, rough cobblestones of the older lanes in London's East End. When he descended into an area where evening clothes were hardly common, the driver no doubt believed that the artist intended to solicit a streetwalker.

Behind the closed door of a public privy, he took ordinary clothes from the leather bag, put them on, and folded his theater garments into the bag. As he continued along increasingly shabby streets, he found stoops, nooks, and alleys in which he dirtied the common clothes he now wore and smeared his leather bag with mud. He entered a filthy mews clean-shaven, with light brown hair, and left it wearing the yellow beard and wig. His collapsible top hat had long since been put in the bag, replaced by a weathered sailor's cap. The ship carpenter's mallet was now in a pocket of a tattered sailor's coat.

In this way, the artist occupied two hours. Far from being tedious, the attention to detail was pleasurable, as was the opportunity to reflect upon the great composition ahead. Through the concealing fog, he came within sight of his destination, a mediocre shop that sold clothing to merchant sailors who frequented this area near the London docks.

He paused on a corner and glanced at his pocket watch, taking care that no one saw it. A watch was so unusual in this impoverished area that anyone who glimpsed it would suspect that the artist wasn't the sailor he pretended to be. The hands on the watch showed almost ten. Everything was on schedule. His previous visits had revealed that the area's policeman passed along this street at ten fifteen. Punctuality was part of the job, each patrolman navigating his two-mile route every hour. The time it took for the constable to reach this point seldom varied.

The only person in view was a prostitute, whom the chill night had not encouraged to go back to whatever cranny she called home. When she started to approach, the artist gave her a sharp look that made her stop abruptly and disappear in the fog in the opposite direction.

He returned his attention to the shop, noting that its window had a film of dust that dimmed the glow of a lamp inside. A man's shadow stepped out and swung a shutter into place, closing as usual at ten.

The moment the shadow went back inside, the artist crossed the empty street and reached for the door. If it was already bolted shut, he would knock, with the expectation that the merchant wouldn't begrudge the further five minutes necessary for a final sale.

But the door wasn't locked. It creaked as the artist pushed it open and stepped into a shop that was only slightly warmer than the street.

A man turned from lowering an overhead lantern. He was perhaps thirty—thin, pale, and weary-eyed. He wore a black shirt with a band collar. One of the shirt's buttons didn't match the others. The cuffs of his trousers were frayed.

Does a great work of art require a great subject? Does the murder of a queen create a grander impact than that of a commoner? No. The goal of the art of murder is pity and terror. No one pities a murdered queen or prime minister or man of wealth. The immediate emotion is one of disbelief that even the powerful are not immune to mortal blows. But shock does not linger whereas the sorrow of pity does.

On the contrary, the subject should be young, hardworking, of low means, with hope and ambition, with sights on far goals despite the discouragement that wearies him. The subject should have a loving wife and devoted children dependent on his never-ending exertions. Pity. Tears. Those were the requirements for fine art.

"Just about to lock up? Lucky I caught you," the artist said as he closed the door.

"The missus is getting dinner ready, but there's always time for one more. How can I help?" The lean shopkeeper gave no indication that the artist's beard didn't appear genuine or that he recognized the man, who in another disguise had visited the shop a week earlier.

"I need four pairs of socks." The artist glanced behind the counter and pointed. "Thick. Like the kind you have on that shelf up there."

"Four pairs?" The shopkeeper's tone suggested that today they would be a sizable purchase. "A shilling each."

"Too much. I hoped to get a better price buying so many. Perhaps I should go somewhere else."

Behind a closed door, a child cried in a back room.

"Sounds like somebody's hungry," the artist remarked.

"Laura. When *isn't* she hungry?" The shopkeeper sighed. "I'll add an extra pair. Five for four shillings."

"Done."

When the shopkeeper walked toward the counter, the artist reached back and secured the bolt on the door. He coughed loudly to conceal the noise, aided by the hollow rumble of the shopkeeper's footsteps. Following, he removed the mallet from his coat pocket.

The shopkeeper stepped behind the counter and reached for the socks on an upper shelf, where the artist had noticed them a week earlier. "These?"

"Yes, the unbleached ones." The artist swung the mallet. His arm was muscular. The mallet had a broad striking surface. It rushed through the air and struck the shopkeeper's skull. The force of the blow made a dull cracking sound, comparable to when a pane of ice is broken.

As the shopkeeper groaned and sank, the artist struck again, this time aiming downward toward the slumping body, the mallet hitting the top of his head. Now the sound was liquid.

The artist removed a smock from his bag and put it over his clothes. After stepping behind the counter, he drew the razor from his pocket, opened it, pulled back the shopkeeper's now misshapen head, and sliced his throat. The finely sharpened edge slid easily. Blood sprayed across garments on shelves.

The overhead lantern seemed to brighten.

A fine art.

Again, the child cried behind the door.

The artist released the body, which made almost no sound as it settled onto the floor. He closed the razor, returned it to his pocket, then picked up the mallet next to the bag and reached for the second door, behind which he heard a woman's voice.

"Jonathan, supper's ready!"

When the artist pushed the door inward, he encountered a short, thin woman on the verge of opening it. She had weary eyes similar to the shopkeeper's. Those eyes enlarged, surprised by both the artist's presence and the smock he wore. "Who the devil are *you*?"

The passage was narrow, with a low ceiling. The artist had seen it briefly when pretending to be a customer a week earlier. In the cramped area, to get a full swing, he needed to hold the mallet beside his leg and thrust upward, striking the woman under her chin. The force knocked her head backward. As she groaned, he shoved her to the floor. He dropped to one knee and now had space to raise his arm, delivering a second, third, and fourth blow to her face.

To the right was a doorway into a kitchen. Amid the smell of boiled mutton, a dish crashed. The artist straightened, charged through the doorway, and found a servant girl—someone he had seen leave the shop on an errand a week earlier. She opened her mouth to scream. In the larger space of the kitchen, he was able to use a sideways blow that stopped the scream, shattering her jaw.

"Mama?" a child whimpered.

Pivoting toward the doorway, the artist saw a girl of approximately seven in the corridor. Her hair was in pigtails. She held a ragdoll and gaped at her mother's body on the floor.

"You must be Laura," the artist said.

He whacked her skull in.

Behind him, the servant moaned. He slit her throat.

He slit the mother's throat.

He slit the child's throat.

The coppery smell of blood mingled with that of boiled mutton as the artist surveyed his tableau. The rush of his heart made him breathless.

He closed his eyes.

And jerked them open when he again heard a child's cry.

It came from farther down the corridor. Investigating, he reached a second open door. This one led into a crowded, musty-smelling bedroom, where a candle revealed a baby's cradle, its wicker hood pulled up. The cries came from beneath the hood.

The artist returned to the kitchen, retrieved the mallet, proceeded to the bedroom, smashed the cradle into pieces, pounded at a bundle in the wreckage, and slit its throat.

He rewrapped the bundle and put it under a remnant of the cradle's hood.

The candle appeared to become stunningly bright. In absolute clarity, the artist noted that his hands were covered with blood. His smock was red with it, as were his boots. Finding a cracked mirror on a drab bureau in the bedroom, he determined that his beard, wig, and cap were unmarked, however.

He went to the kitchen, filled a basin from a pitcher of water, and washed his hands. He took off his boots and washed them also. He removed the smock, folded it, and set it on a chair.

After leaving the mallet on the kitchen table, he stepped into the passageway, admired the servant's corpse on the kitchen floor, and closed the door. He shut the door to the bedroom also. He walked to the front of the store and considered the artistry of the mother and the seven-year-old girl in the blood-covered hallway.

He closed that door also. The shopkeeper's body could be seen only if someone looked behind the counter. The next person to enter the shop would encounter a series of surprises.

Terror and pity.

A fine art.

Abruptly someone knocked on the door, making the artist whirl.

The knock was repeated. Someone lifted the latch, but the artist had made certain that the bolt was secured.

The front door did not have a window. With the shutter closed on the main window, whoever knocked on the door could not see inside, although the lamplight was evidently still detectable through cracks around the door.

"Jonathan, it's Richard!" a man shouted. "I brought the blanket for Laura!" More knocking. "Jonathan!"

"Hey, what's the trouble there?" an authoritative voice asked.

"Constable, I'm glad to see you."

"Tell me what you're doing."

"This is my brother's shop. He asked me to bring an extra blanket for his baby girl. She has a cold."

"But why are you pounding?"

"He won't open the door. He expects me, but he doesn't open the door."

"Knock louder."

The door shook.

"How many people live here?" the policeman's voice asked.

"My brother, his wife, a servant girl, and two daughters."

"Surely *one* of them would hear you knocking. Is there a back entrance?"

"Down that alley. Over the wall."

"Wait here while I look."

After grabbing his bag, the artist opened the door to the passage, stepped through, and remembered to close the door. The risk made his heart pound. He hurried past the bodies of the mother and child, almost lost his balance on the slippery floor, and unlocked a back door. Stepping into a small outside area, he again took the precious time to close the door.

The fog smelled of chimney ashes. In the gloom, he glimpsed the shadow of what he assumed was a privy and ducked behind it, just before a grunting man pulled himself over a wall and scanned his lantern.

"Hello?" The man's voice was gruff. He approached the back door and knocked. "I'm a policeman! Constable Becker! Is everything all right in there?"

The constable opened the door and stepped inside. As the artist heard a gasp, he turned toward a murky wall behind the privy.

"God in heaven," the constable murmured, evidently seeing the bodies of the mother and the girl in the passageway. The floor creaked as the constable stepped toward them.

The artist took advantage of the distraction, set his bag on top of the wall, squirmed up, grabbed his bag, and dropped over. He landed on a muddy slope and slid to the bottom, nearly falling in slop. The noise when he hit seemed so loud that he worried the constable must have heard him. The legs of his trousers were soaked. Turning to the right, he groped along the wall in the foggy darkness. Rats skittered.

Behind him, he heard a distinctive alarm. Every patrolman carried a wooden clacker, which had a handle and a weighted blade that made a rapid snapping sound when it was spun. The constable now used his, its noise so loud that it couldn't fail to be heard by other patrolmen on their nearby routes.

The artist reached a fog-bound alley, guided by a dim street-lamp at the far end.

"Help! Murder!" the policeman shouted.

"Murder? Where?" a voice yelled.

"My brother's shop!" another voice answered. "Here! For heaven's sake, help!"

Windows slid up. Doors banged open. Footsteps rushed through the darkness.

Nearing the light at the end of the alley, the artist could see enough to hide the razor behind a pile of rubbish. A crowd rushed past in the fog, attracted by the din of the constable's clacker.

When the crowd was gone, the artist stepped from the alley and went in the opposite direction, staying close to the obscured buildings, prepared to vanish into an alcove if he heard anyone running toward him. The babble of the mob became a faint echo behind him.

He found a public privy, pulled off the yellow wig, and dropped it down the hole, then did the same with the beard. Five minutes later, in an alley near the edge of a better district, he removed his sailor's clothes and put on the theater clothes that he'd folded into the bag. He tossed the sailor's clothes, including the cap, into a corner, where someone would gladly take them in the morning. The mud-smeared leather bag he dropped among garbage a little farther on. It too would readily find a new owner.

In the better district, he followed the noise of hooves through the fog until he arrived at a main street. An empty cab waited at a stand near a restaurant. The driver looked down from his perch and assessed the artist's evening clothes, deciding that he was a safe passenger at this late hour.

As the driver took him to a music hall in the West End, the artist used a handkerchief to wipe mud from his shoes. He established a presence at the music hall, pretending to be just another theatergoer who wanted mellower entertainment after the bloody climax of *The Corsican Brothers*. Then he hired a final cab and went home, wondering if Titian, Rubens, and Van Dyke had ever felt as satisfied by their fine art as *he* did.